ADDLESTONE

THE ADDLESTONE CHRONICLES

BOOK 1

OCTOBER 1ST 1934 - JULY 20TH 1935

DOUGLAS KUEHN

authorHOUSE

AuthorHouse™ UK
1663 Liberty Drive
Bloomington, IN 47403 USA
www.authorhouse.co.uk
Phone: UK TFN: 0800 0148641 (Toll Free inside the UK)
      UK Local: (02) 0369 56322 (+44 20 3695 6322 from outside the UK)

Published by AuthorHouse 05/18/2022

ISBN: 978-1-6655-9873-6 (sc)
ISBN: 978-1-6655-9874-3 (hc)
ISBN: 978-1-6655-9872-9 (e)

CONTENTS

ACKNOWLEDGMENTS

I wish to thank the many friends who have supported my efforts at fiction and have critically proofread earlier versions of this novel. Amongst those, I include Colin and Jenny Day, Dex Marble, Linda Howe, Lynne Olds and Linda Holst Long. All have provided their skills, wisdom, and encouragement to this embryo project as it has developed over the last four years. The cover photo of the King's College was taken by Linda Holst Long in July 2017. I also wish to offer heartfelt thanks to my nephew, Bart Sears, not just for his encouragement but also for providing the tech support necessary to get this published via Amazon.

INTRODUCTION

The inspiration for this novel began some 25 years ago when I purchased a volume titled 'The Bride's Book' at an antiquarian book fair in Westminster, London. The volume was written and edited by Dorothy Stote and only published for three years between 1935 and 1937. The book offered advice to upper middle-class brides on various topics including the appropriate Trousseau, Jewellery, Beauty Tips, Holiday Destinations, and so forth. Photographs, graphics, and advertising were included to illustrate the correct styles and norms of an upper-class wedding in the 1930's.

I found this an interesting curiosity and put it on a shelf to be forgotten until 4 years ago. In an idle moment, I pulled it out again and, looking at the back, I discovered the pages labelled Wedding Guests, and Wedding Presents had been filled in by hand. It described a large wedding that occurred on July 24th 1937 at St. Paul's church in Addlestone, Surrey. The bride, Rose Betty Gregory and the groom, Humphrey Norman Paine both lived in Addlestone. Rose was 33 years old at the time of the wedding and Humphrey was 37. Both were obviously upper-class judging by their addresses, the size of their households, number of servants and Humphrey's position in a London shipping company. All told, there were over 200 wedding guests, a number of whom were titled. Over 200 wedding gifts were received and were detailed in the back pages of the Bride's Book. On top of that, £329 in cheques were given as wedding gifts and banked by Rose and Humphrey. That sum is in excess of £25,000 in today's prices. The descriptions and wedding gifts and size of some of the cheques were particularly impressive, remembering that this was at the height or rather the depths of the Great Depression when the Second World War was only two years away.

THE ADDLESTONE CHRONICLES
OCTOBER 1ST 1934 - JULY 20TH 1935

"If you want the present to be different from the past, study the past."

Baruch Spinoza, 17th century
Dutch philosopher of
Portuguese Sephardi origin

1

MONDAY, OCTOBER 1ST, 1934, KING'S COLLEGE, CAMBRIDGE

After parking his Railton in front of the Mitre public house, he entered his college for the first time since mid-June. The gilded clock set into King's neo-Gothic gateway showed it had just gone half eleven. He was rather pleased with himself having covered the 80 miles from home in under an hour and a half. His gyp acknowledged his arrival with a deferential touch of his forelock and began to unload his luggage.

Powell, the Head Porter, approached from his office to the left, tipped his bowler, and handed him an envelope. "Begging your pardon sir, I'm instructed, this should be brought to your attention immediately upon your arrival."

The missive required him to present himself at the Provost's study at half three prompt.

Today he would begin his final year reading Mathematics. He looked forward to seeing his mates at Goldie Boat Club whose company offered a pleasant respite from the commitments associated with his degree. However, his first priority was to see Louise de la Béré after their three-month separation. She'd spent the summer on a grand tour of seven European capitals as part of her Modern Languages degree course. She planned to return to Newnham College tomorrow morning.

Two servants carried his bags to his second-floor rooms in Bodley's Court. While his gyp unpacked his cases, he speculated about the highly unusual summons to meet with the administrative head of King's.

At three thirty, he knocked and entered through the elaborately carved oak door on the ground floor of Gibbs' Building. The Provost, John Tresidder Sheppard, was taking tea with the Bursar, John Maynard Keynes. He had not formally met either, but recognised both on sight. He had been obliged to attend the Provost's addresses at the start of each term and had audited a number of Keynes's lectures on mathematical economics and political economy.

Keynes was a legend at Cambridge not only for his academic achievements but also for his financial acumen. Despite the Depression and negative inflation, he had contrived to make better than 8% annual real rate of return on the college's endowment by speculating on stock and commodity markets. He also had a reputation for his closeness to the sharp end of international politics.

Sheppard motioned him to be seated in a comfortable looking Art Deco chair. "Let me get straight to the point. Your tutor has been granted leave of absence in order to undertake some essential work for His Majesty's Government."

Before he could continue, there was a quiet tap on the door. The Provost shouted, "Come," and a short, somewhat rotund, middle-aged man entered the study. He was reputed to be one of the finest mathematical minds in all of Cambridge. "Dr Chillingworth has agreed to act as your tutor. You may use my office to get acquainted while Keynes and I take a stroll in the Fellows' Garden to discuss some pressing college business."

His new tutor sat and poured himself a cup of tea. "I know it goes against all the usual conventions, but I'd like you to call me Richard since we will be having quite a close relationship over the course of this academic year. How should I address you?"

"Do use my Christian name."

"And that is? I ask because you seem to have quite a number of names attached to your double-barrelled surname. I see here on your admission application, you're listed as William James Humphrey Rawnsley Harcourt-Heath."

"Sir, I usually go by James."

"So that's how we'll begin. But take note, this familiarity can only exist when we're alone."

Dr Chillingworth paused to take a sip of his tea and selected a biscuit from the silver tray. "Do you mind if I ask a few questions, some of which might be of a personal nature?"

James stumbled over the familiarity unheard of between staff and students. "Not at all, sir, er... Richard."

"I see from your file, you're a bit older than our usual final year undergraduates."

"I was seven at the start of the 1918 Spanish 'flu pandemic and had just entered Dulwich College in their First Form. When I fell ill that November, I was sent home and had to re-enrol the following October."

"Interesting. I expect you know, Sheppard is also a Dulwich College Old Alleynian, being the first non-Etonian to become Provost at King's."

James wasn't aware of this tidbit of trivia and couldn't see how it could possibly be relevant to this interview.

"Might I know why your parents aren't listed on your application?"

"They died in May 1915. They were passengers on the Lusitania when she was torpedoed by a German U-Boat on her return voyage from New York."

"Ah, yes. That tragic event galvanised the anti-German rhetoric in the early stages of the Great War. From your birth date, it appears you'd just turned four."

"My maternal grandparents took charge and raised me and my sisters."

"So, you've siblings?"

"It's somewhat of a family jest, I'm an only child with two sisters. One is older and the other is my non-identical twin."

"Where are they now?"

He paused, unable to see how his family could be relevant to his maths degree. "Marjorie is married to a Lieutenant Commander in the Royal Navy. They live in Bristol with their two children. My twin sister Beatrice lives with our grandparents."

"Tell me, why the only child quip?"

"Before my parents sailed for America, they renewed their wills. As the male, I'd inherit the capital in trust while my sisters would receive lifetime incomes from our family's investments. I believe my grandparents fully approved of this arrangement based on the medieval principle of primogeniture."

Richard flipped through more pages of his file. "I see they reside in Addlestone, Surrey."

"After my parents died, my grandparents took over the family pile at Woburn Park Farm. Our estate produces crops and beef for sale at auction."

"How's that going?"

"We're in rather a sticky patch, what with the current drought affecting southern England. Last summer, our estate manager showed me how it functions as a business."

"Is that how you imagine life after Cambridge, retiring to the depths of Surrey to become a gentleman farmer?"

"I have a duty of care to our workers and to my sisters so they can enjoy the fruits of their inheritance. With wealth comes responsibility."

Richard proceeded to sort through other pages in his file. "Your former tutor informs me you have the potential to be counted amongst the finest undergraduate mathematical minds in all of Cambridge. Having said that, your academic achievements can best be described as modest. Why do you suppose he placed that assessment in your file?"

James felt exposed by the question and squirmed a little in his chair. "I've come to accept I'll never be allowed to pursue my interests in maths because of that unfortunate will."

"I understand you're taking advantage of everything Cambridge has to offer in terms of social and sporting activities. I've also been informed you regularly attend lectures in contemporary politics, economics, and political economy."

He was absolutely certain this wasn't in his file since lecture attendance is never monitored. "With respect, I don't understand your interest in my non-academic activities."

"For that, I've Keynes to blame. You might know he often does work for our government both formally and unofficially."

James was none the wiser and couldn't see any connection between the Bursar and this interview. What followed, left him even more bewildered.

"I expect you're aware of Keynes's views on the 1919 Treaty of Versailles. David Lloyd-George, our Prime Minister at the end of the war, was amenable to moderating the Treaty conditions. It was the French who insisted on the draconian provisions and swingeing reparations. Presently, the Germans are ignoring the limits imposed on their military. They've also shown they're not serious about meeting the financial obligations embodied in the Treaty. In May, 1921, the London Ultimatum required Germany pay reparations of two billion Goldmarks, that's German currency convertible into gold. That was an enormous sum in excess 130 million Pounds Sterling. Additionally, they were required to annually remit 26% of the gross value of their exports. In order to amass that amount of hard currency, they were forced to sell the Mark on the foreign exchange markets. Naturally, its value plummeted.

"This was the beginning and indeed a primary cause of the hyperinflation experienced under the Weimar Republic over the following three years. It's hardly surprising, the financial and military emasculation embodied in the Treaty remains a sore point with the Germans. Just now, they're rearming as Keynes predicted in his 1919 pamphlet, *The Economic Consequences of the Peace.*"

Richard paused to pop the last slice of teacake into his mouth. "Keynes wasn't alone as regards his concerns about the Germans. In the closing months of the Great War, Field Marshal Ferdinand Foch was appointed Supreme Commander of Allied Forces. In 1919 he predicted the Treaty would result in an armistice of only twenty years. The Ministry of Defence now fears his prescience might well prove accurate. By the way, Foch's rationale was that Versailles was an outright capitulation to the Germans."

James was uncertain as to where this conversation was going and paused before replying. "I'm aware of Keynes's contribution to the post-war political debate and I can infer his views as regards the current and growing threat from the continent. I didn't know about Foch's assertion but I can understand his perspective since he's French. In the Great War, the German military wreaked havoc on his country and his people. With great respect, I'm not at all clear what this has to do with me or my degree."

"Obviously, I'm here in my role as your tutor. I'm also speaking with you as a representative of His Majesty's Government to offer you a job."

"I'm afraid I don't understand. I'm not seeking employment. After my Tripos exams, I'm committed to managing my family's agricultural estate and our London residential properties."

"Before I explain, we'll need to speak further. I'd like to know a bit more about your politics and your loyalties. Would you meet me in my rooms in Gibbs' tomorrow morning at ten? If you don't like the direction this conversation has taken, you must tell me then. In any case, come prepared for your first tutorial."

2

TUESDAY, OCTOBER 2ND, KING'S COLLEGE

The following morning, James walked across Back Lawn, passed through the archway and entered Gibbs' Building using the gatehouse entrance. In his second floor study, Richard directed him to sit in one of the comfortable looking leather Victorian armchairs opposite his enormous oak desk. "I trust you've considered my proposal."

"Actually, I've thought of little else."

"Before we can proceed, I'll require some assurances concerning our meetings."

"Assurances?"

"It's really quite straightforward. Apart from our preparation for your June Tripos examinations, what passes between us, must remain within these walls. To ensure you understand this, we require your written acknowledgment that should you disclose details of our non-academic discussions, it will be tantamount to treason. Mind, this is not a threat; it's just the nature of things. If you're prepared to sign the 1911 Official Secrets Act, British law compels you to abide by its strictures. Failure to do so would be a felony punishable by a maximum sentence of fourteen years' imprisonment. I know this sounds quite formal, but I'm obliged to use those precise words to ensure you fully appreciate the significance of what you might be signing."

"With the utmost respect, I'm now seriously confused. I'm just a country gent who enjoys life as a student and an oarsman and who apparently has some aptitude for maths."

His tutor pushed a single sheet of foolscap across his desk. "You mustn't let your first contact with officialdom put you off the idea of working for your country. If you're prepared to agree to these conditions, we can continue."

After reading the single-page document, he signed and dated it in the requisite slots. His tutor also signed and waved it in the air to dry the ink. He placed it in an envelope, put it in his desk drawer, and turned the key.

"Now tell me, what are your feelings towards the Bolsheviks?"

James paused at this abrupt change of direction. "Actually, I've total sympathy with the struggle for human rights in post-revolutionary Russia. In *Das Kapital,* Karl Marx offered some progressive ideas concerning individual freedom and the redistribution of wealth aimed at creating a more egalitarian society. Prior to the collapse of the Tsarist autocracy in 1917, the Russian people had been de facto slaves for centuries, working on land owned by the corrupt and decadent Romanov hegemony. Indeed, the young Queen Victoria had close family connections with the Romanov's which she promoted during her first 10 years of her reign.

Historically, serfdom slavery been the norm in Europe for centuries and here I include Germany, Italy, Spain, and Portugal. Nearer home, the English establishment have acted as absentee landlords in Scotland, Ireland, and Wales, supressing the indigent populations for their own financial gain. Having said that, I can't abide revolutions that exchange one form of tyranny with another, accompanied by loss of life and destruction of property. That's precisely what happened in Tsarist Russia when Lenin formed the Soviet Union in 1922."

"What about fascism?"

"Extreme nationalism is used to justify both domestic suppression and external aggression. Fascism is a virulent cancer inevitably accompanied by racial, cultural, and religious discrimination. I fully support the efforts of the progressive movements taking place on the continent."

"Is Germany really fascist? One might argue, the current regime simply reflects populist support for strong government to stabilise, revitalise, and return their country to the political and economic position they enjoyed prior to 1914. I'm sure you're aware, the Weimar government that controlled Germany between 1919 until Hitler took power in early 1933, was utterly dysfunctional. The various political factions were polarised on party lines and seemed unable to negotiate compromise. Hence, they were unable to address the pressing economic issues that emerged at the end of the war. Indeed, I expect that stalemate led to the populist revolution that allowed Hitler to assume power. Democracy requires negotiation and compromise to thrive. What's more, no advanced trading economy has been immune from the effects of what the British economist, Lionel Robbins, recently termed the Great Depression. In any case, German leaders claim to be socialists. Remember, the Nazi party's full name is the National Socialist German Workers' Party."

James paused before he replied. "Time will tell. Don't forget, last month Hitler banned all opposition parties in order to consolidate his power base following Von Hindenburg's death in 1933. He declared himself President and Chancellor and his first executive order was to appoint Joseph Goebbels head of the newly created Ministry of Popular Enlightenment and Propaganda. Apparently, its primary purpose is to disseminate a consistent message through a government controlled press. Indeed, in 1925 and 1926, Hitler described in Main Kampf his proposal to promote what he called the 'Big Lie'. In his two-volume autobiographical manifesto, he wrote, "If you tell a lie big enough and keep repeating it, people will eventually come to believe it."

"The Nazi's word for this principle is Gleischaltung. Newspapers that disagreed with the party line have been attacked, boycotted, and summarily closed. Hitler even went so far as describing contrary press coverage as emanating from the Lügenpresse, which translates as the lying press.

"There are those who argue Britain should welcome a stable Germany and even form political and military alliances. I'm thinking of Oswald Mosley and the British Union of Fascists. It's common knowledge, the BUF enjoys financial and editorial backing from Lord Rothermere, owner of the Daily Mail and the Daily Mirror. I'm sure you're aware, many titled members of our so-called ruling classes have offered Hitler endorsements and financial support."

James found it a simple matter to discredit the idea of rapprochement with Nazi Germany. "Mosley's Blackshirts are East End rabble who enjoy dressing up in pseudo-uniforms to terrorise minorities. Because xenophobia is Mosley's primary message, BUF rallies often turn violent. Despite being encouraged by such rags as the Mail and the Mirror, I doubt they'll ever amount to much. As regards support from some sections of the aristocracy, I expect they're simply monarchists who wish to maintain the status quo, nostalgically looking back at our 19th century colonial dominance."

"So you don't envisage an internal threat to British democracy?"

"I don't. Domestic Marxists and Fascists are fragmented and bound to lose their popular support. Our democracy has a long history dating back to 1215 with the signing of the Magna Carta. Germany has only been unified for the last sixty years and their leaders and the electorate have no similar experience with democratic processes. When Bismarck formed the Second Reich in 1871, they were like Russia, essentially a collection of feudal states. Their only real attempt at representational democracy was the dysfunctional fourteen years of the Weimar Republic. Given that experience, it's hardly surprising Hitler was able to assume power. He promised the masses he'd establish a strong government whose primary aim would be to return Germany to the position of international greatness they enjoyed prior to the war."

"What about external threats to our national security?"

James thought Richard was finally getting to the point of this interview. "I'm fully cognizant of the economic power, determination, and anger of the Germans. It's especially relevant now they've a charismatic leader who panders to the electorate's basest instincts. In the Great War, they demonstrated the industrial and military might to take on any nation or group of nations. If there's a threat to British democracy, I expect it'll come from the Nazis."

"That's our thinking as well."

Richard made no attempt to explain his use of the plural possessive. "We're now prepared to offer you a position as trainee agent with MI5."

"MI5?"

"I'm not surprised you've not heard of us. It stands for Military Intelligence, Section 5. It's under the control of the Ministry of Defence and overseen by the Home Secretary, Sir John Gilmour. We're part of the Secret Intelligence Service, or SIS that also includes MI6.

"Let me outline our plans for you. Carry on with your maths lectures and our tutorials and continue to enjoy the social and sporting activities available to a final year student. We'd also like you to become a member of the Apostles."

"Wait now, I've heard about them. Aren't they some sort of elitist debating society? Surely one doesn't simply knock on someone's door and say, please, might I join your club?"

Richard offered him a withering glance. "Indeed not. Keynes is an Apostles' Angel; that's one who's no longer an undergraduate. He's proposed you for membership and you've been accepted.

Somewhat unwisely, he decided on a cheeky response. "I'm sure that sounds delightful."

Richard ignored his pathetic attempt at irony. "Keynes rarely attends meetings and has little to do with undergraduates. We'd like you to be our eyes and ears at their gatherings. Keynes abhors Marxists and believes some members have Stalinist leanings. Because of their elitist position in British society, he feels the Apostles might eventually pose a threat to national security."

James nodded, embarrassed by his immature response and therefore unable to think of anything useful to say.

"As regards your academic progress, we'll meet every Tuesday morning at ten. Next week, I'd like you to write a critique of the Gauss-Bonnet theorem. Ensure your analysis contains a precise statement of the formula in its local form and a discussion of its potential applications. Here are some related problems I'd like you to attempt. Might I suggest you attend the two lectures on linear algebra I've circled on this week's schedule?"

He expected an assignment, but wondered what he was getting into with this spying lark?

Instead of returning to his rooms, James walked the half-mile southwest towards Newnham College. At the Porters' Lodge, he handed his card to a college servant. "Could you see if Miss Margaret Louise de la Béré has arrived?"

Ten minutes later, she skipped down the left staircase and threw herself into his arms. Facing each other, they held hands and smiled in silence. Louise saw a tall, fit, handsome man with broad shoulders, wavy, sandy brown almost blonde hair, and deep blue eyes. She guessed he was at least 6'3" and some fourteen stone. James held the hands of a tall, slim, and beautiful twenty-three-year-old. She had short light-brown hair, an olive complexion, hazel eyes, and a boyish figure.

After this private moment, James said, "I'm a tad peckish. How's about a spot of lunch at the Three Horseshoes at Maddingly?"

As it was some six miles away, she suggested they take her Hillman Minx. Undergraduates were not permitted to keep motorcars but she and several of her final-year friends bent this University rule. Like James, she stored hers in a rented garage a few streets away from the Newnham grounds.

Finding a table, he ordered a pint of bitter and she asked for an orange barley water. Over a pub lunch of bangers and mash, they began to get reacquainted. She told him about her European experiences and he talked about his summer at Woburn.

James reached for her hand. "You know my dearest, your letters and postcards didn't come close to making up for your absence. Can we agree, never to have such a long separation?"

"Do I detect the merest hint of an emotional commitment?"

Even after three months apart, it surprised him how much he enjoyed her company. He was aware of her social idiosyncrasies, but with his other lady friends, there was always tension and misunderstandings. That was especially true this summer when he dated a number of rather silly ladies from Cambridge and North Surrey. Louise was witty and at the same time teasingly perceptive as evidenced by converting his comment into a pseudo-proposal. Not for the first time, he realised he had much to consider in terms of his future.

Once back at King's, he went to his rooms to sleep off the long lunch. He hoped a nap would help him process all that had happened over the last twenty-four hours.

He woke to the sounds of a quiet tapping on his door. His gyp entered and passed him a note. It was from one Guy Burgess of Trinity. He'd been invited to an Apostles' meeting Saturday next.

3

SATURDAY, OCTOBER 6TH, TRINITY COLLEGE

This week was devoted to academia. After writing the set essay and solving the assigned problems, he turned his attention to linear algebra. Lectures were, of course, optional. The primary requirement for undergraduates is to complete work set by their tutors. Nevertheless, he attended a lecture on Political Economy given by a Girton College tutor, Mrs Joan Robinson and another on Welfare Economics delivered by King's Professor, Arthur Pigou.

James found academic work a time-consuming distraction to all the other issues swirling around in his head, foremost of which was Louise. Earlier in the week, he arranged to meet her at King's Chapel for Sunday morning choral Matins. Having spent hours thinking about their relationship, he changed his plans and on Thursday morning, rang his grandfather.

All day Saturday, he'd been nervous at the prospect of being in a room full of intellectuals. At the same time, he was curious to see what the Apostles were about. When he arrived at Guy Burgess' large flat at Trinity, he found it filled with some twenty young men dressed in outfits that could best be described as flamboyant. Wide colourful silk ties and scarves seemed to be de rigeuer.

Guy took him by the arm. "Let me offer my congratulations. We've just had a show of hands and you've been accepted into the Apostles."

A ceremony followed involving signing the membership diary known as The Book. Afterwards, and for the second time this week, he was instructed to swear an oath of secrecy. He was given a long-stemmed flute of Champagne and formally toasted by the assembled members.

The next phase of the meeting involved the presentation of a discussion paper. The speaker argued the case for maintaining colonial control over what he referred to as the world's primitive races. He asserted, the primary objective should be to exploit their labour and natural resources for the benefit of the mother country. At the same time, he supported the separation of the various social strands within, what he termed, the civilised countries of Europe. He stressed this was both a desirable goal in itself and necessary to maintain the balance of European and global political power.

James thought his arguments were confused, self-serving, and littered with contradictions. The discussion that followed was lively, witty, and sometimes biting. In the end, there was general agreement that the greatest threat to civilised society was the dilution of the purity of the various European ethnic strands. He refrained from comment and was content to listen and nod at what he supposed were appropriate times. Afterwards, more Champagne was produced to wash down their snack of sardines on toast, which they called whales. James was amongst the first to leave. It appeared most planned to continue the soirée into the wee hours. He heard champagne corks exploding as he put on his overcoat.

Under his bedclothes, he had difficulty falling asleep thinking about this evening. He was certain they realised he was an outsider. Perhaps when he reported his impressions, Richard would accept he wasn't up to this, or indeed any level of subterfuge.

With that thought, he was taken into the arms of Morpheus. It might have been the sardines but his dreams were more like nightmares. Louise was being seduced by a roomful of gaudily dressed beautiful young men. He awoke in a lather accompanied by a determination to get his life back on an even keel. He vowed to focus on Louise, his Addlestone responsibilities, rowing, and maths in that order. Additionally, his thoughts kept returning to Richard's proposal and his expressed concerns about national security. In this half-awake state, he arrived at a decision.

4

SUNDAY, OCTOBER 7ᵀᴴ, ADDLESTONE

He met Louise outside King's Chapel. "Instead of Matins, I propose a day out in the country and I won't take no for an answer."

"Darling, you know I'd never deny you your desires."

He knew she held exceedingly strong views on pre-marital intimacy so appreciated she was flirting. "I'm taking you to Addlestone to meet my family."

He drove south with the soft top down. When he entered Woburn's elaborate Georgian wrought iron gates, his family and staff met them on the flagstone courtyard.

Louise approached James's grandmother and offered her hand. "Mrs Harcourt-Heath, I'm so glad to finally meet you."

"Do call me Dorothy. My grandson has often spoken of you."

She was tall and slim with a healthy country glow after this unusually dry and sunny summer. Given what Louise knew about James's deceased parents, Dorothy and the Colonel were likely in their mid-seventies, although neither looked their age.

James's grandfather was over six feet, tanned, and robust. Louise extended her hand. "I'm pleased to finally meet you, sir. You appear to be the most important person in James's life."

"Well now, I suppose I am. You must call me Humphrey and none of that sir or Colonel nonsense. That's reserved for estate workers and tradesmen. You should know, after our only son was killed, James has become our genetic legacy."

Louise was unnerved by his oblique reference to future offspring and quickly turned to greet James's sisters.

"Hello, you must be Marjorie."

"Please call me Margie. Everybody does. I must tell you, I'm so glad my brother has finally found an intelligent companion."

Next, James introduced Beatrice. She had fine features but dressed simply and to Louise's eye, somewhat dowdily. Her short blonde hair was unpermed and parted in the middle.

"James has mentioned your charity work. I've been so looking forward to meeting you."

"Do call me Bea. I volunteer at the Addlestone Village Home for Female Orphans. Our charges need all our help to overcome the trauma of being abandoned and raised in an institution. I'm also on the board of the Chertsey Mother and Baby Home. We help young women who find themselves with child but lack the emotional and financial support of family or the biological father."

James introduced the butler who stood tall and erect and had greying mutton chop sideboards. "This is Jarvis. He pretty well runs things now my grandparents are slowing down."

Humphrey obviously overheard and offered James a withering glance. A middle-aged ladies' maid, a young footman, Cook, and two kitchen maids comprised the rest of the household staff. The women servants primly curtsied and lowered their eyes and the men bowed slightly.

The formalities completed, Humphrey took Louise's arm and escorted her into the library. Instead of paying attention to what he was saying, she took in the details of this enormous space. The walls were filled, floor-to-ceiling, with leather-bound books. The centre of the room was dominated by a long rectangular mahogany table surrounded by eight mahogany Regency chairs. At the far end, two matching Victorian chesterfield sofas faced each other, between which resided a low inlaid oriental teak table. A chaise lounge covered in red silk damask was placed near the left wall. A Bösendorfer baby grand piano rested to the left of the doorway and an enormous mahogany writing desk sat below the central mullioned window facing the front drive. To its right was a Georgian cast iron

Fireplace insert surrounded by an elaborate carved oak and white marble mantelpiece. The floors were herringbone patterned oak parquet covered by silk Persian carpets. She looked up at the ceiling cornice and admired the crisp egg-and-dart mouldings. Hanging from two elaborate ceiling roses were matching electrified crystal chandeliers.

Humphrey had stopped talking and she was brought back to the moment when the butler and the footman served small glasses of Fino sherry. Twenty minutes later, a gong sounded and Jarvis announced, "Luncheon is served."

The dining room was the mirror image of the library. Being on the south side of the house, it had loads of daylight streaming in from its mullioned windows. The French polished mahogany dining table could seat at least twenty.

While starters were being served, Louise asked a question directed towards no one in particular.

"Do tell me about Addlestone. James has offered such glowing descriptions."

Humphrey took up the conversational chalice. "Addlestone dates back to at least the 10th century Saxons. Our landmark is the Crouch Oak. Legend has it that Queen Elizabeth stopped in its shade and had a meal whilst on a journey sometime in the 1560's. Experts at the nearby Royal Horticultural Society gardens at Wisley estimated it to be at least 900 years old. Our parish church is St Paul's. It's really quite modern, having been completed in 1836, a year before Queen Victoria's coronation. It has beautiful proportions and some impressive stained-glass windows.

"Here at Woburn Park, we've part of the ruins of Chertsey Abbey. That Benedictine order owned these and surrounding lands from the mid 7th century until the dissolution of the monasteries in 1536. Woburn manor and the estate came into Dorothy's family in the last century. Prior to the arrival of the railways in 1848, Addlestone was pretty much a motley collection of farms and cottages, communications and trade being maintained using the Thames.

"Louise, I hope you like beef. Our cattle are grass fed and allowed to roam free in our pastures. I've found a bottle of 1920 Château Margaux in our cellars. I'd value your opinion as it's still young."

For starters, Jarvis and the footman served salmon mouse accompanied by a 1924 Puligny-Montrachet. As regards both wine selections, she expected James had alerted the family that she considered herself a connoisseur of French wines.

Conversation waned while they attacked the roast beef, haricot beans, roast potatoes, and Yorkshire pudding, all of which were served along with a silver boat of rich gravy. Louise praised the fare and complemented Cook in her absence. She meant it since Newnham meals could best be described as adequate.

After lunch they adjourned to the library. James and his grandparents returned to the chaise, presumably to discuss family or farm business. James's sisters sat with Louise on one of the leather sofas. Margie began the expected interrogation. "We'd like to know a bit more about you."

Louise bit the bullet. She had no secrets she wished to keep from his family, but was aware she needed to choose her words carefully so as not to appear boastful. "I was born in Winchester in June 1911 so I'm a few months younger than your brother. What's more, we all share a similar background. My parents died when I was a baby. As an only child, my guardian and trustees look after my financial interests and act as pastoral advisors until I reach the age of twenty-five. At that point, the trust is dissolved and my parent's assets revert to me. Then, I suppose, I'll be what you might call a lady of independent means."

"But what happened?"

"My father and mother were passengers on the maiden voyage of that unsinkable Titanic. I was less than a year old so I rely on my mother's photo album to create and nurture my memories."

Bea asked, "Is your surname French?"

"It is. My father was born in France and, like me, was an only child. My guardian told me his family had once owned a large vineyard somewhere in Burgundy. Accrued debt and the French wine blight in the late 1870's forced the sale of the property. My grandparents moved to Winchester where my mother had distant relatives."

"After that?"

"After that, my father was sent to Eton and Oxford where he read Law. His ambition was to become a lawyer and he did his pupillage at Gray's Inn. Two years later he was invited to become a barrister. A decade later, he took silk and was appointed King's Counsel. My mother was the daughter of his Head of Chambers so I expect that's how they met. Shortly after I was born, they took a second honeymoon to visit the New World while I remained in Winchester with my nurse. My grandparents on both sides had passed away before I was born so after that, I was truly an orphan."

James's sisters remained silent and in the hiatus, Louise turned to Margie. "I'd like to ask you a question. When we met outside, you said you were glad James had finally found an intelligent companion. Might I ask what prompted that comment?"

Margie looked embarrassed. "I must apologise; that was uncalled for. Bea and I have discussed this on numerous occasions. He's had a string of unsuitable partners over the last few years. All were attractive and some might even say beautiful. To our minds, they were floozies and gold-diggers."

Before Louise could ask further questions, Humphrey rose and suggested a stroll around the estate in what remained of the afternoon sun. Bea demurred and said she'd remain behind to write some letters and spend time with Frédéric Chopin.

Louise borrowed a Barbour waxed jacket and Hunter boots from the mudroom. She welcomed the respite, feeling uncomfortable hearing references to James's previous liaisons.

Some outer walls, arches, and tiled floors were evident in the impressive Abbey ruins. Humphrey acted as her tour guide. "As part of his Reformation, Henry VIII disbanded Chertsey Abbey and had these buildings demolished. Locals removed stones for their own houses and barns and rubble was used to raise the level of the roadways, always prone to winter flooding from the Thames. Our house is late Georgian and rumoured to have been erected on the Abbey's foundations. What you see here, were the monk's living quarters. Just over there is the Abbey's tithe barn. It's our showpiece and very much intact. Presently, its only occupants are colonies of bats which fortunately help us keep down the cattle fly and mosquito populations."

Louise said, "I assume Addlestone is primarily agricultural."

"Not at all. We've a thriving market town and a few modern industries scattered about. The Air Navigation and Engineering Company assembled aeroplanes here during the Great War and after that, produced the

Blériot-Whippet cycle car. Their factory is still on Station Road. By 1918, Addlestone had become Britain's largest aircraft manufacturing centre. Vickers Aviation is nearby and Laing Propeller is less than two miles away in Weybridge. What's more, Brooklands racetrack and aerodrome lie just over that hill to the south. We may be country folks, but we're in the 20th century when it comes to aviation. During the war, I held down a Ministry of Defence desk job with responsibility for coordinating aircraft production at Brooklands."

Back at the front steps of Woburn Hall, Louise recognised Chopin's Nocturne, opus 9 as it came through the open library window. James put his arm around Louise's waist. "Darling, my grandmother has summoned us to stay for supper."

They left their footwear in the mudroom as they'd suffered the expected travails of a stroll through cattle pastures. As they approached the library doorway, the music ceased abruptly and they heard the piano fallboard close with a bang.

While the ladies took tea, James and his grandfather went to the billiards' room for a game and a chat. "Grandpapa, you can rest assured I'll mind the estate after my June exams."

"Never doubted it my boy, but it's nice to hear it from the horse's mouth."

"I'm ever so pleased you've taken to Louise. I wanted you to meet her because I've decided she's the one. I know my mother stopped wearing her engagement ring after her marriage. Could you ask grandmama to bring it down so I can propose properly at supper?"

"It's high time you ended your dalliances. Dorothy and I agree she's a keeper."

They shook hands, which turned into an embrace. That hadn't happened since he was a child of seven on Armistice Day.

The family were seated around the library table when Jarvis and the footman served their choices of pre-dinner drinks. Conversation focussed on last month's Nuremburg rally. James knew a bit about it as he had watched the propaganda film made by Leni Riefenstahl after a Political Economy lecture.

Humphrey led the discussion. "As a military man, I view the expansion of the German army and this Herr Hitler fellow as a danger for continental Europe and therefore for Britain. I'm President of our local branch of the Comrades of the Great War, which some bugger in Whitehall decided to rename the Royal British Legion. None of us wish to see another confrontation with the Hun, if you'll excuse my vernacular."

Margie nodded in agreement. "The last thing I want to see is my husband go to war. That doesn't mean I wish to appease the Nazis. Rearmament has its risks, but we must stop Hitler and sooner rather than later."

Humphrey invited Louise to comment, possibly to test her politics. "Margie's spot on. For us to stick our heads in the sand just won't wash. Of course, everybody abhors war, but if it's a matter of our survival, we must rearm. You might remember, last year the idea was floated that the now independent Poland should join with France to initiate a pre-emptive war against Germany, the aim being to stop Hitler before he became too powerful. Unfortunately, the plan came to nothing. Last June, Hitler adopted the title, Oberster Richter des Deutschen Volkes, calling himself the Supreme Judge of the German People. That followed the Röhm Putsch or what we now call the Night of the Long Knives. That was when his Brownshirt thugs organised the brutal murder of the head of opposition politicians and outspoken Catholic lay leaders."

James was surprised by her interest in European politics not to mention this somewhat incongruous lecture over pre-dinner drinks. He decided it was probably because she had recently returned from her European travels.

The gong sounded and they made their way into the dining room. Over desert, Louise turned to Bea and asked about her work at the orphanage. Before she could reply, they heard a series of clinks. James stood, holding his wine glass in one hand and a dessert fork in the other. She supposed he was about to offer a few comments about the family's weekend reunion. Indeed, he began by thanking his grandparents and sisters for what he termed, answering the call. "I couldn't be happier to be surrounded by those who are dearest to me and whom I respect, admire, and love. For that reason, I've chosen this time and this setting to ask Louise to be my wife."

This was the last thing she expected, although she'd hoped this moment might one day arrive.

James turned to his left, knelt on his right knee and handed her a small box. "My darling, will you marry me?"

Opening it, she admired the most beautiful ring she'd ever seen. "With your family as witnesses, I accept."

He slipped it onto her third finger left hand. Central to the ring was a large emerald and a trio of diamonds on each side of the stone.

"How did you discover my finger size and where did you find such a stunning ring?"

"This was my mother's engagement ring. As for it fitting perfectly, let's regard it as an omen of good fortune."

Jarvis, entered with two chilled bottles of Moet & Chandon and the footman carried five crystal flutes on a salver and a glass of barley water for Bea.

5

MONDAY, OCTOBER 8TH, CAMBRIDGE

His engagement gave him renewed enthusiasm for his studies. This morning, he reviewed the notes he'd taken for tomorrow's tutorial. He also organised his thoughts concerning the Apostles. Louise had made it clear she would be busy preparing for her regularly scheduled tutorial on Thursday morning. Nevertheless, at five he rang and they agreed to meet for supper at the Eagle just off Bridge Street.

Louise said, "My two closest friends spotted my ring and I couldn't deceive them. Have you told anyone?"

"Not a soul. I've been cloistered all day prepping for my tutorial."

"I hope you don't mind, I telephoned Dorothy. She's arranged to place our engagement announcement in The Times, The Telegraph, The Morning Post, The Surrey Advertiser, and The Surrey Mirror. I suggested she include The Cambridge Chronicle Journal."

"Well done. And you're right, we must make a start on the wedding arrangements. Bea has offered to help, but I don't want to put too much responsibility on my grandparent's shoulders."

"What about the ceremony?"

"As a student at King's, we could be married in our Chapel. It would be a beautiful venue but I'd really prefer Addlestone's St Paul's. I'd like to wait until July when our exams are over and we've had our final waltz at King's May Ball. What say we go down this weekend and get my family's thoughts on the reception and guest list?"

"I'm sure I can gain permission from my tutor to be absent from College. By the way, I expect you noticed, I've been elected Captain of the Cambridge ladies golf team. I've told all my Newnham friends in case they missed the announcement in the Varsity."

James made no comment as regards her self-serving boast. After a pause, he added, "If we left Friday morning, you might like to bring your clubs. Humphrey is a fixture at St George's Hill."

The fresh air was a welcome respite after the smoke-filled public house. At Newnham gates, they embraced but the bitter east wind soon got the better of them. James asked, "Darling, how 'bout a bite at the Eagle Thursday evening?"

"Brilliant."

Back in his rooms, he stepped over an envelope that had been pushed under his door. He'd been invited to a meeting of the Apostles Saturday next. He'd have to decline and wrote a note to that affect to be delivered tomorrow by a porter. He was too excited to sleep and felt fully prepared for tomorrow's tutorial. Instead of going to bed, he slumped down in an easy chair with Agatha Christie's latest novel, 'Murder on the Orient Express'.

His Tuesday tutorial focussed on linear algebra. Richard read his essay without comment and together they examined the solutions he provided for last week's assignment. "For next week, I'd like you to review the current developments and practical applications of number theory. Here are twenty problems you should attempt to solve. Before you leave, tell me your impressions of the Apostles?"

"It was obvious I was an outsider and the discussion paper was distinctly off-putting. Having said that, it was consistent with a Marxist perspective. I didn't catch the name of the speaker, but he seemed to hold rather extreme views regarding racial and cultural integration."

"He's one of ours and rather convincing, don't you think?"

"Wait now, if you already had someone keeping an eye on them, what was I doing there?"

"We wanted to find out if you were able to use your social graces to integrate within this disparate group. By our reckoning, they saw you as a fellow traveller."

"You must be joking. I sat there like a lump and hardly opened my mouth."

"I'm told your presence went pretty much unnoticed, which is the test of a successful spy. Did you form any other impressions?"

"Most appear to prefer the company of men."

"Excellent. You're sensitive to their homosexuality without feeling threatened."

"They've invited me to their meeting next Saturday, but I've had to decline. I plan to drive to Addlestone on Friday, assuming I can secure your permission to be away from college."

"Attend their meetings when you can. If you feel you're on top of your studies, by all means take the weekend off. Forget about future furtive activities and enjoy your final year at Cambridge."

"I assume that means you've decided I'm not up to the job?"

"Quite the opposite. We've rather more pressing uses for your talents. By the bye, let me congratulate you and Miss de la Béré on your engagement."

"How did you hear about that?"

"That would be telling."

6

FRIDAY, OCTOBER 12TH, WOBURN

Friday morning, he stowed her case and clubs in the Railton's boot and headed south. Since Humphrey greeted them at the door, James presumed he'd been sitting at his library writing desk when the roadster entered the forecourt.

His grandfather beamed when he saw her golf bag. "Now I know we'll have a splendid weekend. I warn you, my dear, I play off seven on a good day."

Louise turned her head and focussed on the chestnut tree in the front garden. "Actually, my University handicap is four."

James had not forgotten her tendency to call attention to her accomplishments, often in socially inappropriate situations. She seemed to need to be the acknowledged expert on all sorts of topics ranging from etymology to French wines. He decided it couldn't be because she was insecure. She was a wealthy, beautiful, highly intelligent linguist, and a talented sportswoman. What's more, she always appeared indifferent to what others thought of her. Her apparent arrogance combined with lack of eye contact made no sense.

Jarvis instructed Sprott, the ladies' maid, to carry Louise's bag upstairs and accompany her to the room she'd used last weekend. The servant helped her unpack and Louise asked her to press her evening dress.

Over lunch, James suggested they might all take a walk this afternoon to view the Crouch Oak and St Paul's. With that in mind, he raised the topic of their wedding. "Grandpapa, we've decided we'd like to be married at St Paul's."

"Jolly good show. In that case, Dorothy and I will host the reception. Have you thought about numbers?"

"We don't have much in the way of extended family, apart from a few cousins and aunts in London. I've several village friends I'd like to invite. Do you remember meeting Norman Paine? He's older than I but he taught me to ride and we've been hacking together since I was ten. There are also my Cambridge pals, mainly from King's and Goldie Boat House and I've kept in touch with a few school friends from Dulwich College. Louise tells me she has some distant relatives in the south of England and then there are her Newnham College ladies and possibly school friends from St Swithun's."

Humphrey said, "On our side, we've our landowning neighbours and my golf and Dorothy's bridge club members. I suppose we should plan for a couple of hundred. St Paul's could just about handle that number if some of the men stood at the back. In terms of accommodation, close family will stay here and non-local guests can secure rooms in nearby inns."

The trip down and the unaccustomed midday imbibing made Louise drowsy. She excused herself and retired to her room for a nap. She awoke with a start and felt disoriented. Smiling inwardly, she realised she was staying with those who'd soon become her family.

Dressed in comfortable clothes and sensible shoes, she went downstairs just as tea was being served in the library. As they put on their coats, Bea said she wouldn't join them. "I need to attend to correspondence with some of my orphanage leavers and I've been ignoring Robert Schumann for the last fortnight."

After crossing Weybridge Road, they approached Addlestone station. Since no trains were due, the gates were open to allow the public to walk across the tracks. To Louise's eye, Station Road wasn't terribly interesting. For the most part, it was lined with shops and businesses. There were a few late Victorian detached houses that had been converted into flats. They passed the police station just before reaching Crouch Oak Lane. Louise started to turn right, but Dorothy insisted they continue and view the church in the afternoon sun.

St Paul's was laid out in the traditional cruciform with the tower to the north and the chancel to the east. She found it both enchanting and intimate unlike the great cathedrals she had visited in England, Germany, France, and Italy. She especially loved the way sunlight illuminated the stained glass windows to the west.

As it was getting late, they retraced their steps and turned left into Crouch Oak Lane. The trunk was hollow and some twenty feet in girth. One branch was propped up with an iron post much like a crutch.

Louise asked Humphrey, "Is it dying?"

"No, just ancient. Experts from the nearby RHS gardens at Wisley were here last year. They said it'd see us all out."

As previously arranged, the footman arrived with the Daimler to take them back to Woburn. At the station, the gates were down preventing traffic from using the level crossing. A small group of pedestrians, a number of bicyclists, and several motorcars waited while two commuter trains passed heading south to New Haw and Byfleet. Another made its way north to London Blackfriars.

After changing for dinner, they met up in the library and found a cheerful blaze bubbling away in the corner fireplace. Dorothy looked tired after the long walk. Bea was nowhere to be seen. Jarvis explained she's gone to the orphanage concerning some sort of crisis.

Over aperitifs, Humphrey discussed tomorrow's golf match. "Since the War, we've allowed ladies on the course weekdays and Saturdays but obviously not on Sundays. Two chaps have challenged me to a contest of four-ball match play. Tee time is half nine so I'm going to have an early night."

Once alone, they sat in front of the remains of the fire. Louise leaned her head against his shoulder. "My darling James, I can't tell you how happy I am. For the first time in my life I feel I belong."

"You do, my dearest. You belong with me and will forever be part of my world and my family."

Louise thought he couldn't have put it better. She was particularly glad he hadn't said you belong to me.

7

SATURDAY, OCTOBER 13TH, WOBURN

As the shooting season began on October 1ˢᵗ, pheasant was on the menu. Humphrey said, "Smalbridge, our farm manager and his son, bagged this brace on our land at Chertsey Meads."

In the library after dinner, Humphrey recounted their golfing triumph. Before their match, he told Louise to keep an eye on their opponents who had a reputation for bending the rules whenever they had half a chance.

"When I collected my winnings, they actually accused me of cheating by bringing in a ringer. I told them Louise was about to become my granddaughter."

Just as Louise was settling into her bed with de Balzac's *La Comédie Humaine*, she heard a quiet tap on her door. After a long embrace, they sat together on the sofa at the end of her four-poster.

"I'm not sure you realise how much today's victory meant to my grandfather. Those two scoundrels regard him as an easy mark. Thanks to you, he's got his own back and what's more, fleeced them, royally. Those golfing spivs apparently thought having a woman as his playing partner would ensure their victory so they trebled their usual ten Guinea bet."

"Let's not talk about those bounders. Just hold me while I take in the reality of having fallen in love with you and being accepted into your family."

She stretched her feet out on the couch and rested her head on his lap. James bent down to kiss her. They remained there until both were nodding off.

James said, "This won't do. In the morning, we've got to look presentable to meet the vicar."

"My love, I'm just happy to be falling asleep with you holding me in your arms."

He carried her back to her bed, tucked her in, and kissed her goodnight.

Following breakfast of kippers, soft-boiled eggs, and toast, the footman drove them to St Paul's. By this time, she'd learned his name was Peets. Humphrey led her to the family's box pew while the church filled with at least a hundred worshipers. Bea had donned her robes to join the Chancel Choir.

Dorothy put her gloved hand on Louise's arm and whispered, "Reverend Paterson has been with us only four years. It's his first appointment."

Louise found the sermon surprising for this rural and presumably conservative setting. His themes were sharing, universal education, help for the poor, tolerance towards other religions, and non-violence. He was forthright when he asserted, "War is incompatible with the teachings of Jesus."

And later, "A true Christian should never support nor justify violence."

She knew there was a substantial school of thought within the Anglican Church that viewed war in this way. Another part of the C of E establishment supported the Augustinian Just-War Theory. She wondered how Humphrey, as a retired army Colonel and local leader of the Tory party, viewed the vicar's staunch defence of pacifism. When the choirmaster chose Onward Christian Soldiers as the final hymn, she accepted there was a schism within the parish establishment, the young vicar opposing the more traditional views of the curate and obviously the organist. These were confusing times, but she found comfort that there was at least a dialogue occurring that could impact the congregation.

After the service, the family stood in front of the church greeting local friends while James had a quiet word with Rev Patterson. The vicar said, "I've a few minutes just now. If you'd care to join me in my vestry, we can discuss your wedding plans."

Once in his office, the minister shook hands with Louise. "I'm pleased to welcome a new face in our congregation."

"I so enjoyed your lesson. I must say, I'm glad to hear the Church's views expressed so eloquently."

"I fear my sermons are somewhat modern for Addlestone."

Humphrey objected. "Not at all, sir. For those of us who've experienced war, we'd do anything to avoid another."

For some minutes, Humphrey and the vicar discussed the consequences of war and possible justifications for armed conflict. Louise smiled inwardly, enjoying the interchange and eventual common ground found between a pragmatist and a pacifist.

James returned to the purpose of their visit. "We were thinking of mid-July next year for our nuptials."

The vicar opened a leather bound diary headed 1935. "Saturday July 13th and July 20th are both available."

"Can you give us a week to decide?"

"Of course, I doubt there'll be a rush of applications fully nine months ahead."

Peets drove them to the George Inn for a post-service drink. The main bar had low ceilings and blackened oak beams so that James and Humphrey had to duck their heads as they entered from the car park in the rear. As it was Sunday, it was packed with patrons. Humphrey introduced Louise to the landlord, Charles Hall. He nodded towards a corner table by the front window that had just been vacated by a group of locals.

Humphrey said, "Charles, good of you to find us a place."

James knew full well the men had been shifted and made to stand at the bar. The landlord followed them to their table. "Well, sirs and ladies, what can I get you?"

Humphrey and James ordered pints of Weybridge bitter while Dorothy and Louise chose dry sherry. Bea opted for a glass of barley water and asked Louise about their meeting with the Vicar.

"We've been offered two dates in July."

"Would you mind awfully if I were to invite a few of my unmarried lady friends? I'd really like to ask my closest friend Rose Gregory who lives just down the road on Woburn Hill."

"You must, but if it's of any interest to the ladies, James will be inviting some strapping young fellows. Some are from his first and second boats, his pals from King's, and a few of his old Alleynian schoolmates."

"You do realise so many young officers perished in the Great War."

It was obvious Bea was embarrassed discussing dating and men. James changed the subject and asked her about the flap at the orphanage.

"Oh, it was nothing. I'd lost contact with two of our leavers. Letters I'd sent were returned unopened. When I checked their files, they'd changed jobs and digs from those I'd arranged. I'll look them up when I get the chance."

After lunch, they went upstairs to pack and returned carrying their overnight bags. When Jarvis fetched her clubs, she thanked him, noticing her shoes and clubs had been cleaned.

8

MONDAY, NOVEMBER, 5TH, CAMBRIDGE

Over the last three weeks, James and Louise had become constant daytime companions apart from those times when academic commitments took precedent. Long walks along the Backs and meals at country pubs made the time pass quickly. He'd attended a few meetings of the Apostles and decided Keynes's concerns were groundless. He found them a rather silly lot with little intellectual devotion to Marxist-Leninist dialectical materialism. His tutorials were progressing at a ferocious pace and he'd mastered many of the areas he'd struggled with last year. What's more, he was glad Richard hadn't mentioned anything further about spying.

Tonight, was Guy Fawkes Night. Throughout the week, local children pestered everybody in town by shouting, 'Penny for the Guy', as they dragged hastily constructed effigies of the traitor in wagons. In 1605, Fawkes attempted to destroy the Houses of Parliament by placing barrels of gunpowder in a rented basement room. For some bizarre reason, this so-called Gunpowder Plot had become an annual celebration.

They arranged to meet at dusk at Scholars' Place, a field on the far side of the Cam behind King's. Locals had gathered beams and branches to erect a huge bonfire. As the flames took hold there was an enormous explosion, sparks shooting thirty feet into the air. Louise's eyes rolled back into her head, her legs buckled, and she collapsed in a heap. James helped her up and held her in his arms. When he asked about her fainting spell, she shivered but was unable to reply.

By the time the bonfire had been reduced to embers, she had returned to her usual self. They walked the half-mile to Newnham where staff served mulled wine to celebrate the occasion. Louise introduced James to a number of her friends and also to Miss Sybil Fergusson, her Modern Languages tutor. He also met the Principal of Newnham College, Miss Joan Strachey. After the usual formalities, Miss Strachey led him towards a sofa in a quiet corner of the reception room.

"James, I understand you and Louise are engaged to be married. I wanted this little chat, partly to ensure you've the best of intentions towards her. You must be aware she's quite fragile and that's not simply because she's an orphan. I expect you've noticed, she appears to exude strength and determination almost to the point of arrogance."

"I've found that puzzling, although I know what it's like to lose one's parents at an early age. Do you think that explains her haughty attitude?"

Miss Strachey declined to comment. Instead she said, "I've done my own snooping and discovered you're a forthright young man with a fine academic reputation. I also hear tell you're never short of female companionship. From now on, I trust you'll devote your undivided attentions to Louise. What she desperately needs is stability in her life and somebody she can place her trust. I'm sure she'll eventually learn to embrace the more usual social graces that are expected of women these days. If I may, I'd like to offer my blessing on your engagement and future marriage."

"We've now settled on July 20th and hope you'll attend."

"I wouldn't miss it for the world. She's one of my favourite young ladies, although I'm not supposed to express preferences."

Louise approached and put her arm through his. "The party's breaking up so you really should return to King's."

He nodded, aware that his tutorial was only a few hours away. They said their goodnights and embraced just inside Newnham's gatehouse. Walking back, he realised he was glad to have met both Miss Ferguson and Miss Strachey. However, the Principal's comments raised more questions than answers. The same was true of Louise's reaction to the gunpowder explosion. He decided that without further knowledge, it was fruitless to speculate as to the causes of her petit mal seizure.

Two weeks later, he had his final tutorial of the Michaelmas term. It was spent working on topology since he'd attended four lectures on that subject over the past fortnight. Richard handed him a detailed schedule of topics and problems he should tackle over the Christmas break.

"Before the New Year, we'd like you to visit Vienna, Munich and Berlin. You should provide us with a written report of your impressions of both countries."

"Normally, I'd be happy to oblige, but I plan to spend the vac with Louise. She has no family and I wouldn't wish to abandon her during the holidays."

"Then invite her along. Let me remind you, you're not to let on you're working for HM Government."

9

FRIDAY, NOVEMBER 30ᵀᴴ, PARIS

They encountered only light traffic on the north circular on their way down to Woburn. Louise said, "Darling, don't you think it's time you told me why you insisted I bring my passport?"

"I know you love surprises. I'm taking you to Vienna to celebrate our engagement."

"If you've no objections, I'd love to spend the first night in Paris?"

A week later, they motored to Dover and took the ferry service launched a few years ago by Captain Stuart Townsend. Using a decommissioned minesweeper, the company transports passengers and their motorcars between Dover and Calais.

After checking into their suite at the George V, they went downstairs to the magnificent Salon Louis XIII dining room. When the waiter arrived, James used his rusty schoolboy French to order Kir Royales. Examining the menu, both decided to start with six Brittany oysters followed by the hotel's famed chateaubriand.

Louise intercepted the carte des vins the waiter offered to James and spent some minutes examining the choices. "While I greatly admire your grandfather's cellar, I've spotted a couple of interesting possibilities. Could you beckon the sommelier?"

A rather distinguished gentleman arrived at their table. A silver tastevin hung around his neck by a red silk ribbon. Louise asked his opinion about two Burgundy wines, the 1920 Gevrey-Chambertin Grand Cru and the 1924 Morey-Saint-Denis Premier Cru. After some discussion, she opted for the '24.

James said, "I understood most of that, but why did you chose the wine with the inferior classification?"

"The sommelier felt that although 1920 is a marvellous year for clarets, 1924 Burgundies are now being rated as outstanding with the potential of becoming the vintage of the century. I've also read Morey-Saint-Denis produces some interesting wines but I'm not sure where that hamlet is located in the Coté d'Or."

Back in their suite, they stared at the large four-poster.

"James darling, we need to get a few things clear now that we're about to share a room."

"I understand perfectly. I plan to sleep on the sofa in our salon."

"You are a silly goose. I've decided it's time we find out if we're suited to marriage."

Paris is aptly called The City of Light. It is also known as The City of Love. For him this seemed apropos given he had just experienced the most emotionally fulfilling night of his life.

After he'd gone into a deep sleep, Louise remained awake. 'He's an experienced lover. He's gentle and knows how to attend to a woman's needs and satisfy her desires. I must accept the past is over and focus on our future life together.'

10

SATURDAY, DECEMBER 8TH, PARIS

As dawn broke through the lace curtains, James leant on his left elbow and stroked her hair, her neck, and then her back. She turned towards him and they made slow and relaxed love before dressing for the day.

Over breakfast, he proposed plans for this morning. "Let's ride the hydraulic lift to the top of the Eiffel Tower. We can lunch at the Jules Verne restaurant and admire the Parisian skyline."

"You go if you want. I'm spending a few hours with the impressionists at the Louvre. As I very much doubt that's your cup of tea, I'd prefer to go on my own and not be rushed."

He found this abrupt, but was inwardly relieved since he had little interest in representational art.

He asked, "What about lunch?"

"I've read the Grand Louvre dining room specialises in Gascony cuisine. That would be duck or goose and their marvellous foie gras. Meet you there at two?"

After he put her into a taxi, he strolled down the Champs-Élysées and purchased yesterday's edition of the New York Herald Chicago Daily Tribune. At Rond-Point, he ordered coffee with calvados and scanned the headlines.

The lead story focussed on next month's plebiscite to be held in the industrialised and coal rich Saar. This would allow the region to become self-governing after being jointly administered by Britain and France as a condition of the Versailles Treaty. This election would pit the National Socialists against their left-wing opponents and the outcome would determine whether Hitler's power base was complete.

In Leningrad, Stalin's purge resulted in the murder some 2000 party officials.

Mussolini's forces had invaded Abyssinia and Emperor Haile Selassie lodged formal protests with the League of Nations.

US unemployment was still running at more than 20% despite the extensive New Deal programmes introduced by President Roosevelt nearly two years ago. Strong economic growth had returned after four years of recession that persisted throughout Herbert Hoover's entire term as President. In 1931, Hoover undermined any possibility of recovery by insisting Congress focus on fiscal austerity. His budget proposal demanded cuts in government expenditures to compensate for falling tax revenue. Not surprisingly, he was roundly defeated in the 1932 election, only carrying six states, and getting less than 40% of the popular vote. It was generally accepted his policies were directly responsible for the severity of what is now being called the Great Depression. James knew Keynes had visited Washington on several occasions and persuaded FDR it was flawed monetary and fiscal policies that had created the worst downturn since the Panic of 1893.

Everything appeared surprisingly normal as the capital prepared for the Christmas festivities. Historically, Parisians controlled enormous wealth although French unemployment was running at a quarter of the labour force. Factories had closed and rural poverty was widespread as agricultural prices continued the decline that began early in the last decade. Socialists had organised protests some of which had turned into violent confrontations with the gendarmerie.

He left his newspaper on the table and continued on to Place de la Concorde, down the Allée Centrale, through the Jardins des Tuileries, finally arriving at the Musée du Louvre.

Louise was waiting at the entrance to the dining room holding today's edition of Le Figaro. They were shown to a table with a view of the gardens leading down to the Seine.

Back at the George V, they had a light supper and took coffee in the hotel's lounge.

Louise said, "When you suggested I bring my passport, I decided I'd try to persuade you to take me to Burgundy. I'd dearly love to find where my family lived in the last century. I've brought along my mother's scrapbook and found a photo taken at what might be my grandparent's wedding."

She extracted a small tintype photograph from her handbag. It showed a couple in front of a building called Hôtel le Cep. On the reverse side was written, Beaune, June 1867.

11

SUNDAY, DECEMBER 9TH, BEAUNE

On the way into the breakfast room, James asked the receptionist to try to book a room at the Hôtel le Cep in Beaune for this evening. He seriously doubted this would be possible. The hotel might not be standing after the wartime destruction. If the building had survived, it might no longer be a hotel given the photograph must have been made nearly seventy years earlier.

While Louise went to their suite to finish packing, he returned to the front desk to pay the bill and collect their passports. In addition to their room, the tariff included meals and drinks as well as miscellaneous charges including local taxes and telephone calls. He was pleasantly surprised when the receptionist confirmed his Beaune reservation.

One of the uniformed staff brought his car to the sheltered forecourt. James ensured the cloth top was secure and turned the heater to its maximum setting. Rain and sleet accompanied them on their four hour journey.

After checking in to the Hôtel le Cep, they found the dining room almost deserted. That gave the headwaiter time to answer Louise's queries. "I'm looking for my family's former estates located north of Beaune. I've no idea of the name of the property, but I believe the vineyard had an impressive château."

She accepted this might be fantasy, invented by a lonely little girl trying to imagine and perhaps glorify her roots. When their waiter returned with the cheese trolley he was able to consider her question. "You should head to the Côte de Nuits. That appellation lies to the north."

After he returned to his duties, she muttered under her breath, "What a cretin. Everyone knows the Côte de Nuits is north of Beaune."

James gently suggested they might visit a local notaire. "They handle all French property transactions and might have some information concerning large estates sold sometime in the 1870s."

In the morning, the receptionist gave them directions to one of the oldest notaire in the city. A middle-aged gentleman dressed in black greeted them in the reception foyer. After Louise explained the purpose of their visit, he suggested they meet his father. James thought it highly improbable a man approaching eighty might still be practicing the laws of conveyance.

A wizened gentleman sat behind his oak desk, stacked high with papers and files. Steel rimed half-moon spectacles hung off the end of his Gallic nose.

After years of neglect, James was getting his ear tuned to the rhythm of the French language, although the local dialect had misled him on several occasions. The lawyer said he was certain his firm hadn't handled the transaction although, as a young man, he well-remembered the phylloxera outbreak. He spoke to Louise in slow, precise but somewhat strangely accented French.

"I suggest you drive to Nuits-Saint-Georges and speak with my friend, Monsieur Le Rouvillois. He's the only notaire in that village and his files date back to the Revolution."

Half an hour later, they arrived in Nuits-Saint-Georges. James spotted the Notaire's oval brass plaque over the doorway of a two-storey building. A middle-aged assistant was at his desk in the front reception and directed them to the office of Monsieur Le Rouvillois. He appeared to be approximately the same age as his Beaune colleague. James idly wondered if it was somehow embodied within Napoleonic law that French notaire were required to be octogenarians.

"My name is Louise de la Béré and this is my fiancée James Harcourt-Heath. My father was born somewhere in the Côte de Nuits but moved to England with his parents following the phylloxera outbreak in the last century. I believe they owned a château and a substantial vineyard somewhere north of Beaune. We're hoping you might have some record of local property transactions around 1880."

The elderly gentleman smiled, slumped back in his chair and appeared to fall asleep. After several minutes, James thought if he didn't move or say something fairly quickly, he should summon assistance from the outer office.

The notaire opened his eyes. "I've just reviewed my mental files and I'm familiar with the name de la Béré. My father handled that transaction when I was his apprentice. As I recall, there was a legal hiatus. Eventually, the château and much of the surrounding land was sold so family members could realise their inheritance and emigrate. The vineyard was called Clos des Chênes."

Louise was visibly excited by this news. "Could you direct us there? I'd love to have a look and make some photos."

"Bien sur, Mademoiselle."

There was a map on the wall behind his desk. He swivelled his chair and used a silver letter opener to point out the two vineyards called Clos des Chênes in the village of Morey-Saint-Denis.

"Two?"

"The present owners of the larger estate occupy the 17th century château. They wished to keep the original name, as did the owners of the smaller property. Each produced a wine called Morey-Saint-Denis, Clos des Chênes. Although that caused some confusion with amateurs, connoisseurs and négociants are well aware of their very different character. A compromise was reached after the war. The larger operation now labels their wine Château Clos des Chênes and the other uses simply Clos des Chênes. To my palate, the wine from the smaller estate is far superior to that of the larger, more commercial operation. My grandson believes the differences are solely attributable to the skills of the winemakers since the land is essentially identical."

Back in the car, Louise reminded him that the wine they enjoyed at the George V was from Morey-Saint-Denis. "If nothing else, I'll get a chance to explore this hamlet I've only read about in wine reviews."

When they entered the village, they'd spotted a large sign showing the location of each vineyard in the commune. Noting the position of Château Clos des Chênes, James reversed the car and drove to the property. Not

43

surprisingly, the gates were closed fast this time of year. When he persisted in ringing the bell and sounding his horn, a middle-aged workman approached and tipped his beret.

Louise got out of the car and spoke with the labourer. "We're English and wish to meet with the owners of this fine estate."

James noticed she'd slightly changed her accent from the one she'd used in Paris.

"Je suis désolé. Ils hivernent à Cannes."

She thanked him and they returned to the car. In case James hadn't caught the man's rapid and locally accented patois, she explained the owners were wintering in the south of France. Fetching her Kodak Brownie, she took snaps of the dormant vines and several more of the château. James's interest was in the fortified structure. It had two corner circular towers and impregnable limestone walls. It appeared to be well-maintained, no doubt with the profits from winemaking.

"Thank you, my love. You don't know how much this means to me to have found a bit of my heritage. Now, I'm done. We can return to our hotel and prepare for the next stage of our journey."

James embraced her and noticed a tear running down her cheek. "What say, we find the other vineyard? While we're here, you might make a photograph or two of the smaller operation for your scrapbook."

From his memory of the sign in the village, he found the single-track road where a faded sign read Clos des Chênes. Geographically, the two estates backed onto one another but their entrances were at opposite ends of the contiguous land.

The two-storey stone house was substantial but unpretentious. Golden brown limestone outbuildings formed an aesthetically pleasing close within the large walled and granite cobbled courtyard. James rang the bell and eventually a robust man in his sixties opened the gates.

"My name is Louise de la Béré. I'm searching for my family connections from the second half of the last century."

He stared at her in stony silence with his jaw agape. Louise was nonplussed and glanced at James. "Do you think he's mute or perhaps somewhat simple?"

Eventually, the man broke his silence. "I am Michel de la Béré. My wife would love to meet you." After a pause he added under his breath, "Revoir."

They shook hands and Louise introduced her fiancé. James was mildly surprised they shared a surname. He had no idea how common de la Béré was in France. It might be like Smith in England, Jones in Wales, or Singh and Patel on the Indian subcontinent.

Inside, a woman stood at the kitchen sink preparing vegetables for their midday meal. She turned, wiped her hands on her apron, and greeted their visitors. "My name is Louisa de la Béré. Please be seated at our table."

What transpired left everybody stunned. Louise explained what she knew about her family history. Michel shook his head and corrected her on virtually every detail. Most importantly, she learned her father wasn't an only child.

"Your father and I were identical twins. Clos de Chênes was once a single estate that had been in our family for four generations. Phylloxera and accrued debt forced the sale of the château and the bulk of our property. Only this house, barns, and the surrounding few hectares belong to us. The dispute was so fundamental, my parents separated. My mother remained here to raise me and my father took my brother and moved to England. We never spoke again. As for our business, we've a few permanent workers but produce only a modest amount of wine for sale. We've no family left in Burgundy or indeed all of France. Our two sons died as teenagers in 1916 at Verdun."

Louisa invited them to share their midday meal of coq-au-vin. While it was cooking, Michel showed them around the property. At this time of year, the hillsides were barren apart from the carefully pruned vines. Louise fetched her Brownie and made more photos. The tour lasted about an hour and they ended up in an outbuilding.

The 19th century equipment was totally different from the scores of French établissement vinicole she'd visited. There was an ancient and enormous beam press and a huge blackened oak fermentation cask. Everything looked neglected but presumably functioned to produce wine in the traditional manner. Michel entered the cave whose ceiling was festooned with cobwebs. He lit a candle and returned carrying a bottle.

Despite the wintry conditions, their dining room was cosy. A fire blazed at the far end of the room creating a welcoming atmosphere, scented with the aroma of roasting chicken, garlic, and rosemary.

The bottle Michel selected was without a label but he said it was their '06. Louise believed it was amongst the best Pinot Noir she had ever tasted. After their meal, all were in a reflective mood, stunned by what they had learned.

They thanked their hosts and returned to their hotel. Before a light supper, they walked to the town centre to admire the magnificent Hospices de Beaune.

Louise said, "One day this might become our market town."

He had an inkling as to what might have prompted this comment. This led him reflect upon Morey-Saint-Denis. He guessed there were fewer than 600 inhabitants even if one included the outlying farms and vignoble. It was an ancient hamlet with half-timbered buildings, many with cut stone entryways and granite lintels. The streets were cobbled and the kerbstones granite. Significant wealth had been here for centuries, but the excesses of the French aristocracy, so obvious in Bordeaux and along the Loire valley, hadn't spoilt the village. Morey-Saint-Denis was a working town whose primary business was winemaking.

In bed, she leant her head on his left shoulder while they discussed her family's history. She accepted the story had been altered to place her grandfather's relationships in a better light. She had learned from novels, it was not uncommon for families to sugarcoat the past omitting disparaging events such as suicide, divorce, or terminal diseases such as cancer.

"Michel and Louisa are my closest relatives. Any I might have in England are perhaps second cousins or great-aunts. Could we return in the morning? I'd like it if we were to approach our trustees and propose an investment in a vineyard in Burgundy."

"I thought you might have that in mind. It would give us an excuse to spend more time in France. What's more, it would be a project that would be ours alone, rather than a legacy from your parents or mine."

12

TUESDAY, DECEMBER 11ᵀᴴ, MOREY-SAINT-DENIS

In the morning they returned to the vineyard. Louisa didn't seem surprised and invited them into the dining room for coffee and pain perdu.

Louise said, "If you're willing, we'd like you to attend our wedding in mid-July."

Michel smiled. "Of course, we'll be there. July is quiet for us. Our permanent workers can manage any tying-in or spraying. Mid-September onwards is another matter. That's when the vendange, pressing, and primary and secondary fermentations occur."

"Michel, I'd like to know what you meant when you said Louisa would like to meet me again?"

He paused and looked down at his hands. "I hadn't meant to say that. Let me explain. It broke my heart when my brother encouraged the sale of the bulk of our property. I believe it's imprinted onto our French souls, land is always meant to remain in the family. After you were born, we were invited to your christening but I refused to go. I just couldn't bear to see my brother again. Louisa insisted she'd attend to represent our family. We had a terrible row that came close to ending our marriage. I've regretted that decision for the last twenty years."

Michel picked up his serviette, wiped a tear from his eye and took a deep breath to regain his composure. He reached for his wife's hand and they exchanged smiles.

"Louisa travelled to Winchester and was welcomed by my brother and his wife. Our father had passed away some years previously, as had my mother. Last night I found the photograph of your christening."

Michel opened a photo album sitting on the dining table. He showed them a picture of an infant swaddled in a lace christening gown. She recognised her parents in the photograph from other images in her album. Standing next to them was a man dressed in clerical robes she assumed was the Bishop of Winchester. Louise was stunned and wondered why this photo was not in her scrapbook. She was about to learn why.

Michel then showed her the christening announcement and invitation. These were new to her as well.

Louisa explained. "You were ten months old when I made that photograph. Your parents were so pleased I'd attended, they named you Margaret Louise. So, it's no coincidence we share a Christian name. I can't tell you how moved I was by that gesture. As you can see from the invitation, the ceremony took place Sunday, April 7th, 1912. The Titanic set sail the following Wednesday. They told everybody they'd leave for Southampton that evening to join her maiden voyage. When we read of the tragedy, I naturally assumed you'd gone with them. To offer our condolences, I wrote to their Winchester residence."

She pulled out a yellowed sealed envelope from a pocket in the back of the photo album. It had been returned unopened and was stamped in bold lettering, NOT KNOWN AT THIS ADDRESS.

Michel said, "One more thing you should know. As we were your nearest blood relatives, Louisa agreed we would serve as your godparents."

With tears in her eyes, Louise stood and embraced her aunt and uncle. She'd brought out her own photo album and asked about the couple in front of the Hôtel le Cep.

Her uncle put on his spectacles. "Those are my parents on their wedding day."

Michel showed her other photos of her grandparents as well as her father as a child. Louise decided the time was right to broach their proposal. "Because James was orphaned when he was four, family is extremely important to us. We'd like to invest in your vineyard so the equipment can be updated and production increased. James has experience of the financial side of running a working agricultural estate. After our wedding we could spend part of the year with you, helping out, primarily by transferring funds, as you felt necessary. Our overriding objective would be to keep Clos des Chênes in our family forever. How that comes about will be up to you and your legal advisors. I know this appears presumptuous but I can assure you we're not dilettantes."

Looking directly at James, Michel issued a caution. "Si vous voulez faire une petite fortune dans le commerce du vin, commencer avec un grand."

James wasn't able to follow his rapid French so Louise explained. "He's warning us to make certain of our motives. The direct translation of this aphorism is, if you want to make a small fortune in the wine business, you'd best start with a large one."

Louise turned to Michel. "While we're speaking about wine, could you arrange for a couple of cases of your pre-war Pinot to be shipped to James's grandfather's house."

James handed Michel his card. "Please charge me for the wine, shipping, and insurance."

Michel consulted a leather-bound ledger. Once the price for two cases of 1900 was determined, James handed over a bundle of francs and they shook hands. "I'm going to add a case of our '24 to the shipment as a wedding gift to my niece and her future husband."

13

WEDNESDAY, DECEMBER 12TH, MUNICH

At his final tutorial of the Michaelmas term, Richard had instructed him to report his impressions of Munich, the Nazi's spiritual homeland. While they snuggled in bed, James said, "Munich is about halfway to Vienna. What say we stop there tomorrow night?"

"Brill. My Hochdeutsch is excellent, but my Bavarian accent and idioms can always use a brush-up."

After breakfast, the receptionist booked a suite for them in a top-class hotel in central Munich. While James fetched the car, Louise completed their packing and had a porter take their cases to the front lobby. When he settled the bill, he idly noted the inclusion of meals, local taxes, and telephone charges.

Within the first hour, they'd passed through Dijon and by lunchtime reached the Vosges mountains. After that, they skirted Switzerland and crossed the Rhine into Germany.

At the border, it was sleeting heavily. Several armed soldiers brusquely ordered them to stand aside while they searched the Railton and their luggage. As they returned to their car, the guards raised their right arms in the air, palm forward and shouted in unison, "Heil Hitler."

James and Louise were too dumfounded by this mechanical action to even consider what it might signify or how they should react.

Once in Munich, they spotted a soldier in a smart black uniform. Louise asked if he could direct them to the Hotel München Palace. He did so, saluted, and barked, "Heil Hitler."

"James, I didn't once encounter that bizarre greeting last summer. I expect that raised arm salute with the palm forward has its roots in the pomp and circumstance of the Roman Empire. Do you know what else is strange? It's identical to the Bellamy Salute. That's what American school children are required to use every morning when they pledge allegiance to their flag. Might the Nazi's have pinched it from the Americans?"

Louise knew Bavaria was staunchly Catholic so wasn't surprised when the hotel receptionist frowned when inspecting their passports. Upstairs, James rang room service and asked for a bottle of Champagne. Louise grabbed the 'phone and added toast and liverwurst paté to the order. After finishing their snack and the Taittinger '24, they made love while listening to the comforting sound of rain beating against the windowpanes.

Bavarian breakfast is nothing if not hearty. On offer were boiled, salted, and smoke-cured ham plus a baffling array of hard cheeses. These were served with sliced semi-sweet hard black bread. Louise said this rye bread from Westphalia is called pumpernickel. Although he found this breakfast odd, he had no complaints since they'd missed dinner.

Over coffee, James asked, "Join me in a stroll around town?"

"Thank you, no. I'm in dire need of some culture. I plan to visit the Glockenspiel at the new town hall and then the 14th century Munich Residenz, a former royal palace of the Wittelsbach monarchs."

James remained silent. He was not well-pleased his suggestions had twice been dismissed out of hand. They arranged to meet at noon at the entry gates to the Englischer Garten where the hotel's receptionist said they could find restaurants and Bierstuben.

James first walked to the Angel of Peace (Friedensengel) bronze monument and crossed the Isar river. He was struck by how many uniformed men were out and about despite the freezing temperatures. These ranged from officers in black uniforms to the earth-brown garb of enlisted men. There were numerous male children also in uniforms.

Individuals and groups greeted each other with the same straight-arm salute and shouts of "Heil Hitler".

When he didn't respond in kind, he was given sour looks and was even berated by an old woman. He passed several boarded up shops, which struck him as odd given the apparent prosperity of the regional capital. Stopping for a stein of lager in a Bierstube, he noticed two signs posted at the entrance: Juden Werden Hier Nicht Bedient and Juden Zutritt Verboten. He'd an inkling of their meaning but as with the salute and the shuttered businesses, he'd ask Louise over lunch.

When they met in a small restaurant, both ordered bratwurst and sauerkraut. While waiting for their meal, he asked her about the signs and the closed shops. "The posted notices prohibit Jews from being served or even entering the premises. The shuttered businesses were likely formerly owned by Jews and had been closed down by SA riff-raff."

"SA?"

"It's the initialism for the Sturmabteilung which translates as Stormtroopers. These Brownshirts form the paramilitary wing of the Nazi Party. They're a violent and bigoted lot who assault protesters at Hitler's rallies and are encouraged to actively, independently, and illegally rid the country of foreign influences. This has been primarily directed at Jews and Romas, their homes, and businesses."

"What about that bizarre Heil Hitler greeting?"

"I've just read an editorial in this morning's Nazi party's propaganda newspaper Völkischer Beobachter. It was apparently mandated a few months ago and is called the Hitlergruß. Special courts are being set up to fine those who fail to comply."

"I also saw a number of boys in uniforms."

"They are the Hitler-Jugend, much like the Boy Scouts in Britain and America. Actually, I've read that last year, Hitler banned the Scouts as well as Catholic boys' groups."

Over dinner he raised his glass of wine to her health. "Next stop, Vienna. It's a magical city especially at Christmas. There are concerts and, of course, the Vienna Boys' Choir."

"My darling, I'm blissfully happy to be looked after. I've always had to make my own travel arrangements and never dared share my experiences with anyone. Travelling with my lover has been my dream for as long as I can remember."

14

FRIDAY, DECEMBER 14ᵀᴴ, VIENNA

Neither was interested in the hard cheese, ham, or black bread on offer at breakfast. While Louise had a bath and finished packing, James asked the receptionist to reserve a suite in a top-class hotel in Vienna. Richard had instructed him to take the pulse of the fiercely independent Austrians explaining that last January their government banned the Nazi Party. His tutor intimated, they would likely provide a major challenge to Hitler's oft-stated goal of uniting the German speaking Europeans. He waited at the front desk while she booked the Hotel Sacher on Philharmonikerstraße. When she presented the bill, he noticed charges had been added for meals, local taxes, and several telephone calls to Vienna.

Although it was snowing heavily, they experienced a twenty-minute delay at the border while uniformed soldiers thoroughly searched their car. When the Hitlergruß was given, they raised their arms in an attempt to imitate the soldier's mechanical actions.

The six hour drive from Munich was a strain due to the perpetual rain and sleet. Along the way, Louise asked, "Might we catch a concert this evening? I've read there will be Christmas music at the Town Hall Saturday afternoon and we must get tickets for the Sunday concert of the Vienna Boys Choir."

Once in their hotel room James reclined on the canopied bed. "I'm knackered. I'm going to have a bit of a kip. Join me?"

"Actually, no. I'm going to the Belvedere Palace to see Gustav Klimt's paintings of his companion, Emilie Flöge. You could come along. I'm certain you'd find his images romantic."

Ignoring her suggestion, he undressed and got under the covers. He was disappointed his amorous invitation had again been spurned in favour of some unknown Austrian dauber. When he awoke, she was sitting on the window seat reading the Wiener Zeitung. She undressed and joined him in bed for the rest of the afternoon.

Downstairs, they approached the concierge. Louise asked if he could procure tickets for whatever music was being offered at the Philharmonic across the street. The receptionist shook his head, explaining tickets were impossible to come by during the holidays. When James slipped him several silver five-schilling pieces, he nodded and made a telephone call. Smiling, he told them tonight's concert was Brahms's, 'Ein Deutsches Requiem'.

He dressed in black tie and she wore an evening dress with a mink stole to protect against the elements on the short walk to the concert hall. The performance lasted just over an hour. They left in a mood of reflective ecstasy having held hands during the entire seven movements.

Over breakfast, they made plans for today, which would involve Christmas shopping and the carol concert. On Kärntnerstraße they found a small shop that specialised in woollens. As their space was limited, Louise thought scarves would make ideal gifts for the ladies of the family. The Geiger creations were nearly five feet long, made of soft Austrian lamb's wool, and tightly knitted in solid colours. Next, they entered Kohlmarkt, a collection of small specialist shops under the same roof. Near the entrance, they spotted a silversmith whose designs were in the Art Deco style currently popular around the capitals of Europe. Louise selected three brooches with coloured enamel inlay she thought would complement the scarves.

They arrived at the Town Hall after the concert had begun. That didn't seem to matter since people entered and left during the performance. They found seats near the front and listened to traditional seasonal favourites including 'Stille Nacht, Heil'ge Nacht', 'O Tannenbaum', and a beautiful

Austrian lullaby 'Still, Still, Still'. For this last song, local children joined the adult choir. Although it was dark by the time they left, street and Christmas lights illuminated Stephansplatz creating a festive and romantic atmosphere.

Supper at their hotel was well-prepared and delicious. James chose Weiner Schnitzel and Louise opted for Goulach mit Semmelknödel. As had become their habit in Paris, they fed bites to each other, reaching across the table with their forks to share their impressions of each other's choices.

Other diners gave them stern looks but they didn't care. Louise decided this was not only the most romantic day of her life but also her happiest. She and James simply enjoyed each other's company although she had read in novels that travel invariably places strains on relationships. She vowed to be more attentive to his needs and hoped she could keep this promise to herself.

Sunday afternoon they walked to the Hofburg Chapel. Only a pianist accompanied the twenty-five boys dressed in sailor suits. As it was close to Christmas, it was no surprise seasonal music dominated the programme. The final song was Franz Shubert's, 'Ave Maria' sung by a boy soprano.

Walking back to their hotel, they spotted a cosy-looking family restaurant. It was dusk, so they decided to have, for them, an early meal and retire at a reasonable time. Tomorrow they'd spend the entire day in the car to reach Berlin.

Over coffee, she got up the nerve to broach a subject that had dominated her thoughts for years. She reached for his hand across the table as they waited for the bill. "What do you think about children?"

He wasn't sure of her meaning. She had a serious expression so he decided against a flippant reply. "Are you asking me, do I want children?"

"We've never discussed this."

"I have two sisters, but I've always missed my parents. My grandparents were wonderful, but it wasn't the same. So, yes, I'd love to have children, but only with you, my darling."

"I'm certain we'd make good parents. Our devotion to each other would be apparent to the little ones."

She paused with a tear in her eye and said in a barely audible whisper, "I have a confession. When I was thirteen, I was riding my bicycle outside

Winchester. A lorry's nearside tyre burst just as it passed. There was an enormous explosion. A piece of rubber knocked me off the carriageway and I ended up in the verge wrapped around a tree.

"Of course, the driver stopped. He hailed a passing motorist who found a call box and rang for an ambulance. Eventually, I was taken to hospital and treated for abrasions, a broken leg, and some internal bleeding. The attending surgeon said there was a strong likelihood the damage to my pelvis would either prevent conception or I'd be unable to carry a foetus to full term."

He started to interrupt but she stopped him, putting her open hand on his cheek. "My guardian sent me to a Swiss clinic to recover and that's how I lost a year of my schooling. It was those months that fostered my love of spoken languages. I was cared for by Swiss, German, Italian, and French speaking doctors and Spanish and Portuguese nurses. Everybody was so wonderful that I decided I needed to develop my language skills in order to get to know them and thank them properly."

He recalled her reaction to the explosion on Bonfire Night and Miss Strachey's comment about her vulnerability. Seeing him pause, she became fearful of his reaction and tears welled up in her eyes.

"My dear, I do understand. There's always adoption. We know from my sister's work, there must be thousands of orphanage children who deserve to be part of a loving family."

"Please don't hate me."

He was beginning to appreciate the source of her insecurity. "Like every couple, we'll have to take our chances."

She started to speak, but he wasn't finished. "Should we adopt, I'm not of the school that thinks children should be played with like puppies while they're cute and then relegated to a nurse and nanny until they're packed off to boarding school at six. I went through that and I can tell you I've always longed for my parents and family. Mind you, I'm not attaching blame. During the war, Humphrey was away most of the time working at the MOD. He either stayed at Boodles, his London club, or was at Brooklands at all hours of the day and night. At the same time, Dorothy volunteered as a nurse at Weybridge Community Hospital. Boarding school does some good as far as academics go, but it can inflict permanent damage by making children cold and distant. That often becomes a pattern which carries over into their adult lives. At Dulwich, many of my classmates in Blew House cried themselves to sleep night after night."

Louise grasped his hands. "Like you, I was raised by strangers and sent to boarding school at six. I was desperately unhappy at St Swithun's, so much so that I now realise, I erected barriers against my fellow students and teachers to avoid getting hurt or disappointed. I feigned indifference to other's opinions and my Newnham friends tell me that has become an unfortunate habit preventing me from developing close relationships."

James wondered if this was part of the reason, she regularly attempts to impress everybody with her knowledge of wine and etymology to the point of being embarrassingly boastful.

She wasn't finished. "You, my darling, are the very first person I've been able to trust and share my thoughts and feelings about that period of my life. My men friends didn't want to know and I wasn't about to reveal anything personal about myself or my childhood. I simply couldn't trust their motives or their discretion."

She paused to finish her lukewarm coffee. "You are a man and having children might be something you desire for societal reasons. I can't speak for other women, but for me, being a mother has become an emotional and biological imperative. When I was injured at thirteen, I'd already experienced my first episode of the curse, my hips were getting wider, and my breasts were filling out. Physiological and hormonal changes are designed to make us capable of giving birth and nurturing our children. I expect all women recognise from an early age that childbearing is our biological destiny. Even the erogenous zones are there to encourage us to want to have intercourse. The physical changes in men at puberty; more body hair, a deeper voice, and a more prominent Adam's apple are minor as compared with ours. Please try to understand. The likelihood of my inability to bear children, has dominated my thoughts since I was thirteen."

Tears were now flowing down both cheeks. He got up from their meal and tossed some banknotes on the table. He helped her into her coat and they left the restaurant with his arm around her shoulders. Both were aware this evening had been an epiphany in their relationship.

15

TUESDAY, DECEMBER 18ᵀᴴ, BERLIN

They checked into the Grand Hotel Bellevue. Dinner gave them an opportunity to share their first impressions of the German capital. Both agreed the most disturbing sight was the proliferation of large red and black flags with the Hakenkreuz symbol. These were hung on staffs or draped vertically from windows and balconies in front of virtually every building they passed.

After a restful night accompanied by some pleasant intimacy, they dressed in warm clothes and went down for breakfast. It was the usual ham, hard cheese, and rye bread they'd encountered in Munich. James said, "What I wouldn't give for a kipper, a three-minute egg with soldiers, and a nice cuppa? What say, we head for the Brandenburg Gate."

"I'm going to Museum Island. I've read the Altes has the Prussian royal family's art collection and the Bode specialises in paintings and sculpture."

James said nothing and stared at the basket of rye bread. Louise was puzzled by his silence and failed to see why she should alter her plans.

After yesterday's eight-hour drive from Vienna, they agreed to stretch their legs to walk off some of their heavy meals. He joined her as they ambled towards the two museums. About a mile from their hotel, they entered the Tiergarten, a large park in the centre of Berlin. As in Munich, it was filled with numerous young men in uniforms and boys in Hitler-Jugend garb. Despite the freezing temperatures the children wore shorts and knee length white woollen socks. Everybody looked happy and prosperous apart from some elderly men who shuffled along with their eyes cast downwards.

James asked about this apparent incongruity. "After the Röhm Putsch, Hitler put Victor Lutze in charge of the SA. He treats it like his private army. Their mission is to exclude Jews, Romas, and Eastern Europeans from all aspects of German life. Formed at the end of the Great War, the SA now has over three million members, thirty times more than the entire German military establishment. Of course, that's partially due to the restrictions built into the Versailles Treaty."

"They're a bit like Mosley's Blackshirts who regard themselves above British law and regularly terrorise immigrants, Gypsies, and Jews."

"Exactly. Joseph Goebbels, the Minister of Propaganda, is cracking down on Jewish composers and has banned their music. The Brownshirt rabble have been given tacit freedom to burn non-approved books in public squares."

Louise pointed towards group of teenaged girls who walked by in military order. "They're the Bund Deutscher Mädel, much like the Girl Scouts in the US and UK. The Nazi's have a clear message for women. They're to stay at home to be good wives and mothers while their husbands support the family. The primary and secondary educational system has been adjusted to promote these goals. This discrimination is not unique to Germany. During the current Depression, the Marriage Bar has been the custom the US and the UK. Despite the fact that women's pay is only half that of men for the same job, it's become an accepted practice that women aren't hired if there are qualified men available. Indeed, women teachers are being forced to resign when they marry. I've also read, the German government is offering subsidies to enable elite Nazi Party families to aim for four children. Orphanages are state funded and adoptions are being encouraged so older couples can reach this quota."

Apart from the obvious gender discrimination, James thought this might have a sinister side. Richard had once suggested that as Germany expanded its borders, Hitler would need more Aryan Germans to populate the acquired territories. For obvious reasons, he had his eye on the fertile lands, raw materials, and industrial infrastructure to the east. Louise said this strategy had been promoted in the German press and called Lebensraum or living space.

He was surprised by her interest in these developments until he remembered her strong condemnation of the Nazis last October.

It was as if she read his thoughts. "Tell me, James, is there any reason you're paying such close attention to European politics?"

"I suppose it's an idle diversion from maths."

He knew his reply was pathetic. He found this duplicity intolerable and vowed to raise his concerns at his first tutorial of the Lent term and, if necessary, resign from MI6.

James had no interest whatsoever in any royal family's art collection so begged off from her first museum. He bought the Sunday Telegraph and found a cosy Bierstube to kill time. As arranged, they met on the museum steps and headed towards the Bode.

As they'd walked miles, it seemed natural to stop for a midday meal. The museum was reputed to have a top-rated dining room so they opted for this rather than the usual sausage available in a tavern.

While Louise viewed the exhibits, he walked around looking at the building's interior and especially admired the magnificent domed ceiling. Glancing back, he noticed her chatting with various strangers and assumed it was connected with her interest in spoken German.

They walked towards their hotel just as council workers were lighting the gas streetlights. Louise was in a pensive mood. "I don't like this Germany. It's so different from last summer when I immersed myself in their language, culture, and music. Their overt militarism scares me."

They stopped at a small restaurant. While the waiter filled their wine glasses, Louise asked, "Have you heard of Konrad Lorenz?"

"Isn't he a German who conducts research into animal behaviour?"

"Actually, he's Austrian and has become the darling of the Nazi Party. His study of wolves focusses on pack hierarchy. Female wolves become the property of the alpha male who establishes his authority over the lesser-ranked males through fights and snarls. Lorenz asserts this benefits the species as a whole since the pack leader's presumed superior genes are passed onto the next generation through his mates' offspring. The Nazi Party has embraced his publications to support their idea of the natural order of society. They regard Aryan Germans as genetically destined to control the inferior races to the east which includes Jews, Gypsies, Slavs, and presumably everyone else."

"I wonder if that's even an accurate description of wolf pack behaviour. Who's to say an aggressive wolf is smarter or hardier? He may just be a nasty piece of work, demented, or even rabid. Despite the fact that Jews and Romas represent less than 1% of the German population, Hitler has apparently selected them as convenient targets."

"James, my darling, I've had enough. Can we leave in the morning?"

"Right you are."

After paying the bill, they walked towards their hotel. It was dusk, the shops had closed, and the streets were becoming deserted apart from the usual groups of drunken soldiers, shouting slogans and singing as they swaggered down the centre of the pavement. James and Louise were forced to either step into the gutters or press themselves against the adjacent buildings to let them pass.

Safely back in their suite, Louise unfolded the Michelin map on the duvet. "Do you think we could make it to France tomorrow?"

"That'd be a push. It must be some 500 miles. Even under ideal conditions, it would take at least ten hours. Don't forget it's winter and the roads might be dicey and then there's the usual delay with border inspections. We could try but it'll mean a very long day in the car."

"I don't care. I simply can't bear to spend another night in this dreadful country."

Louise punched her finger on the town of Metz. "It's just over the French border and has a 3000-year history. I expect you'd like St Stephen's Cathedral. It's 13th century Gothic."

Given their early bedtime, they were up and dressed before seven. Downstairs, James asked the receptionist to book a hotel in Metz. He smiled when she recommended the Hôtel de la Cathedrale. He told her to make the reservation as he paid their bill.

16

THURSDAY, DECEMBER 20TH, METZ

After eleven hours on the road and the expected delay at the border, they crossed the border into France. They checked in to their hotel and once in their room, she flopped backwards onto the duck down duvet.

"You know, James, I've always admired the Prussians. Their music, art, culture, scientific innovation, and industrial technology have led the world for centuries. Did you know Germans have won 39 Nobel Prizes since the first one was awarded in 1901? Top of that list is Albert Einstein who won the physics prize in 1921. Of course, he and many other laureates were Jews. Right now, Germans follow Hitler's every whim, even though it must be patently obvious, the party's message is socially divisive and culturally racist. I simply don't understand how this could happen in what is historically a blink of an eye. They're neither sheep nor fools."

He repeated the argument he'd put to Richard last October. "Perhaps it's their lack of experience with democratic processes."

"Yes, I see. Hitler seems to possess the cunning of a huckster. He's able to tap into their collective anger at having been defeated in the war and their humiliation at Versailles. Hitler was released from jail in 1924 after serving a nine month sentence for high treason. This was for his attempted coup d'état, for what's called the Beer Hall Putsch. It was while he was incarcerated at Landsberg Prison, he wrote Mein Kampf. He promised his semi-literate SA followers he'd make Germany great again by reclaiming Germany for what he termed the Herrenvolk."

"Herrenvolk?"

"The direct translation is Master Race."

James paused and asked, "Have you heard of George Santayana?"

She shook her head.

"He was a Spanish philosopher who taught at Harvard for a number of years. Prior to that, he lived in Berlin. At the end of the last century, he spent three years as a student at King's which is where I ran across his aphorisms. What springs to mind is: Those who cannot remember the past are condemned to repeat it."

Louise thought for a moment before replying. "That certainly applies to Nazi Germany. What's more, I believe he's suggested a universal truth. Politicians rely on the electorate having short memories. They seem willing to choose war as a diplomatic option when historical experience should convince them of the folly of that course."

After breakfast, they made a quick tour of St Stephen's. As has become their habit in churches and cathedrals, they embraced for some minutes in the light that filtered through the east-facing stained glass windows.

On their arrival at Woburn Park, the kitchen provided a light supper. Sprott helped her with her cases and Louise instructed her to launder her intimate items and iron and press her dresses and blouses so they would be ready for the morning.

Breakfast was kippers, fresh bread, and Darjeeling tea. She reminded him they still needed a Christmas present for Humphrey. "His clubs are almost antiques. I've read, Selfridges has a resident golf professional. I'm fed up sitting in a motorcar, so let's take the train to London."

They got the 11:02 to Waterloo and caught a taxi to Oxford Street. She knew the new chrome steel shafts had become popular in America a few years ago and hoped they'd have been deemed legal by the R&A. The professional confirmed her information and said that replacing the usual dimples with grooved clubfaces added accuracy, distance, and backspin. Louise thought this was just what Humphrey needed to compete with the younger members at St George's Hill. Even the names of the clubs had changed. She selected a four-wood and a driver to replace his play club and baffy. She also chose a pitching-wedge to replace his jigger and a seven iron to replace his mashie niblick. Back on Oxford Street, they agreed to go their separate ways to do some Christmas shopping and meet at the Ritz for afternoon tea.

James headed to Tiffany & Co on Old Bond Street. Scanning the array of sparkling jewellery, his eyes landed on an Art Deco sapphire, diamond and platinum bracelet. The stunning lines of square cut blue stones tapered from a larger rectangular cut sapphire in the centre.

Louise was finding it difficult to find him a personal present. Clothes were out and he already had the Rolex Oyster Humphrey gave him for his 21st. Then she remembered him dressing in black tie for the concert in Vienna. His cufflinks and studs were really quite plain and possibly hand-me-downs from his father. She headed directly for Cartier's on New Bond Street and found a set made of mother of pearl and white gold. As she was leaving, she spotted James coming out of Tiffany's. Together they walked to Piccadilly for high tea.

Back at Woburn, they found Humphrey at his desk writing a letter. "Dorothy has arranged a family dinner to celebrate your escape from enemy territory."

Just then they heard the front door bell pull. Jarvis announced the arrival of Margie and her husband, Jonathan. In front of them were two small boys of approximately equal size, each holding a hand of a middle-aged woman, obviously their nanny.

James introduced Louise and they moved into the library while Jarvis and Peets took their cases upstairs. When the ladies excused themselves to change for dinner, Nanny took the boys to the nursery on the top floor where the kitchen would supply their supper.

The men remained in the library for pre-dinner drinks. James said, "I say, Jonathan, tell me about your command."

"My ship is the HMS Harrier, a Halcyon-class mine sweeper. We patrol the Channel and the North and Irish Seas with our sister survey ship, a minehunter. We're always on the lookout for problems for passenger and merchant shipping from Kriegsmarine minelayers."

"Will you be able to stay for our Christmas celebrations?"

"After seven weeks at sea, we've been given shore leave until January 1st"

"The boys will be pleased. By the way, I know they're non-identical twins but I'm embarrassed to admit, I can't tell them apart."

"The slightly shorter one is Peter, named after my grandfather and the other is Humphrey, named after yours."

When Jarvis sounded the gong, Humphrey rose from his chair. "After all your fancy European dining, Dorothy and I thought you and Louise would like a traditional meal of roast beef, roast potatoes, Yorkshire pud, honey roasted carrots, parsnips, and apple crumble for afters."

"Just the job. French cuisine was fabulous, but Germanic grub should be avoided like the plague."

"My boy, I have a confession. I opened one of the wooden boxes that arrived addressed to you, just to have a peek, don't you know? The label says it's from Morey-Saint-Denis. I've decanted a couple of bottles. It's ten years old and I hope it goes well with the starters and our beef."

As the evening came to a close, the ladies went to their rooms. Humphrey invited James and Jonathan to join him in the library for snifters of cognac.

Humphrey asked Jonathan, "Do you think war inevitable?"

"My Admiralty briefings suggest we should expect some sort of overt German aggression possibly against their eastern neighbours. Certainly, another continental conflict that included Germany, Russia, Italy, and France would be difficult for us to ignore. These days, the Channel offers little protection against the tools of modern warfare."

"That much is clear from my stint at the MOD and Brooklands. I've known two wars at first-hand. We must do all we can to stay out of any European conflict. If the German people can't stop Hitler by reason or if international diplomacy fails to temper his aggression, then war it must be. I seriously doubt he'll stop after annexing eastern European neighbours for his so-called Fatherland. German aspirations will, once again, turn west towards the wealth of France and Switzerland. After that, he'll think, why stop there when that prosperous, complacent, and unarmed little island is just waiting across the Channel?"

17

SATURDAY, DECEMBER 22ND, WOBURN

James found Humphrey at the breakfast table reading The Times. "My boy, where did you find that marvellous wine?"

He told him about Louise's uncle and aunt and their run-down vineyard. "We hope to take a stake in the business."

"How would you manage that?"

"That will be up to you and my other trustee. For now, Louise and I would just be investors using our savings and trust incomes to upgrade and modernise the equipment."

"I suggest you contact Sir Ronald Featherstonhaugh. He was your father's colleague and your other trustee. For my part, I've no objections whatsoever should you wish to invade the capital."

"I'll ring him but only on a tentative basis. Her relatives haven't decided whether they even wish to take on partners. They have agreed to attend our wedding, but I doubt they speak any English."

"My schoolboy French is obviously a trifle rusty having been ignored for the last sixty years. Never fear, I'll be my usual cordial self."

After breakfast, James discussed plans for the day. "Louise and I are driving into Sutton to do some Christmas shopping. Bea, care to join us?"

"Yes, please. I haven't even started. I've been so busy with the orphanage's holiday preparations and the church choir."

A shopping area had just opened called Shiners Arcade. The town was also was known to have a good selection of antique shops that might provide a present or two.

The Arcade was crowded with shoppers and James tailed the ladies around a toy store. He made a few suggestions which both ladies deemed to be age inappropriate. By mutual agreement they arranged to meet at the nearby Hope public house at one o'clock.

James pottered around several antique shops just off the High Street. For his grandfather, he bought an ancient hickory shafted golf club with R. Forgan & Son, St Andrews, stamped into the wooden head. It was strangely shaped and the dealer said it was called a long-nose spoon. In another shop he purchased a pewter hip flask for Jonathan. On the front, it had the enamelled insignia of HMS Dreadnought.

At the Hope, he snagged a table and ordered a pint of bitter. Fifteen minutes later, Louise and Bea entered, burdened with packages. Louise asked for a gin and tonic and Bea requested her usual barley water.

"James, don't ask about the presents, they'll be revealed in all their glory on Christmas Day."

"Louise, our family opens presents on Christmas Eve. Grandpapa has adopted the custom of Queen Victoria's family."

Back at Woburn, Humphrey suggested the family dress for dinner. Louise donned the evening gown she'd worn in Vienna and James came down in black tie. They were now seven at the dinner table as Nanny and the twins were taking their meal in the nursery. Bea informed them that tomorrow's church service included both the adult and children's choirs and would start earlier at half ten.

When the ladies retired to the library, the dinner table conversation returned to the prospect of war. James wanted Jonathan's take on the current political situation. "Do you think the Americans would support us if we were dragged into a European conflict?"

"I've had several Admiralty briefings on precisely that question. American politicians seem to regard the rise of fascism as continental Europe's problem. The same isolationist factions that resulted in their belated entry into the Great War are still at work. Did you know their Congress just passed a series of Neutrality Acts effectively prohibiting the

US military from entering any European conflict? What's more, there's a political movement in the US using the slogan America First. They've the backing of Henry Ford, Ezra Pound, and Charles Lindbergh. In Lindbergh's speeches, he regularly attacks Jews for lobbying for a declaration of war against Germany. It's become apparent, all three men are outspoken Nazi sympathisers and anti-Semites."

When they joined the ladies in the library, James continued the political discussion. "Our National Government's platform is simply stated. Instead of engaging in an arms race against Germany and possibly Italy, Labour Party leaders propose we disarm to inspire other countries to do likewise. To my mind, that strategy is straight out of cloud-cuckoo-land. Nothing will stop the rise of fascism unless Britain, America, and the Soviets intervene to promote diplomatic solutions. Unfortunately, I seriously doubt there's sufficient popular support in America to enter a European conflict. We know nothing about Bolshevik intentions or how they might use a European conflict to their advantage. What's more, I've no idea about the strength of the anti-war feeling in Britain. If parliament choses neutrality, I fear for our small island and our way of life."

Louise slowly put down her demitasse and took a sip from her glass of Grand Marnier. "James, do pay attention. I seriously doubt appeasement has widespread support. The memory of the Great War is permanently imprinted in our psyche. Nearly a million British Empire soldiers died and there's hardly a family that didn't lose a loved one. That's not to mention those incapacitated by mustard gas, lost their eyesight or limbs, or are still suffering from shell shock. Everybody is surely aware of the Nazi threat. The Times and Telegraph editorials focus on it almost every day."

"My dear, editorials in Lord Rothermere's Mail and Mirror regularly propose either alignment with the Nazis or support the idea that we remain neutral. Their daily circulation is over four million."

Louise glared at him and left the room. He knew she hated to be contradicted.

18

SUNDAY, DECEMBER 23RD, ADDLESTONE

⸻

The Christmas service at St Paul's was well-attended, so much so that number of men were forced to stand at the back and along the west side. After the lesson, the children's choir assembled in the Sanctuary to the left of the altar. Joining the Chancel choir, they sang a cappella, 'Angels We Have Heard on High'.

Following the service, they went to the George and found their usual Sunday table unoccupied although the pub was overflowing into the back garden. The men ordered pints of local ale. The twins demanded fizzy lemonade and Nanny asked for a sweet sherry. Louise, Margie, and Dorothy requested Dubonnet and lemonade. When Bea said she'd like try one as well, there was mild surprise. The family knew she had never touched an alcoholic drink her entire life.

After the midday meal, James proposed a stroll around Victory Park. They entered the elaborate memorial gates, dedicated to the Addlestone soldiers who had died on Flanders Field in Belgium. James coaxed Louise to walk ahead of the rest of the family who were being slowed down by the boys.

"What have you done to bring Bea out of her shell? She seems like a different person, smiling and laughing more than I can remember. She's acting like a lady in her early 20's rather than a middle-aged single woman."

"She told me because of the decimation of the young officers in the Great War, there were a number of what she refers to as 'us spinsters', living in Addlestone, Chertsey, and Weybridge. There are few unattached gentlemen of her class and those of a suitable age and background had already been bagged by others.

"I'll give her a few tips on make-up and dress fashions. I told her we knew a number of Cambridge men with whom she might strike up a friendship. Also, that apart from Newnham and Girton, all the others are men's colleges. Graduate students and recently appointed Fellows regularly find it difficult to secure partners for social events. I also promised to take her up to London so we could examine the latest fashion trends and get her outfitted for Cambridge nightlife."

"You're marvellous. Since she left James Allen Girls' School, her life has been dominated by her charity work and minding our grandparents. By the way, I intend to pay you a visit this evening."

When Louise looked sceptical, he added, "We've oodles of wrapping, you know."

They returned home after only a few minutes in the park. It was cold and breezy and the twins were in a grisly mood.

After cocktails, they sat down to a light supper. For the fish course, Humphrey produced a fruity Riesling. "Since Hitler has assured the world the Alsace has finally and forever been returned to France, I don't mind drinking this Germanic style wine."

Over port, Humphrey organised the morning's activities. "After breakfast, James and Jonathan should find Smalbridge. He'll know where you can find a fir tree about eight feet tall on our estate."

Jonathan said, "My lads would love to join in. By cutting down their own tree, I expect they'd remember this Christmas for years to come."

The men joined the ladies in the library for coffee and digestives. Before Nanny took the children upstairs, they did their rounds giving each of the adults a hug and a kiss. Louise caught herself smiling at the sight of the twins behaving in such an affectionate and grown-up manner.

James kissed Louise goodnight at the top of the stairs and both returned to their own rooms. Twenty minutes later, she heard a quiet rap on her door. He entered carrying several small packages and the golf clubs. She threw herself into his arms and they held each other for some minutes simply enjoying the closeness of their bodies.

71

"Louise, my darling, I can't tell you how much I've missed you. With all this company, we've hardly had a chance to chat about anything."

"We'd better deal with the wrapping before anything else or it might not get done at all."

19

MONDAY, DECEMBER 24TH, WOBURN

Cook produced the classic English breakfast. Kippers, soft-boiled eggs, bacon, fried potatoes, pork sausage, wild mushrooms, and fried tomatoes were all available in heated silver salvers on the sideboard.

After bundling up against the winter weather, the 'men' found Smalbridge at his cottage. He fetched a bow saw and led them to a stand of Scots pines. After cutting one down, he led them to the old apple orchard where the boys could pull down mistletoe from the lower branches. Back at his cottage, Smalbridge made a sturdy base for the tree.

James said, "I trust we'll see you Wednesday morning."

"Since I returned from the war, Hattie and I haven't once missed Boxing Day at Woburn Hall. The Colonel said I could bring my lad along now he's turned eighteen."

The twins were whinging. They were cold, tired, and probably hungry. As they approached the house, it began to snow. It was a windless morning and large dry flakes settled on their shoulders and wool hats. They left the fir tree on the front steps and entered via the mudroom, shedding boots, gloves, and heavy wool coats.

The household had been busy. Branches from the English holly hedge hung over doorways and placed on the upper bookshelves. Dorothy knew the berries were slightly toxic and children could be attracted to their bright red colour. Louise took a sprig of mistletoe from Humphrey minor, raised it above James's head, and planted a kiss on his cold lips.

Everybody agreed they were now in the holiday spirit so Humphrey asked Jarvis to fetch a couple of bottles of Dom Perignon. The twins were served fizzy lemonade in flutes so they could pretend to join in. Bea said she'd rather like to have her first taste of Champagne.

Jonathan placed the tree next to the piano and hoisted his boys, one under each arm. "Now to work, me hearties."

Cardboard boxes were opened and decorations hung on the tree. Louise sat on the leather couch sipping her drink. She thought to herself, 'Last year I spent Christmas with a college friend and her parents. Now I've found my aunt and uncle and James's family will soon be mine.' She was nearly overwhelmed with tears of joy but managed to keep her composure by focusing on her fiancé as he chatted while hanging decorations on the tree.

After a light lunch, the house went silent for a few hours. Once downstairs, the family found the library fire roaring away. Looking out the window, six inches of dry snow lay on the ground. The bare branches on the horse-chestnut tree to the left of the front drive were stacked with an inch of snow. Louise wound her arm in James's and leant her head against his shoulder. Porch lights illuminated the picture postcard Christmas scene in the front drive.

In the dining room, the overhead chandelier was turned off and the pair of Georgian silver candelabra provided the only illumination. Humphrey carved the roast goose with flair and precision. While doing this, he informed everybody he'd decanted a double magnum of 1909 Pauillac from Château Lafite.

Louise felt it necessary to say, "You might not know, but experts have rated this as one of the top years for claret."

Jarvis carried the sliced fowl to the sideboard to be put on pre-heated plates while Peets brought in sterling silver salvers of honey-roasted parsnips, roast potatoes, and carrots with grated parmesan.

When the dishes were cleared, Jarvis entered with the traditional brandy-soaked Christmas pudding. He used a silver douter to extinguish half the candles just as Humphrey put a taper to the desert. The twin's eyes nearly popped out of their heads when they saw blue flames rising more than a foot above the table. The pudding was accompanied by a bowl of brandy butter that even the boys were allowed a taste.

Jarvis relit the candles using a match he extracted from a silver case kept in his waistcoat pocket.

As previously arranged, Jarvis, Peets, Sprott, Cook, and both kitchen maids entered the dining room. The family stood and applauded while Humphrey wished the servants a happy Christmas.

Back in the library, Humphrey announced it was now time to open the presents. The twins were given theirs first. Paper and ribbons flew in all directions, after which they clutched their cache and toddled upstairs with Nanny.

Humphrey opened his long and slender package and smiled when he saw the chromed steel shafted clubs. "But what should I do with this hickory contraption?"

"If you hang it on the wall of your estate office, you could pour a shot of Glenmorangie as a toast to a lower handicap in 1935."

"James, I'll do just that. You do know, it's every senior golfer's dream to shoot their age and I might make it with these new-fangled clubs. But Louise, my dear, I'll need a lesson or two."

"When the snow melts, I look forward to a round with my grandfather."

After the others exchanged gifts, Louise handed James a small box. When he opened it he said, "If you consent to be my date, I'll wear these studs to the King's May Ball."

When Louise unwrapped James's gift, she gazed at the beauty of the Tiffany creation. "Where did you find this? It's perfect. How did you know blue is my favourite colour and sapphires my favourite gemstone?"

After this long day, the rest of the family said their goodnights and went upstairs to their rooms. Louise leant her head on his shoulder as they snuggled in front of the dying embers of the coal fire. She was in a pensive mood, realising there remained a serious impediment to their marriage. She hoped this could be resolved in the New Year.

20

TUESDAY, DECEMBER 25TH, WOBURN

The house was awakened at 7:00am by the twins playing a raucous ball game on the stairs.

Over breakfast, Humphrey said to Louise, "Today is for family but not so tomorrow. It's been our Boxing Day tradition since the war that we welcome our estate workers along with a few local tradesmen. Servants have the day off so we'll be fending for ourselves. In the afternoon, local friends will join us for another round of hospitality."

Bea announced, "I hope you don't mind, this year I've invited a few of my fellow spinsters who will be on their own over the holidays. Louise, you must meet my dearest friend, Rose Gregory."

Humphrey asked Dorothy, "I say, what's on the dinner menu for tomorrow?"

"You must wait and see, but everybody must pitch in."

"Of course, my dear, don't I always step up on the 26th?"

"You do until you've had a few drinks with the local worthies and your golf club cronies."

Smalbridge, his wife and son were the first to arrive. Fifteen other estate workers and their wives were lined up behind them along with Joseph Hodges, their village butcher and their builder William Gosden. Humphrey passed a tray of hors d'oeuvres the kitchen had prepared yesterday. James and Jonathan were placed in charge of serving drinks.

At midday, Humphrey stood by the piano and addressed his guests. "Because of the drought in southern England, we've had to buy in fodder from Yorkshire and sell off some of the Angus steers before they'd reached their optimum weight. I'm indebted to you all for your loyalty and hard work throughout 1934. As a token of our appreciation, please accept this modest gift to see you through the holidays."

He handed an envelope to each estate worker. James knew Humphrey had doled out similar Christmas boxes to Jarvis, Peets, Sprott, and the kitchen staff. After this ceremony, their guests left to enjoy their own holidays since no estate work was ever conducted on Boxing Day.

"Well, I guess that went well. I find this lord of the manor nonsense a trifle awkward, but it seems they expect it. Now we have a break before our next guests arrive. We should tidy the drawing room, clear the empties, and prepare lunch."

"My dear, was that the royal we? You know you won't be lifting a finger. Just make sure we have some suitable wine."

"It would help if I knew the main course."

Louise stepped up, adopting the role as resident wine expert. "You should select a light Burgundy, perhaps from the Côte de Nuits."

"Say no more. James, care to join me?"

He knew he wasn't needed, but did want to see the cellar again. He hadn't been down since 1919 when he explored the house after he was forced to take the year off to recuperate from the Spanish 'flu. They went through the pantry and descended the slate steps. This enormous space extended the entire footprint of the manor house. It was separated into sections by stone pillars, each of which supported a complicated array of dark oak beams. It was as he remembered, cold, musty, dimly lit, and foreboding.

"My boy, I wanted to have a quiet word."

He wondered what was on his grandfather's mind. His intention was, at some stage to broach the idea of sharing his room with Louise. In the end, that didn't happen.

Humphrey led him to a section of the cellar where enamelled plaques labelled Côte de Nuits were attached to several bins. He pointed to bottles of Domaine Faiveley Musigny Grand Cru, 1920.

"I remember this from some years back but it wasn't ready."

James carefully lifted two from the racks so as not to disturb the sediment. They were covered in black mould and cobwebs but the étiquette was still legible, having been stored with the label downwards.

In the pantry, Humphrey prepared to strain the contents of both bottles into a lead crystal magnum decanter. He poured the wine through a muslin cloth placed over a glass apothecary's funnel. This was a slow process and by the time it was completed, lunch was ready. The surprise meal was partridge with spiced apple and walnut sauce and Fettuccini Alfredo.

As Humphrey poured the wine, he offered his usual toast. "To our family."

All helped clear the plates to prepare for the arrival of their next guests. Their local friends knew their own houseguests were welcome so they might expect between fifty or a hundred and possibly more.

When the bell rang, Humphrey answered the door showing visitors into the library and the drawing room. The folding mahogany doors between the two rooms were open which created an enormous space. This was the only time of the year this was needed.

A young lady, dressed in a low-cut sleek red silk dress, put her arm through James's and guided him towards the mistletoe hanging between the library and the drawing room. She embraced him with her hand behind his head and gave him a lingering kiss. James visibly froze but seemed at a loss as to what to do.

Louise rushed over and put her arm through his. "Darling, would you fetch me another glass of bubbles?"

She led him back towards the family but the woman clung to James's other arm before reluctantly releasing her grip. Louise smiled sweetly at her over her shoulder but was livid. She was certain she'd raise this embarrassing spectacle later this evening.

Bea introduced James and Louise to her best friend in the village, Rose Gregory. In turn, James introduced both to his riding partner, Norman Paine. Although Rose and Norman lived locally, they hadn't previously met socially.

Humphrey had known many of the guests since before the war and made sure James was introduced as his successor at Woburn. He was welcomed like the prodigal son. Everybody wished for continuity in what they realised was a changing world.

Humphrey guided James towards what he called his boffin friends, who were designers and engineers attached to Brooklands. He introduced Barnes Wallis, George Handasyde, and Reginald Mitchell and their wives. "Barnes designs airframes and George designs gliders. Reginald is the chief aeronautical engineer for Supermarine Aviation Works."

Humphrey then introduced a shy Canadian physicist called Beverley Shenstone. "Beverley is designing the unique elliptical wing of the prototype fighter aircraft."

By seven, the last of the guests had departed for their own celebrations. Nanny put the boys to bed and Dorothy suggested a few hands of bridge. After one rubber, Humphrey took Dorothy's hand and said goodnight. The rest of the party went upstairs and James held Louise back for their usual evening cuddle and chat.

"When my grandfather and I went to the cellar, he told me they thought we were being rather Victorian in our sleeping arrangements since they were sure we shared a bed while abroad. In other words, my dear, they've instructed me to invite you to my room."

"I'm ever so glad. These public meetings and chaste embraces are driving me barmy. I'm seriously impressed they understand that couples need to be together in these uncertain times."

21

TUESDAY, JANUARY 1ST, 1935, CHELSEA

They'd been invited to a New Year's Eve party in London hosted by Ran Lawrie, the Cambridge stroke. Louise persuaded Bea to join them and lent her one of her evening dresses since they were approximately the same shape. Bea asked for a few hints on conversational gambits and help with her makeup. It was obvious she was nervous about going to parties. "Just be yourself. You're a beautiful, intelligent, and talented woman. No man could desire more."

They arrived at Ran's parents' house in Chelsea an hour before midnight. James decided he wouldn't drink as he'd be driving back to Woburn in the early hours. In the crowded drawing room, Bea became the centre of attention for a gaggle of young men and fought off invitations to dance. Gramophone music included a fox trot and a quickstep: 'Oh! You Sweet Thing' and 'Go Into Your Dance' and then a slow ballad by Connee Boswell, 'Smoke Gets In Your Eyes'. James noticed his sister knew the latest steps and presumed she'd practiced with her Surrey lady friends.

The radiogram was turned on so they could count down as Big Ben sounded twelve times. After toasting the New Year and singing 'Auld Lang Syne', the young men queued to give Bea a kiss.

At two in the morning, they made their excuses and had to coax Bea away from her admirers. As James drove back to Woburn, the ladies whispered in the back seat. He politely tried not to eavesdrop over the engine noise.

New Year's Day was spent quietly at Woburn with the remaining five taking a long walk to the western edge of the estate.

Over lunch, Humphrey mentioned the depleted state of his wine cellar. "Dorothy and are thinking of driving to France to restock."

Louise asked, "When would that be?"

"I suppose mid-March when the weather has improved and the days are longer."

"In that case, we'd like to join you. The Lent term finishes on March 15th."

Louise abruptly stood and asked James if she might use the telephone. "Of course, my dear. In future you needn't ask."

"Bea and I are planning to take the train up to London to do some shopping. I know it'll be crowded given the January sales, but I thought I'd combine it with some academic business. My Modern Languages tutor, Miss Sybil Fergusson, is in town staying with her parents in Belgravia."

After making her call, she returned to the library. "Tomorrow, we'll take the 10:12 to Waterloo and then go to Oxford Street to select Bea's new look and wardrobe. I'll meet my tutor, while Bea looks at jewellery on Bond Street. I expect you'll find something to amuse yourself."

"Don't worry about me. I'm still trying to get my head around the calculus of variations."

Peets left to take them to the station. James settled down in the library and began scribbling on a legal pad. At his final Michaelmas term tutorial, Richard suggested he should attempt Hilbert's twenty-three problems over the Christmas vac. David Hilbert was a German mathematician who posed these questions in 1900, most of which remain unsolved.

On the train, Louise asked about the woman who kissed James on Boxing Day. Bea blushed, looked down at her hands but remained silent.

Louise pressed her for an answer. "James dated her last summer. I believe they spent several weekends down in Brighton. In July he broke it off describing her as clingy. I expect she'd targeted my brother as a potential marriage partner."

Louise stared out the rain streaked carriage window. When she calmed down, she decided it would accomplish little to confront him, thereby exposing her jealous streak.

At Waterloo, they hailed a taxi and went to several fashionable dress shops on Oxford Street. Bea chose three evening dresses and several more that were smart, but also suitable for daytime functions. They instructed the shopkeeper to send her purchases to Woburn Park by courier.

Shoes were next so they took a taxi to Regent Street. They selected several styles and the assistant took moulds of her feet so footwear could be made and delivered to Woburn. At a haberdashery, Louise helped Bea choose four hats suitable for parties in the summer season.

Louise hailed a taxi, leaving Bea to look at jewellery on Bond Street

At Selfridge's café, Louise handed Miss Fergusson several packets she had received from her French, Austrian, and German contacts. She also passed her a sealed envelope containing her resignation from MI5. They spent the next twenty minutes discussing her dilemma.

Louise asked, "So, what should I do now?"

"I suggest you catch up with your reading."

"You must realise, I've little appetite for 18th and 19th century European literature. My real passion is the spoken word, regional dialects, patois, and etymology. It was only when I arrived at Newnham, I discovered those formed no part of the Modern Languages syllabus."

"Perhaps you should have read something else, English or PPE, but it's too late for that now."

When Bea entered the café, Louise stood and made her excuses.

In the first-class carriage, Bea showed Louise the earrings she'd purchased along with a classic pearl necklace. Walking back to Woburn Park from the station, they chatted about fashions, parties, and men.

Louise found James in the library surrounded by screwed-up sheets of foolscap. Clearly, the calculus of variations was not treating him kindly. She approached from behind and threw her arms around his neck. He stood, gave her a lingering kiss, and a hug that nearly knocked the wind out of her.

"Successful shopping trip?"

"Bea's ready to take on the Cambridge men in style. I agree with you, she's very happy right now. I hope she isn't disappointed when she discovers relationships require hard work and compromise and aren't simply made in heaven."

"And what about academia?"

"Tell you later."

22

THURSDAY, JANUARY 3RD, WOBURN

When they were snuggling in bed, James again asked about her meeting with her tutor. "I've been constrained by the Official Secrets Act from disclosing details of my work for Britain."

He thought she might be making some sort of joke, perhaps a rather oblique reference to their premarital lovemaking. But not once had she displayed a sense of humour in the two years he had known her. Seeing her serious face, he sat bolt upright.

"I've been an MI5 agent and courier for the last eighteen months. It was actually quite fortunate your choice of destinations coincided with my appointments. I had coded messages and several small packages to deliver and others to collect. At the Louvre, my instructions were to carry Le Figaro in my left hand. I met my contact by Monet's Waterloo Bridge and we exchanged messages as we shook hands.

"Thereafter, I used our hotels' telephones to arrange times and places for my meetings. I doubted German and Austrian switchboards were secure so my rendezvous were always set to be an hour and a quarter earlier than agreed by 'phone. In Munich, my connection identified me as I was instructed to carry the Grafinger Zeitung. In Vienna I met the British agent at the Belvedere Palace by Klimt's painting, The Kiss. This time the protocol was to carry the Wiener Zeitung. A simple handshake accomplished the transfer of a small package. I received a packet in return on both occasions."

James started to interrupt, but Louise put her hand to his lips. "You must let me finish. At the Altes Museum, I met my Berlin contact. This meeting had the greatest risk. We chatted while looking over each other's shoulders to ascertain whether we were being watched. There were uniformed soldiers about and no doubt plainclothes Geheime Staatspolizei as well. When we were satisfied it was safe, we shook hands and messages were exchanged."

"What's this Geheime Staatspolizei?"

"The direct translation of the term is Secret State Police. The Germans use the initialism, Gestapo."

"I did notice the telephone calls on our hotel bills but assumed they related to hotel reservations for our next destinations."

"Yes, that wasn't ideal, but it was my only opportunity to use the 'phone in private. I hated this deception but was sworn to secrecy by Miss Fergusson. As I expect you now realise, she is my MI5 controller. When I met her in London, I informed her I found this duplicity intolerable and formally submitted my letter of resignation. I withdrew it when she told me you were also working for MI5."

"Yes, well, apart from attending some student meetings, I've done bugger all. On this trip, I was instructed by my tutor, Dr Richard Chillingworth, to take note of my impressions of Austria and, of course, Germany. I was also told to keep you in the dark. This deception bothered me and I vowed to raise it at my first tutorial."

He pondered this new information. "Was your European tour last summer part of your work for MI5?"

"It was."

"Ah, there's another mystery solved. I couldn't for the life of me work out how Richard knew about our engagement. You said you'd only told a few friends at Newnham. Obviously, our tutors are in close contact. We now know both are MI5 agents and recruiters. I suspect that explains why they designed my itinerary to coincide with your meetings. It appears we were being tested."

23

FRIDAY, JANUARY 4TH, WOBURN

Dorothy was sitting in the library with her knitting. "Louise, my dear, what are your plans before the start of term?"

"We've loads of swotting, but perhaps we should begin work on the wedding guest list?"

"Bea and I have discussed this. Your nuptials are going to be quite the social occasion in North Surrey."

"When we get back to Cambridge and let our friends know, we should have a fair idea of numbers. By the way, where's Bea?"

"At the orphanage, of course. Seems there's been another drama."

Just then, Bea entered the library still wearing her black cashmere coat and her charcoal Geiger scarf. She stood immobile in the doorway, dropped her bag and burst into tears. "Grandmama, I'm so very frightened. I simply don't know what to do."

James helped her out of her coat and asked Jarvis to fetch a gin and tonic.

Bea sat on a leather sofa and did her best to control her breathing. "You might remember there was a difficulty last October. I thought it was sorted so I put it out of my mind."

She raised her voice between sobs. "Well, it's far from sorted. My senior girls are in danger."

Dorothy held her hand while Bea dried her eyes with her handkerchief. "Let me explain. Most of our charges are orphans but some come to us

86

from abusive families. Because of the current Depression, adoptions are rare, so most girls remain at the orphanage until they're sixteen. After that, they go out into the world with some training to become useful members of society."

James asked, "So, what's the problem? Is it to do with excessive corporal punishment or bullying by staff or other senior girls?"

"It's far worse than that. My girls are being abducted."

James said, "Steady on, old girl. Why would you think that?"

"One of my roles is to find employment and accommodation for our leavers. Last October, I tried to visit two I'd arranged jobs and rooms in Ottershaw. They'd made no attempt to contact me and my letters weren't answered. When I sought out the paperwork, handwritten additions were added to their files indicating they'd moved and changed employers."

"So they were just thoughtless."

"That's not it at all. Last week, I took note of their new positions in Chobham. I drove there this afternoon and no such factory exists and their addresses were false. They've vanished into thin air."

"Isn't it possible they wanted to break all contact with the orphanage? After all, they're legally adults and can go where they wish and do as they please. I expect the young women themselves provided the false information."

"I hadn't thought of that. They're both strong-willed and looked forward to their lives outside the orphanage. Just now, I'm going mad with worry and I've no idea how to find them."

"I doubt this is a police matter and, what's more, your leavers are entitled to their privacy. If they don't want to be found, it's no concern of ours."

He saw Bea was distraught. "Look, Louise and I might know some people who have access to all sorts of records using the Post Office and Inland Revenue. They'll have the resources to discover their new addresses. If they've gone abroad, the General Register Office would have records of passports issued and possibly details of their destinations. Go to bed and leave this with us."

Later, Louise said, "I haven't found your sister prone to hysteria. I wonder if she's spotted something amiss."

"Hang about. Isn't it likely both girls wished to start new lives without the burden of their employers or workmates knowing they were raised in an orphanage? This is well outside our brief with MI5. I suppose I did promise to follow this up and I'll do so if only for her peace of mind."

24

TUESDAY, JANUARY 8ᵀᴴ, LONDON

Over Sunday lunch, James mentioned, he and Louise would be taking the train up to London the day after tomorrow. They'd meet with their tutors concerning some academic matters.

Bea said, "Could I tag along? I'd really like Louise's advice."

They shared a taxi to Oxford Street so Louise could help her select cosmetics as well as some intimate items of apparel. After that, they went their separate ways and agreed to meet up at the Savoy for lunch.

In Selfridge's café, they joined Richard and Sybil at their table. "You'll be pleased to know, I've come clean with James. We're happy to act as a team and undertake whatever tasks you have in mind."

Richard was obviously annoyed. "I trust that's not why you've summoned us down to London on this bitterly cold January day. Over the Cambridge station tannoy, they announced that trains aren't running to schedule because of frozen points and the wrong sort of leaves on the tracks."

James said, "We'd like to raise a matter that doesn't directly concern MI5."

"If it's academic, couldn't you have waited until the beginning of the Lent term? We've more important matters on our plates than final year nerves."

James pressed on, ignoring Richard's irritation. "My twin sister, Beatrice, volunteers at the Addlestone Orphanage for Foundling Girls. She has no specific role, but mentors the girls and offers advice and support. Most are orphans but some have been rescued from abusive domestic situations. Bea uses our family's Surrey connections to arrange jobs and accommodation when they leave at sixteen."

"Go on."

"Just now, she's in a right state. She believes something has happened to two of her leavers."

"If it's a police matter, she should lodge a formal complaint with the Addlestone Constabulary."

"Actually, it's a bit of a mystery. Bea tries to keep in touch with her former charges to ensure they're surviving and hopefully thriving in the outside world. She told us she's lost contact with several orphanage leavers. They never arrived at the jobs or lodgings she'd arranged."

"And how might that concern Sybil and myself?"

"We accept this isn't SIS business but we'd like you to arrange for a Home Office official to come down to Addlestone to interview Bea. They'd have the resources to locate the missing young women and reassure Bea her worries are groundless."

Richard looked down at his folded hands, occasionally exchanging sideways glances with Sybil. "It's highly irregular for MI5 to approach the Home Office with this or indeed any request. You do realise, it's the responsibility of local police to locate missing persons. However, because you two are valued as proto-agents, we'll see what we can do."

Sybil asked, "And Louise, what about your studies? I don't suppose you've managed to open a book since the end of the Michaelmas term."

"James has been working on maths, but for my part, you're right. I intend to spend the next three weeks on some serious revision. When the Lent term begins, both of us plan to adopt a regimen of study and sports in that order."

Richard said, "Now I'd like to raise another issue. The powers that be have recently made us aware both of you are in the habit of keeping motorcars in private parking arrangements. Personally, I don't give two hoots, but I'm afraid University officialdom is taking a rather strong line."

"We're both in our final year and a bit older than the usual undergraduates so we felt this might be overlooked."

"Well James, it's not been. Before you get in a flap, we've stepped in and procured special exemptions. Do keep this under your hat so you don't encourage others to bend the rules."

"I suppose you realise we're breaking another regulation by leaving Cambridge during term-time."

"Sybil and I regard that as minor. As long as we know where you are, you can take it you have our permission. But there's a caveat. You must treat your studies rather more seriously than you've done over the last two years. James, unless you knuckle down, you're destined for a second class degree."

"I'd like to raise another matter. For the same reason I hated keeping Louise in the dark, I'd like your permission to tell my grandparents about our MI5 positions. I'm sure they thought it curious that we spent time in Germany and they'll surely think it odd if we arrive with some Home Office official to interview Bea. My grandfather was an officer in the Boer war and rose to the rank of full Colonel during the Great War. He worked at the MOD as a Liaison Officer responsible for aircraft production at Brooklands."

"We're well-aware of all that. They were thoroughly vetted before you were recruited. Permission will be forthcoming, but you must only let them know of your roles in a general way. No specifics, mind."

Richard asked them if they'd written their reports on their impressions of Austria and Germany.

Each handed their tutors a sealed envelope. Their business apparently concluded James stood to help Louise with her chair.

Richard motioned them to remain seated. "One final question. Do either of you know how to use a handgun? Amongst his other accomplishments, your grandfather is a certified weapons' instructor. Take this package and ask him to teach you to use this tool safely."

25

FRIDAY, JANUARY 11TH, WOBURN

Jarvis called James to the 'phone as they were having breakfast. Richard was on the line. "As regards informing your grandparents of your work with the SIS, MI5 have granted formal permission. As far as that other matter we discussed concerning your sister, our masters thought it was well outside our jurisdiction. However, they've decided to trust your judgment."

"I have to thank you for your support."

"I still have serious doubts. It was Sybil who persuaded our superiors. She has a very high regard for Louise's instincts and analytical thinking. So here's what will happen. A Mr Donald Hutchinson from the Home Office Missing Persons Bureau will arrive at Addlestone on tomorrow's midday train. Make sure Beatrice is home so he can interview her."

At noon, they met the Home Office official on the platform. From his accent, Louise immediately identified him as a cultured upper-class gentleman. He was well over six feet, but perhaps a little shorter than James. He'd jet black hair, a swarthy complexion, and was lean and fit in a chiselled sort of way.

"Mr Hutchinson, I have to thank you for taking the time to deal with my sister's concerns."

"First of all, you must call me Donald. I'm here informally as a friend to collect first-hand details so my colleagues can trace the young women."

"Isn't this an unusual situation?"

"You'd be surprised. Scores of English girls are reported missing every year and many more if you include Wales, Scotland, and Northern Ireland."

"What happens to them?"

"Obviously, we've no idea which is why they're classified as missing. Some might be victims of violent crime, but it's likely most are runaways escaping unhappy domestic situations. They tend to migrate to big cities, find jobs, and start new lives. Some are at risk of adopting prostitution as a way of surviving while others might change their names or even go abroad. If they don't appear on any official registers, we've literally no means with which to trace them. To be blunt, if a body turns up, the best we can do is to go through our records to see if the description matches one of those on our lists."

"So there may be nothing suspicious about James's sister having lost touch with a couple of orphanage leavers."

"I'm afraid that's right. What's more, if they don't want to be found, it's neither a police matter nor a Home Office concern. Your tutors told me some of the girls at the orphanage were from abusive families. If those who've disappeared are amongst that category, it's perfectly understandable they'd wish to leave no trace, lest one of their biological parents attempt to find them."

"It appears you've made a wasted journey."

"Not at all. I look forward to enjoying a bit of the Surrey countryside."

When they arrived at Woburn, they heard Bea practicing on her piano. James held them back in the front hall. He rarely had the opportunity to hear her play because she was extremely shy about performing in front of anybody. Louise recognized the piece as Beethoven's Pathetique.

Donald didn't move a muscle. He closed his eyes and was transfixed by the beauty of the music. After a couple of minutes he stuck his head around the corner to see who was playing. Bea slammed down the fallboard, let out a cry, and covered her face with her hands. When she recovered her composure, introductions were made before they sat at the library table.

Donald asked, "Beatrice, could you tell me about your responsibilities at the orphanage?"

"Of course. As a volunteer, I've no specific duties. When my senior girls leave, I find them jobs and lodgings and try to keep in touch to see how they're faring on the outside. Normally, I'm quite good at this. I've about sixty young women with whom I'm in regular postal contact. Sometimes they ask for help but mostly they just want to let me know they're thriving, developing social contacts, and even getting married and having children of their own."

"Have you managed to kept in touch with many of your leavers?"

"All, without exception. That is, until last summer. Five girls left our care at about the same time. They were close friends, having been together at the orphanage since they were four. Two have gone missing and neither I nor the other girls have a clue as to where they might be. Even if they didn't want to keep in contact with me or the orphanage, I'm absolutely certain they wouldn't drop their lifelong companions."

"I hear what you say. Would it be possible for you filch their files?"

"I've free run of the Record's Office. Leaver's dossiers are stored in a separate filing cabinet not used for our current charges."

"Have you mentioned your concerns to anyone at the orphanage?"

"I haven't. Last October, I tried to sound out our local bobby, PC Adler. He made me feel quite silly and instructed me, in no uncertain terms, to drop it. He stressed, it wasn't police business as the girls are of legal age and can go wherever they wish and do as they please."

Bea left in her Jowett Kestrel and returned twenty minutes later with five fairly bulky folders. Donald studied each in turn, taking notes on a yellow legal pad. When he'd finished with one, he passed it along the library table to Louise and James. The first two were the missing girl's dossiers. Their names were Winifred Elizabeth Bradford and Kathleen Mary Fawcett.

Bea said, "Betty and Kitty's fathers were killed on the Somme and their mothers and siblings died in the 1918 London influenza pandemic. After that, they were taken into local authority care and in 1921 placed with us. As regards the other leavers, two are orphans, but the fifth's parents are still alive, one in Wandsworth prison for burglary and aggravated assault and the other a prostitute."

"Return the files and I'll let you know when we locate them."

"Mr Hutchinson, I'm ever so grateful you believe me. I truly think something dreadful has happened. I trust you'll join us for lunch."

"That's an exceedingly kind offer, but I'd best return to London to file my report."

He put on his overcoat and asked James for a lift to the station. Louise grabbed her purse. "I'll come along. I've a couple of things I need at the shops."

Louise sat in the back seat. As they approached the station, she tapped the Home Office official on his shoulder. "Did you spot anything unusual about the two missing girls?"

He paused, turned his head and looked her in the eye. "So you noticed."

James asked, "Noticed what?"

Louise said, "Both girls were blonde and according to their records, also had blue eyes. Lebensborn comes to mind."

"That's certainly a possibility. MI6 has recently learned suitable pregnant young German women are being admitted to an institution where they can have their babies in seclusion to be put up for adoption by SS families. Our analysists believe the Nazis are encouraging pregnancies amongst these so-called superior types to populate the lands they intend to acquire to the east. At this stage, there's no reason to suppose hair and eye colour are anything but coincidence."

The train was due to depart so Donald sprinted to the platform and boarded the first-class carriage.

"Louise, what on earth is Lebensborn and what's this SS?"

"The literal translation of Lebensborn is the wellspring of life. It's a Nazi programme aimed at creating a superior race they refer to as Aryans. SS is the initialism for Schutzstaffel. It translates to Protection Squadron. It's a paramilitary organisation set up by Heinrich Himmler in the mid 20's. Now it's one of the most powerful organisations in Nazi Germany with responsibility for domestic security and covert surveillance of Hitler's enemies."

James turned across the level crossing and headed towards the village centre.

"Where are you going?"

"I thought you needed to do some shopping."

"No, James, I just wanted to have this chat with Mr Hutchinson away from the family."

When they returned, Humphrey and Dorothy were in the library. Dorothy was reading *Gaudy Night,* a novel by Dorothy Sayers published earlier this year. Humphrey was at his writing desk with a cut crystal tumbler of single malt at his right hand.

"Are you two busy? Louise and I have something we'd like to share."

Humphrey abruptly rose from his desk. "Under no circumstances are you to tell us you're calling off the wedding."

"Nothing like that grandpapa."

He gently asked Louise, "My dear, are you in a family way?"

"That's not our news. Once we're married, I hope to supply you and Dorothy with more great-grandchildren."

This was hardly the moment to mention it was likely she wouldn't be able to conceive. "Independently, we've been recruited by MI5. James has just begun his training but I've been a courier for the last eighteen months."

"We both thought your country hopping before Christmas was a little odd, but I'd never have believed you were spies."

"We're part-time amateurs learning as we go. More's the point, Louise and I fear a war in Europe will drag Britain into the conflict. If there's anything we can do to prevent that, we've made it clear we're willing to serve. My controller told me you've both been vetted by the Foreign Office. I expect you've passed with flying colours."

"I bloody well hope so. As a full Colonel in the British Army with an OBE, I've served my country with distinction in two wars and have battlefield gongs to prove it. Tell me, was that Home Office chap a spy?"

"Actually, we know nothing about him. Even his name may be something else. As MI5 operatives, we're required to have weapons training. I've been issued a pistol and some ammunition and we'd like your help with some target practice."

"Right you are. In the morning, let's walk to our feed barn on Chertsey Meads. It's bounded on three sides by the meandering Thames so it's not overlooked by housing or farms. Do remember, we've cattle there and you don't want to damage our livelihood."

"One more thing, they said we're not to tell my sisters of our espionage activities. For everybody's protection, the fewer people who know the better."

"A nod's as good as a wink to a blind horse."

26

SATURDAY, JANUARY 12TH, CHERTSEY MEADS

On the way to the barn, Humphrey began their lesson. "Forget everything you think you know about weapons. I'll show you how to use this tool safely and accurately."

Once inside, James handed him the package which contained a Beretta model 1934 and two boxes of ammunition. "This is just a toy. It has no stopping power."

"Grandpapa, it's compact and easily concealed, appropriate for our roles as agents."

"Fair enough, a gun's a gun. Let's have a look."

Humphrey ensured there were no bullets in the chamber or in the magazine located in the grip. He demonstrated the safety, how to release the magazine, and how to insert the seven shells into the spring-loaded clip.

"Now for some preparation. James, you go first. Here's the unloaded gun. Put it in your coat pocket, pull it out and aim at that hay bale over there. Release the safety, then pull the trigger."

James did so and heard a satisfying click.

"Practice that a few times and then pass it to Louise."

She put it into her pocket and repeated the lesson.

"Always ensure there's nothing like a scarf or gloves that could get snagged when you draw your weapon. Now, for some target practice. If you need to use this pocket gun, your quarry will be nearby so accuracy isn't all that important. This is a very small gun carrying tiny bullets. At close range it'll do the job, but it's next to useless for anything over fifty yards."

Humphrey walked towards the hay bales. He stacked one vertically on top of another. Using baling wire, he attached an empty burlap feedbag about chest height on the upper bale.

"Right James, load the gun, take careful aim, and fire at the bag's logo."

He filled the clip and put it in his pocket.

"Stop right there! This is about accuracy. Release the safety, aim at the target and take your shot."

He missed the central design and nicked the feed sack on the right. Humphrey asked for the Beretta. He held it in both hands and took aim. His shot hit the logo dead centre. "Nothing wrong with the sights."

James tried again. This time he imitated Humphrey. Using both hands, he took the shot, but still missed to the right.

"Breathe out then in, hold your breath, and gently squeeze the trigger. Avoid using your hand muscles. If you pull hard on the trigger, your bullet will always veer to the right since you're right-handed."

James tried again with the remainder of the clip and his accuracy improved. Next it was Louise's turn. She hit the logo with each shot.

"She's the marksman. Now we'll practice pulling the gun out of your pocket and taking a quick shot at the target."

James loaded the gun and set the safety. He put it in his coat pocket, took a short breath, pulled it out, released the safety, and fired.

"Much too slow. Don't sight the target. Shoot when the gun reaches chest height. The whole process should take under a second."

James let off the rest of the magazine in single bursts, on each occasion, drawing the gun from his pocket.

"Louise, I expect you're a quick learner. Repeat the exercise."

Again she was rather more accurate than James and offered him a smug smile.

"Let's let the barrel cool down."

They sat on hay bales and Humphrey continued the lesson. "If you feel the need to pull your gun, don't wave it about and threaten to shoot. I know that's what they do in the cinema to add dialogue and suspense. That'll only get you killed. The people you encounter will be well-trained and armed with large calibre weapons. If you decide you need to fire your Beretta, you must do so without hesitation."

Humphrey placed an old galvanized bucket on top of the vertical bale, holding it down with more wire. "Now for the next exercise. Draw the gun, release the safety, and fire. But this time let off two shots. Tap! Tap! If you feel confident, the first one should be at the chest and the second at the head, in this case, the logo and bucket. The Beretta's magazine holds seven rounds, so aim the final shot at the feedbag. James, you first."

He did as he was told and hit the bucket twice.

"Excellent. Louise, it's your go."

They heard the pings as she scored three hits on the bucket.

Again, they paused to let the gun cool off. "I expect neither of you have ever killed another human being and likely never considered the prospect. In a few years, our country will be at war with the Nazis. We know them to be both ruthless and professional. James, what if one of our enemies was a woman? Would you be able to shoot her if you determined it was kill or be killed?"

"Honestly, I've no idea."

"Louise, would you be able to kill a woman or a young man of say, sixteen?"

"Like James, I've never even remotely considered the possibility. I'll process this and try not to hesitate if it's a situation of them or us."

"Good. Now repeat the two shot exercise until it becomes second nature. It looks like I'll need to get Smalbridge to replace that bucket he uses to feed the calves."

Back in the library for pre-dinner drinks, Bea commented on how sympathetic Donald had been to her concerns. Louise's feminine instincts were put on high alert.

27

FRIDAY, FEBRUARY 1ST, CAMBRIDGE

James spent the last three weeks of the vac immersed in his maths' curriculum. He made progress with the calculus of variations and geodesic solutions and solved two of Hilbert's twenty-three problems.

At his first Lent term tutorial, Richard assigned twenty more conjectures associated with the calculus of variations. He also circled several lectures he should attend. Before he left, Richard updated him on the MI5 investigation into the missing orphanage girls.

That evening at the Eagle, he was ordering drinks at the bar when Louise slipped her arm through his. They bagged their usual table in a secluded corner of the snug.

"Richard told me the two missing orphanage girls are creating quite a flap in both the Home Office and the Foreign Office. Apparently, a number of blonde, teenage females have disappeared over the last year."

"Have they found Bea's leavers?"

He looked down at his pint and shook his head.

"How can girls disappear from under our noses and be spirited abroad. That's tantamount to government sanctioned kidnap and rape."

"Steady on. We don't actually know it's anything to do with Lebensborn. They still might turn up."

Friday morning, on their way down to Woburn, they picked up Donald in central London. "I've received permission from my section chief to brief you on my role in this investigation. I expect you've guessed, I'm with MI6 and not the Home Office. Very occasionally, MI5 and MI6 work together when there's an international threat on British soil. I'm also allowed to inform you I'm coordinating the search for the missing girls."

At Woburn, Humphrey looked up from his library desk and greeted Donald. "I hope you intend to stay the weekend. Last Friday you took off like a scalded cat."

"I look forward to spending time with you all."

He said this looking directly at Bea. She was wearing one of her new daytime outfits. Her hair was permed and her makeup done to perfection. With his direct eye contact, she blushed and looked down at her feet in a demur fashion.

Jarvis served drinks while Donald explained his presence. "I must apologise for not being frank with you on my last visit. I'm actually with MI6. Bea's missing leavers have become our top priority. Our primary concern is to prevent further abductions. James and Louise have offered to help, but Bea, you will be crucial since you've inside knowledge of the orphanage."

The gong sounded and they adjourned to the dining room. Donald helped Bea with her chair and after lunch, sat next to her on the chaise.

"Bea, could you filch the files for those staff hired over the last two years?"

"That's no problem. I sometimes rest in our Records Office as it's a quiet place to have a cup of tea."

"Could you go this afternoon?"

Bea returned his smile and grabbed her handbag. She was back within twenty minutes and placed four manila folders on the library table.

Donald studied them and took notes. Louise looked over his shoulder and saw he was writing names, past employment record, references, and previous addresses. After he'd finished with each file, he passed it along to the others.

"Louise, spot anything suspicious?"

"All four are women but Bea told me men only work in the gardens and kitchens and have no access to the girls or the main office. Three are in their 30's and one in her 50's. No surprises there."

"I need more information. Colonel, might I use your telephone? I'll pass on their details to my department and they'll ring if they uncover anything dodgy."

"Do call me Humphrey and feel free to regard Woburn as your operational base."

Donald excused himself and went out to the hall. He was back in the library after ten minutes. "The investigation has begun. I'm hoping we'll have something concrete either this afternoon or tomorrow."

While he was on the telephone, Bea left to return the files.

When she returned, Donald asked, "Any hiccups?"

"The staff are used to seeing me coming and going at odd times."

"Good work."

Bea smiled politely but this time looked him straight in the eye and said, "Thank you, Donald."

Humphrey suggested a walk around the estate. Donald chose to remain near the telephone. Bea said she'd also stay behind to deal with correspondence from orphanage leavers and perhaps get reacquainted with Mozart's piano sonatas. James was visibly surprised since to his certain knowledge, she had never voluntarily played the piano in front of anyone except her teacher.

The others put on heavy coats and Louise said she'd like to see the tithe barn again. "Last time, I was paying more attention to James than your landmark."

Humphrey invited them to find seats on the huge blocks of cut stone that were part of the Abbey remains. He handed Louise a small package wrapped in brown paper and string. "I know you young people believe in equality in your future marriage and I thought it unfair that James take responsibility for protection on his own."

James was aghast. Louise turned her gaze towards the tithe barn unable to understand his meaning. When she opened the box, both understood. Inside, wrapped in chamois leather, was a Beretta model 1934.

"Grandpapa, how'd you find this?"

"I have my sources. By the way, I've replenished your ammunition so you can practice anytime you're down."

It was getting late and the sun had dropped behind the trees. Back at the house they found Donald and Bea on the leather couch enjoying a cheerful fire. Donald quickly stood, obviously embarrassed they were sitting so closely together.

Louise asked, "Any news?"

"We're now focussed on one individual. The woman in her 50's had bogus references. It's a wonder the orphanage didn't spot this. I guess they liked her at interview and that was that."

"What's her name?"

"Betty Smith, would you believe? Betty could be short for Elizabeth, but since her references were phony, I expect it's an alias. MI6 and the Home Office are looking into her background and will telephone when they garnish more information. As she lives at the orphanage, we have no neighbours to approach for background checks. Bea, what are her general duties?"

"She's what we call a house mother in the senior girl's dormitory."

Louise said, "That fits. She'd know a lot about the girls, including whether they'd friends or relatives on the outside who might miss them if they disappeared."

"Good point."

James cautioned him. "Donald, I expect you realise, otherwise honest people have been known to give fake references. Jobs are scarce these days and desperation might trump good sense. Besides, we don't even know if the girls are actually missing. They, themselves, might have supplied the orphanage with false destinations."

"Right on both counts. However, phony references invariably raise red flags. I wonder, Bea, could you arrange an orphanage visit. If your family adopted the role as local philanthropists, you could all see what you make of this Smith woman."

Bea slipped out to the hall to ring the Matron.

While she was gone, Louise said teasingly, "James, my dear, I'm sure you could pass as an upper-class gent if you put on a posh voice."

"Hang about, there's nothing wrong with my accent."

"Please pay attention. You know my expertise is in spoken languages. When you deal with, shall we say, the less fortunate classes, you tend to affect a sort of south London accent, somewhat akin to Cockney. You regularly drop your aitches and I suspect you picked this up from Dulwich dayboys."

Jarvis rang the gong announcing the arrival of the cocktail hour just as Bea returned from making her 'phone call. "I've arranged a tour tomorrow morning at ten."

Donald gave her a big smile. "Well done, Bea."

Jarvis served drinks and the conversation turned to the inclement winter weather.

Bea whispered to Louise. "Can you think of a way to find out if he's married or in a serious relationship? I'd be too embarrassed to ask."

"I say Donald, do you have children?"

"Louise, I'm not married and with my schedule of traveling and uncertain hours, I'm not likely to find a lady who'd put up with me."

28

SATURDAY, FEBRUARY 2ND, ADDLESTONE ORPHANAGE

Staff and girls of all ages were assembled in the orphanage courtyard. At Matron's signal, several hundred children curtsied in unison. James was embarrassed by this display, but Humphrey and Dorothy acted as if it was their due.

Matron introduced her staff. Betty Smith was tall, somewhat overweight, and wore a grey dress, which appeared to be the orphanage uniform. Matron then led them towards a group of teenage girls. Two were standing in front of the others. "Let me introduce you to our Senior Prefects."

One girl had long brown hair and hazel eyes and the other was fair-haired with deep blue eyes. Bea introduced the dark-haired girl as Susan Dutton and the blonde as Lillian Turner.

Louise asked Susan about her plans for the future. "Miss Harcourt-Heath got me a job at a Chertsey bakery."

She asked Lillian the same question. "She found me a position at a newsagent. I turn sixteen next Friday. On Saturday, I'll catch the midday bus to Weybridge."

"Good luck to you both."

They curtsied, turned, and left to go back to the group of older girls. When the tour finished, Humphrey told Matron he strongly supported their work and was prepared to donate an annual stipend of a hundred guineas.

Back in the library, Louise asked Donald if he'd received any news. "It turns out, Betty Smith was formerly Bettina Schmidt. In 1920 she emigrated from a small village east of Munich called Ebersberg, accompanied by her parents and three sisters. Shortly afterwards, she changed her name by deed poll. There's nothing unusual in that since there was and remains substantial anti-German feeling in the Home Counties. Her parents are deceased but interestingly, her sisters work at other Surrey orphanages. These three other institutions have also reported they've lost contact with several fair-haired girls. Complaints to the police weren't pursued since there was no evidence of foul play and the leavers were technically adults."

"How many are you talking about?"

"Hard to tell, perhaps half a dozen. You know Bea, if you hadn't persevered none of this would have come to light."

"I did ask questions, but it was my brother and Louise who believed me."

"Because of the physical similarities between the missing girls, I'm going to tentatively regard these as kidnappings. If that's the case, I've no doubt they are restricted to the four orphanages where the Schmidt sisters work. Unfortunately, it's likely they communicate with each other using public call boxes. That makes it impossible to identify their contacts or learn what they might be planning."

"Orphanage staff are allowed to use the office telephone. We've an honour system and put pennies in a wooden box to pay for our calls."

He rose and started towards the hall telephone. Louise blocked his way. "Stop right there. We were introduced to an orphanage girl called Lillian Turner. She's a blue-eyed blonde and leaves on Saturday."

Donald hesitated for a moment. "Right, protecting her will be my top priority. Just now, I'll get a court order to place wiretaps at all four institutions."

After lunch, James and Louise went to the library to catch up with their studies. Humphrey and Dorothy said they'd take their usual nap. Bea asked Donald if he'd like to join her on a walk around the estate grounds.

Hours later, James was holding his cup of tea while looking out the library window. Bea and Donald were walking towards the front steps holding hands.

Jarvis helped them with their coats and passed Donald a telephone message. "I told your office you'd ring back immediately you returned from your investigations."

After telephoning his section leader, he joined the others in the library. "I've just assigned a dozen operatives to this case. It appears similar disappearances have occurred elsewhere in the home counties. My men will initially interview staff at all four orphanages where the Schmidt sisters work. I can't for the life of me figure why this wasn't spotted sooner. Because of you, Bea, Addlestone is our best chance to catch the kidnappers. Once again, I thank you and our government thanks you."

Bea raised her voice. "Thanks are one thing, but what about Lily?"

"This investigation has received the highest priority from the Home Secretary and I've been promised all the manpower I need."

Louise was livid. "That's not an answer and you damn well know it."

"It's the best I can do for the moment."

James said, "Louise and I have to return to Cambridge tomorrow, but we'll come down next weekend to help out."

"Don't bother. By then, I'll have every angle covered. Humphrey, might I stay here? I don't want to attract attention to myself at a local inn with my men checking in at odd times for meetings. My agents will stay elsewhere and could report to me here during the day."

"Feel free to use Woburn as your command post."

"Arrests should be made by the end of the week, after which we all can return to our former lives."

Bea was visibly stunned. Louise stood and asked to see the purchases she'd made in London last week.

Bea had the presence of mind to reply, "Let's go to my room."

After half an hour, they returned, Louise muttering something about Bea's marvellous taste.

"Donald, it's our custom to attend St Paul's Sunday service. Afterwards we usually pop 'round to our local."

"Humphrey, I'm sure I can be away from the telephone for a few hours. Perhaps you could ask your man to cover for me again."

In their bedroom James asked why they left the library to look at Bea's shopping.

"She's falling for Donald in a big way."

"Is that a problem? He seems a thorough gentleman."

"His lifestyle is such that he'd not make an ideal partner or husband for a lady such as Bea. I was just warning her not to fall too hard until they've discussed a number of issues."

"Issues?"

"Marriage, children, home life, financial circumstances, career demands, fidelity. Women need to be satisfied about these before getting involved in a relationship. I used that same checklist when I decided you might become a suitable partner."

"Surely, it can't be that complicated. We fell in love and that was that."

"James, do try to understand. I would not have allowed myself to fall in love unless I was satisfied about those concerns."

29

TUESDAY, FEBRUARY 5TH, ADDLESTONE

This morning, he had his usual gruelling two-hour tutorial. Before he left, Richard updated him on what MI5 now referred to as the Addlestone Affair. "We congratulate you on uncovering the kidnapping plot. It now appears to be endemic throughout the United Kingdom and seems to have been going on for the last fifteen months."

"We're returning on Friday to help out."

"I'm giving you explicit instructions to not get in their way. Hutchinson is an experienced professional and will have the situation contained."

They drove down to Woburn on Friday morning. Over pre-lunch drinks, Donald updated them on the present state of the investigation. "Our telephone taps have revealed a number of leads. As expected, the four Schmidt sisters are in regular contact. Their conversations are conducted in Bavarian German. What's more, we've confirmed Lillian Turner is their next target."

"I assume they're under arrest."

"James, conspiracy is notoriously difficult to demonstrate, let alone secure a conviction. An attempt to kidnap Lily is another matter. If they're aliens, we can put them on trial and if found guilty, they'll be deported after they've served their custodial sentences. If they're naturalised British citizens, arrests will follow and the criminal justice system will run its course. Just now, we've nothing but recordings of a few guarded telephone conversations in dialect German. Obviously these would be inadmissible in a court of law. I'm afraid we must use Lily as bait."

Bea raised her voice, "But you promised you'd protect her."

"Don't worry, I'll have my team in place so she won't be in any significant danger."

Louise remained silent and stared out the library window.

After lunch, James and Louise walked towards Victory Park.

Louise said, "I'm not at all impressed with Donald's arrangements. Not in any significant danger really has no practical meaning in terms of Lily's safety. I know Richard instructed you to keep your distance, but there's nothing to say we can't be nearby when she catches the Weybridge bus."

Saturday morning, Donald outlined plans for today. "Bea, attend to your orphanage duties as usual and don't worry about Lily. Any attempted kidnapping will occur prior to her boarding the bus and I'll have my team of armed agents around the station. When they try to grab her, we'll disable their cars and arrest the lot."

James drove to the station carpark. They mouched around acting as if they were there to meet the midday commuter train. Just before noon, the omnibus pulled into the station car park. As passengers boarded, Lily walked towards the coach, followed by Bea and Miss Schmidt.

Louise grabbed his arm. "What's Bea doing there? Look, they're all getting on the bus."

They rushed to their car and followed. The coach was a local and stopped every few hundred yards as it headed towards the terminus at Weybridge centre. Passengers boarded and alighted at most halts. It stopped at the end of Victoria Road before turning right onto Woburn Hill, the A317. Lily, Bea, and Miss Schmidt got off and walked towards a car illegally parked at the bus halt. Bea and Lily glanced over their shoulders and appeared frightened and confused.

The bus left without anyone else getting off. Louise wondered why Donald's men hadn't followed and arrested the kidnappers. She dismissed the thought since her immediate concern was Lily and Bea's safety. The car was a powerful Humber Snipe saloon. James followed as it sped towards Weybridge. After a half mile, it turned down a rutted farm track, stopping in front of a neglected stone cottage. James braked when he saw the house through the trees. Two other newish saloons were parked out front.

James said, "We can't stay here. There's obviously others inside. I'll reverse and park on Woburn Hill. If they leave, we can follow and look for an opportunity to take some useful action."

Meanwhile, Louise was scribbling something in her notepad. He parked out of sight behind a white builder's van. After a minute or so, there was a rap on the driver's side window which caused both to reach for their weapons.

Donald and another man stood by their car. "Here's what I think happened. We know Bettina Schmidt received a 'phone call this morning from the Weybridge orphanage. When Bea entered the office, doubtless she was captured along with Lily. As they approached the bus, one of my men saw the glint of a gun in her hand. He signalled the others not to interfere. Two of my team followed them onto the bus, but I guess they didn't blend in. Several members of the gang must have boarded first. When we got here, I realised you'd the same idea of keeping Bea, Lily, and Miss Schmidt in your sights."

"We followed them down that single track lane over there to the right. It dead-ends at a cottage and there are two other cars parked in front besides the Humber."

Louise handed Donald her notepad on which she'd written the cars' make, model, colour, and registrations. He tore off the top sheet, gave it to his partner who dodged traffic and sprinted across Woburn Hill to a telephone kiosk.

He returned twenty minutes later. "I'd assumed all three motorcars would have been reported stolen so license numbers wouldn't help. It appears they might be with their owners since all three have north Surrey registrations."

"They're clearly amateurs. They could have nicked the cars or the plates."

"James, both would have been risky. Remember, we believe this group has been at it for over a year. They'd need transport for their daytime jobs and to carry out the kidnappings. An inquisitive bobby would notice if the vehicle had been reported stolen or if the tax disk didn't correspond with the license plates. My apologies, let me introduce my partner, Harry Pearce."

They shook hands, but Louise wouldn't let up on Donald. "Any more clever ideas now that your brilliant plan has come a cropper?"

"I'll have Harry ring my Addlestone team for back-up. If all three cars leave in separate directions, we'll be able to follow and keep tabs. Meanwhile, my staff will find out everything they can about the registered owners. They'll get addresses from their logbooks and I'll assign men to each location."

Harry dashed across the road to ring for the required assistance. After about ten minutes, two other cars arrived each carrying a pair of agents.

After briefing his team, Donald said, "I expect they'll wait until nightfall before they make a move."

Louise still wasn't satisfied. "So much for your guarantee to protect Lily. Now you've managed to place Bea in peril."

"They'll be safe unless we try to interfere. Lily is valuable as a Lebensborn target and Bettina Schmidt knows Bea is from an important family and could be used as a hostage."

"Damn it, Donald, that's rubbish. You've absolutely no way of knowing that. Both are expendable if they need to avoid capture."

"I'll monitor developments before deciding on my response. In principle, I'll try to isolate each car from the others so they'd feel less secure and more inclined to surrender when faced with armed officers."

Harry rushed back across the road. "Now we're getting somewhere. All three vehicles are registered at Addlestone addresses along with two white three-ton Bedford vans. It's possible they use those to smuggle the girls abroad. I was sure you'd want those houses watched so I ordered three additional teams to be dispatched from London. They'll be in place by early evening."

"Harry, get the Home Office to institute an All Ports Warning. The APW should cover the south coast ports of Dover, Portsmouth, Weymouth, and Southampton. Extend the search to any port large enough to accommodate cargo ships. The girls could have been drugged and put into crates. Focus on ports that send ships directly to Germany. That would include Felixstowe and Harwich. Smaller ones might also handle freight if they transport the girls that way. Finally, get Scotland Yard to instruct Home Counties constabularies to keep an eye out for the vehicles. Relay my thoughts to MI6 and the Home Office."

Harry nodded and returned to the kiosk.

Donald asked, "Is there anything I've forgotten?"

"You've deployed sixteen men in eight vehicles, but you've patently ignored us."

"James, you're novices, trained only in covert surveillance, and you've never had direct confrontation with the enemy."

"Look mate, we're talking about my sister. We're armed and have had weapon's training. Addlestone is obviously at the heart of the plot given all the vehicles are local. Remember, I was raised here."

"Very well, but don't go off half-cocked. Telephone me at Woburn if you discover anything that might affect my planning."

"Just give me the addresses and we'll be out of your hair."

Donald copied them and handed the note to James.

"I know all three streets. We'll be there in two ticks."

He did a three-point turn and sped towards the town centre.

The first address was an oval street of Victorian terraced houses called Fairway. He knew it backed onto an unpaved alley called Fairfields where commercial vehicles were regularly stored. He parked on Free Prae Road and they walked down Fairfields peering into the parking areas looking for white Bedford vans.

At the third yard, they were intercepted by a burly worker dressed in overalls and a tweed flat cap. "Wotcha, cock?"

"Alrigh' mate? My guv'nor is looking for a secondhand lorry. I'm told there's one 'ereabouts for sale."

The man raised his flat hat and scratched his head. "Don't know nuffink 'bout that. My gaffer rents out space to anybody who wants to store his lorry off the streets. The Old Bill is cracking down on them parked in residential areas."

James pointed to the Bedford van whose license corresponded to one of those Donald had written down. "How's about that?"

"You can ask the bloke. His gaff's just 'round the corner, number 27."

"Is he a local?"

"I don't go sticking my nose where it ain't wanted."

"'Course not, but I might know him?"

"Doubt it, guv. He's a Fritz and I know what they sound like. My platoon captured a slew of Jerry at Passchendaele."

James left it at that and they returned to his car. Louise said, "Find a kiosk and tell Donald we've found one of the vans."

Jarvis answered the 'phone and passed it to Donald. After relating their information, he hung up and hoped Donald had gently broken the news of Bea's kidnapping.

When he returned to the car, Louise suggested they drive by the address on Fairway to see if there was any activity. Although net curtains covered the bay windows of number 27, they saw several people sitting at a table in the front room. He found another telephone box and informed Donald, the Fairway house was occupied.

The second address was on Hazelbank Road. James knew this was close to Bridge Wharf where small boats and lighters are moored on the narrow upper reaches of the Thames.

"The girls could have been drugged, ferried to the Port of London and transferred to a larger ship for transport to Germany. I'll ring Donald and suggest he add London to the APW."

Donald was obviously busy but found time to thank him for the update. He didn't volunteer any news and James didn't ask.

They drove slowly past the terraced house on Hazelbank Road but Louise couldn't see any activity through the front bay window. "They could be out back."

James nodded. Both were aware that one of Donald's teams would be there in a couple of hours.

The third address was a market garden business called Bourne Green Farm. It was only a quarter mile northwest of Woburn just off the A317. Being so close to home, James knew it was down a single-track road that dead-ended at the farm. He'd regularly ridden his horse down this lane during the summer vac. They parked in a lay-by and ambled down the rutted dirt track. When they reached the farm buildings, they saw six newish motorcars parked out front. In a dilapidated barn to the left, they spotted a green, mud-spattered John Deere tractor. Next to it, partially obscured by the barn door, was the second Bedford van.

Louise said, "We've seen enough."

They turned to leave, but froze when they heard the click of a bullet sliding into its chamber.

"Halt. Who are you?"

Louise replied in Bavarian German, "Bettina said we could take walks around her land if we felt like getting off the main roads."

"She didn't ask me."

"She's such a dear. We're friends from the orphanage."

He seemed satisfied and waved his gun towards the main road. "Raus!"

On the drive back to Woburn, Louise had her notebook out and was rapidly writing down registration numbers. When they entered the house, the library was a hive of activity with a dozen agents standing around the table littered with Ordinance Survey maps and paperwork.

Donald was using the hall telephone. He saw them enter and held up one finger while he finished speaking. After he hung, up he said, "Well done on your forward intelligence. I've made inquiries at the London Port Authority and they're working on your scenario right now."

James said, "We've found something else."

He described their reception at the farm cottage, the other Bedford van, and the six cars parked outside. Louise handed Donald her slip of paper.

They entered the library and Donald addressed his team. "Right. Listen up lads. Now we focus on Bourne Green Farm. Set up roadblocks on Woburn Hill in both directions and stop cars trying to leave the farm. If we can pick them off one at a time, they'll have no chance to warn the others. I'd like to have the army in on this with their firepower and uniforms. Trouble is, getting them in place would take hours and by then the gang might have scarpered."

Humphrey cleared his throat. "There's a platoon permanently stationed at Brooklands. That's thirty men, a lieutenant, and two NCO squad leaders. You might suggest they arrive with a couple of armoured personnel carriers to make their presence more intimidating."

Donald went to the hall 'phone and told the operator to connect him with Brooklands. When he returned he said, "They'll be in place in fifteen minutes. My agents will be at both roadblocks keeping an eye out for the registrations Louise supplied. Harry, get the soldiers to direct travellers to turn back due to a burst water main."

A few minutes later, Jarvis called Donald to the telephone. When he returned, he briefed his team with the latest developments. "When the bus reached the Weybridge terminus, my men were faced with a hostage situation. A stalemate lasted for several hours. Marksmen were called in and shots exchanged. One of my team was wounded and two civilians and a gang member were killed. The other Nazi surrendered and has been taken to the local nick. So far he's keeping stumm."

An hour later, Jarvis again called Donald to the telephone. This time he was away for twenty minutes. "My agents assigned to the house on Fairway, entered the premises and arrested a Schmidt sister and her husband. A second team broke into the house on Hazelbank Road but found it empty. They discovered a back-bedroom door with a new hasp and a sturdy lock. Mattresses, blankets, cups and dirty plates littered the floor."

A few minutes later, the telephone rang again. Donald took the call himself and after half an hour, returned to the library. "We've captured Betty Smith and several others at that stone cottage outside Weybridge. When the two cars attempted to leave, there was a bit of a shootout. All three have been arrested and are in custody in a local lockup. They denied any knowledge of Bea, Lily, or the Humber Snipe. Obviously, Betty Smith was lying through her teeth. Don't worry, we'll have them singing like canaries by morning."

Nothing of significance happened over the next two hours. The sun had set and the waiting was getting to the family. When the telephone rang, everyone stood while Donald engaged in a conversation lasting some forty-five minutes. He rang off and returned to the library. "Good thing we got our roadblocks in place. The six cars parked outside the farm were stopped on the A317 and twenty-two people have been taken into custody. My men and the soldiers then surrounded the house. Those still inside fired a few shots, but surrendered when they saw the military. We've rescued the eighteen kidnapped girls being held in the cellar."

"For God's sake, man, what about my sister?"

"I'm afraid there was no trace of her, but the girls said she'd been there earlier. I've instructed my agents and soldiers to scour the countryside and alert the Surrey Constabulary. Don't worry, we'll find her."

That assurance satisfied no one, especially not Louise who continued sniping at Donald. "So much for your clever planning."

In an attempt to make the peace, James asked, "How are the young women?"

"Lily and the others appeared unharmed. Remember, I told you they're precious cargo."

"Where are they from?"

"Several were from Surrey but others were kidnapped as far north as Aberdeen and Belfast. Most of those arrested are German and have no civil rights under British Law. Our interrogators will squeeze them until the pips squeak. When we inform them, alien spies can be hanged, it might encourage them to provide details of their operation."

Having calmed down, Louise asked Donald, "If it's not too much trouble, I'd like to talk with Lily tomorrow."

"I'll arrange it for the morning."

Over the next few hours, Donald's team quietly prepared for tomorrow's interrogations which would be conducted at Brooklands. The family's only concern was Bea's welfare. The projected scenarios concerning her safety became more and more outrageous. It was even suggested she might have been taken abroad, or worse yet, murdered as an inconvenient witness and dumped in a ditch.

At midnight they were startled by a knock on the front door. Jarvis answered it and an Army lieutenant escorted Bea into the library. Her dress was torn and muddy. Her hair was soaking wet and she looked exhausted. When she saw Donald another expression crossed her face. She rushed into the room and caught him in an embrace. Donald was embarrassed as this was in front of his team, but this didn't stop him from reciprocating.

"Can I get you anything, my dear?"

"I only need a bath and my bed."

30

SUNDAY, FEBRUARY 10TH, WOBURN

It had gone 2:00am when the last of the agents left. Harry stayed behind to have a final word with his boss. "Listen mate, you must be wacked. In a few hours, we'll need to begin interviewing the prisoners. You'll have to be in top form to coordinate the intelligence. Remember, you're the only one who can question the Germans if they can't or won't speak English."

Jarvis arranged for a sandwich and a glass of beer and Donald slowly climbed the stairs to his room. Before he returned to his Chertsey hotel, Harry spoke to the family. "On behalf of His Majesty's government, we thank you for your contributions to today's operation. Despite our successes, we've a long way to go. Our first task will be to discover exactly how many young women have been kidnapped and how they were transported to Germany. In the interviews, we'll try to get their descriptions so we can update local and national missing persons' files. Next, we'll need to see if our suspects lead us to other cells. Our immediate priority will be to find out if there are other staging areas. We'll do this immediately as we don't want to give them the chance to go to ground when they learn we've shut down their Addlestone base. Eventually, we'll contact our partners at the International Criminal Police Commission, but that will be only after we're certain we've completely dismantled their UK operations."

In the morning, James and Louise joined Donald at breakfast. "So, what's happening today?"

"Louise, our specialist team of interrogators won't arrive for another hour. We're letting the gang stew in their own juices and keeping them separated at Brooklands and in police lockups. I've just arranged for you to visit Lily after the orphanage church services at St Augustine's. She spent last night back in her dorm and will stay there until a Weybridge doctor examines her to see if she's fit to take up her job at the newsagents. Wednesday is early closing and the shopkeepers said they'll collect her in their motorcar."

"I trust you've remembered to arrange for the other young women to be seen by doctors."

"That was done straightaway. We won't receive formal written reports for a few days, but the medics say all are well with no apparent physical injuries. They'll keep tabs on them to ensure there are no lingering psychological issues."

"That's precisely why I wish to talk to Lily. I'd like to see if her positive outlook on life has suffered."

When Bea entered the library, she went straight to Donald and gave him a peck on the cheek. He told her she looked rested and radiant. Jarvis poured her a cup of tea and she joined the family at the table.

Donald asked her, "I'd like to learn all I can about how this lot operates before I begin the interrogations. Are you up to telling us what happened?"

"That's no problem, although I have to admit I was terrified. After Miss Smith escorted us off the bus, Lily and I were driven to a cottage in the middle of nowhere. In addition to the driver, two other men were there. They tied our hands behind our backs and at dusk, the same driver blindfolded us and told us to lie down on the Humber's back seat. Initially it was a bumpy ride so I presume he drove on farm tracks until we reached a tarmacadamed road. When we finally stopped, he led us into a farmhouse, removed our blindfolds, and untied our hands.

"About half a dozen men stood and saluted our driver. I remember, one addressed him as Joseph Housman. That's when the driver called me a bonus. At that moment, I realised I was to be part of their Lebensborn programme. I decided I'd commit suicide before I'd allow myself to be raped to serve as a Nazi breeder.

"Lily and I were taken down to the cellar where I met a number of blonde teenage girls. They were frightened and confused so I reassured them we'd be rescued. To be honest, I wasn't all that confident.

"A few hours later, we heard the telephone ring upstairs. Almost immediately, Housman fetched me up to the sitting room and retied my hands behind my back. He led me to a barn and lifted me onto an old tractor. Now he called me his insurance policy. We crossed some sodden fields until we got to Mead Lane. He stopped the tractor and simply walked off into the night. It was pitch dark and drizzling. After a bit, I managed to tumble down and make my way towards Fordwater Road. I shouted and kicked on a door until the family woke. They untied my hands, gave me a cup of tea, and called the police. Eventually, some soldiers arrived and brought me home."

Louise never suspected Bea had the emotional toughness to recount her dreadful experience in such a matter-of-fact way.

Humphrey stood and hugged his granddaughter. "You're a brave soldier and I'm proud of you. After breakfast, it's St Paul's as usual."

Donald said, "I would have liked to join you, but my team will arrive at Brooklands in a few minutes. I expect we'll be questioning our prisoners well into next week."

Louise met Lily outside St Augustine's and together they walked back to the orphanage. Louise returned to Woburn just as the family returned from the George.

James asked, "How's Lily doing?"

"I expect she'll be fine. She's anxious to get out into the world to see what life brings. I told her we'd be living here after our wedding and we'd always be available should she need help or advice."

Dorothy abruptly stood, went to her study, and returned with a large envelope. "I'm glad you mentioned the wedding. What with all this kerfuffle, I'd completely forgotten that the invitation pro forma arrived last Thursday. Louise, before you leave, you should at least choose the style of script."

"What about the message?"

"Leave that to me. We know the date, time, and location and that's really all that matters. The printer said they'll be ready to be addressed in a fortnight."

31

TUESDAY, FEBRUARY 12TH, CAMBRIDGE

At the end of his tutorial, Richard identified several areas he should tackle and lectures he ought to attend. He was given two sets of ten problems on differential geometry and complex manifolds. Before leaving, James asked about the kidnappings.

"Scotland Yard has arrested more cell members based in the Home Counties including the other Schmidt sisters and their husbands. Donald's MI6 team is still interrogating those we captured last Saturday evening. They've isolated the suspects and used the usual technique of suggesting certain individuals had confessed so all that was needed was corroboration. All were German citizens apart from a few who'd emigrated from Germany and been naturalised. They told us they were trained by SS officers who received their instructions from Generalleutnant Wilhelm Keitel. Apparently, he's been appointed by Hitler to head the Wehrmacht. This newly formed organisation is now part of what they call the Oberkommando or High Command. Keitel is a new name to us. We're trying to learn as much as we can about him from the prisoners.

"Donald's language skills were crucial. Most had only rudimentary knowledge of English. Some outright threats were used including informing them the penalty for treason and espionage could include hanging. Interestingly, several seemed more afraid of being deported back to Germany having made a dog's dinner of their mission.

"We've confirmed the Bedford vans were used to collect the young women from various staging locations around Britain and Northern Ireland. We've also established that Bourne Green Farm was the final UK holding area. From there, they were transferred to German registered merchant ships. It turned out they were gagged and simply escorted up the gangplank at night. Needless to say, Customs and Excise has egg on its face. They've sacked several customs officers and charged them with criminal dereliction of duty. The Home Office is in the process of tightening up UK port security."

"How many girls have been abducted to Germany?"

"They admit to four deliveries of nine at a time."

"Can MI6 launch a rescue?"

"That's not an option. We've few operatives in Germany now they've tightened border controls. We've no idea of their final destination so I'm afraid we'll have to regard them as casualties of war."

James was stunned by this dismissal, but had the presence of mind to ask, "What about other countries?"

"Through secure diplomatic connections, we've contacted representatives of the International Criminal Police Commission and informed them about the UK Lebensborn operation. Unfortunately, Germany is also an ICPC member and the Abwehr will eventually become aware of our direct role in dismantling their British wing. For the present, that's all we can do. Other countries have a duty to protect their citizens."

James absorbed this information with a degree of sadness. Still, they'd saved his sister and nine others from a life of slavery and state-sanctioned rape.

"You just mentioned the Abwehr. What's that?"

"It's the Nazi equivalent of our Ministry of Defence. It's their intelligence organisation designed to gather information both domestically and abroad."

"Why Addlestone? It's a quiet little backwater where nothing much happens."

"James, you've answered your own question. Addlestone is like many Home Counties villages where nobody thinks anything as evil as this could occur. That suits those who wish to commit such atrocities on our soil."

"One more question. Why orphanage girls?"

"Several reasons. First of all, once they left at 16 there'd be no family or friends to report them missing. Secondly, they've lived a cloistered life. They'd be virgins free of any sexually transmitted diseases. Hence they'd make ideal candidates to serve as breeders of Aryan children."

32

THURSDAY, FEBRUARY 14ᵀᴴ, CAMBRIDGE

Louise was first to arrive at the Mitre at opening time and bagged a table. When she looked up, she saw James approaching with a pint in one hand and a Gin and It in the other.

"James, I've reserved a table at the Hotel du Vin on Trumpington Street and I'd like you to join me for dinner. Pack your toothbrush, I've also booked a room."

The restaurant was intimate and their table illuminated by candlelight. She raised her flute of Champagne, "Here's to Saint Valentine of Terni and your 24ᵗʰ birthday."

In bed she handed him a small box. Inside were a pair of gold and cornflower blue sapphire cufflinks.

"I found these on Old Bond Street when I was helping Bea with her shopping."

She turned towards him and they celebrated his birthday as only lovers can.

In the morning, they agreed to bunk off and drive to Woburn. Donald's government issue Austin 6 was parked in the courtyard. There had been rain and freezing fog on the drive down from Cambridge so the corner fireplace offered a welcoming blaze.

While Jarvis took their requests for pre-lunch drinks, James asked Donald for an update on the kidnappings. "We've charged thirty-seven people who've admitted their roles. A few were British born supporters of Nazi Germany. Their information allowed us to detain and interrogate another twenty based in various parts of the British Isles. They've been placed on remand and will be formally charged this week."

"What about Joseph Housman?"

"He's a loose end. Bea looked at photos of German residents but with no success. Trouble is, he's almost certainly not a foreigner. According to Bea, he had a plummy upper-class accent. Did you know she's quite a talented artist? She sketched a likeness which we'll circulate around the south of England."

Louise asked, "Have you found other girls?"

"We've freed another thirty who were being held in makeshift cells around the UK. That makes seventy young women we've rescued thanks to Bea and yourselves. By the way, I've taken Bea into our confidences. This morning, I acted as her MI6 recruiter and she's signed the Official Secrets Act."

Louise congratulated her. "What about your training?"

"At some stage, I'll attend a two-week course in tradecraft in the Midlands."

"Will that involve weapons' instruction?"

"Absolutely, as well as unarmed combat and self-defence techniques. I'll also learn about disguises and covert communication including cyphers and codes. I know a fortnight isn't much, but in my first year in the field, I'll have a mentor. You two have been so successful posing as a pair of young lovers, MI6 has decided Donald and I should do the same."

"I'd be interested to know how much role-playing is involved, if that isn't too personal a question."

"Well, it is rather. But as you've raised the subject, we're now officially a couple."

Jarvis entered the room with two bottles of Dom Perignon and six flutes.

"I'm impressed. Do you always keep a couple of bottles of Champagne chilling in the icebox?"

"Not normally, Colonel. Some of us felt it might be needed."

After lunch, James asked Donald about the European investigation. "It's now codenamed Lebensborn. Through diplomatic contacts, we've confirmed that several other countries have reported similar disappearances of blonde female orphanage leavers. It's apparently endemic in countries bordering Germany, particularly Poland. The good news is we're confident we've dismantled their British based operation."

"I'm glad for that, especially since we were able to play a small part."

"No, Louise. MI6 was effectively working for the three of you. Bea's inside knowledge of the orphanage was crucial. SIS was only alerted because she kept track of leavers and didn't give up trying to find Betty and Kitty. Without her, it might have been months before this came to light, indeed, if ever.

"Louise, your outstanding memory for registrations gave us a head start on identifying the gang and capturing them, as they fled Bourne Green Farm.

"And James, your local knowledge enabled us to arrest the entire Surrey cell and rescue the ten young women held there. Take note, I've included Bea in that total. From our interrogations, we've learned she was to be added to the next shipment to Germany. That was scheduled for the early hours of last Sunday morning which is why there were so many of the gang at Bourne Green Farm. Our Saturday night raid was in the nick of time."

Dorothy changed the subject. "We really must consolidate the wedding guest list to get an idea of numbers. Two hundred engraved invitations have arrived so we should make a start on getting them ready for posting."

With the plan agreed in principle, there was general relief when Donald suggested a stroll into the village. The weather had improved and the sun was out although it was still only in the high 30s.

Donald said, "I'd like to see the Crouch Oak. I read about it as a schoolboy. It's believed to be one of the oldest trees in Britain."

When they returned to Woburn Hall, Humphrey announced the sun was over the yardarm.

After dinner it was obvious Bea had been thinking about the wedding guest list. "Louise, do you think we should write addresses down as well?"

"Hardly. That would be seriously tedious and likely introduce errors of transcription."

Dorothy nodded her agreement. "Once we've got a master list, each of us should be responsible for addressing and mailing invitations to your friends."

33

SATURDAY, FEBRUARY 23RD, WOBURN

This morning, they attempted to create the wedding guest list. This was not going well. Alphabetising the names of titled guests was the primary the bone of contention. Another issue was whether those with double-barrelled surnames should be listed under the initial of their first or second name. Louise insisted de la Béré should be placed under B rather than D. Tempers frayed and on several occasions, sharp words were exchanged between Donald and Louise. This was followed by periods of tense silence. Humphrey called time and demanded a truce.

They went for a short walk around the grounds to admire the snowdrops and crocuses. When they returned, it was agreed they deserved a pre-lunch libation.

While Jarvis served drinks, Louise broke the strained silence. "Is our French trip still on?"

"It is indeed, and I've a surprise. My former commanding officer General Sir Nicholas Gavin-Wheeler and his wife Lady Helen will be joining us. They have a large wine cellar in dire need of replenishing. They live in Dublin and plan to take the Holyhead ferry and catch a connecting train to Euston station in London."

"In that case, Louise and I will take the Railton."

After lunch, they continued the task of creating a master wedding guest list. To everybody's relief, they reached the end of the alphabet just as the sun was setting.

Dorothy oversaw the arrangements. "So far there are 127 invitations to be posted. Louise, we should plan on around 200 guests."

"That many?"

"Most will be couples and there'll be families with children. Also, there's bound to be people we've forgotten. I didn't hear you call out any de la Bérés apart from your uncle and aunt."

"You're right. I'll need to have a word with my guardian."

James said, "My dear, you've an unusual surname. Why not use directory inquiries?"

Donald attempted to make the peace. "Louise, you might wish to leave this with me. I'll have a word with my Home Office contacts. They have access to all sorts of domestic registers."

Louise smiled, "That's a very gracious offer, thank you."

Bea said, "Let me take the guest list to the orphanage. I'll get one of my girls to copy it out twice, one to list details of the posted invitations and acceptances and the other to record the wedding gifts as they arrive. I've in mind one of our senior girls who'll be leaving in August. She has a beautiful hand and has been given secretarial training by one of our staff. I'll pay her, of course."

James asked, "Where will guests spend Saturday night after the reception?"

Humphrey said, "Family will stay with us and that includes yours, Donald. Others who aren't locals won't have any idea about accommodation. I'll have Jarvis make a list of nearby hotels and inns. We can include that with the non-locals' invitations."

When the dinner gong sounded, they went into the dining room for a light supper buoyed by the fact that the tedium of the guest list was now out of their hands. After coffees, they said their goodnights. Bea said they'd remain downstairs as she and Donald had something to discuss.

At breakfast, Bea said they'd like to join them on their French wine trip. Louise caught James's eye. Before they went to sleep, she suggested Bea might be running the idea past Donald. Humphrey pointed out the Daimler wouldn't be able to handle six people and their luggage.

"Donald will take his own motorcar."

James said, "I didn't know you owned one. You always come down here by train or drive those government-issue Austins."

"I don't use it much. I keep it in my mews stable garage."

"What sort is it?"

"It's rather silly, really. I have a seven-seater Packard limousine. I've always liked those big American straight-eights."

"Same here. My Railton has an eight-cylinder Hudson motor. I'd like to see your limo."

"You'll get a chance in three weeks. I say Humphrey, Bea and I could collect your friends at Euston on our way down."

"How would you recognise them?"

"James, I'm an experienced agent trained to know things and ferret out information. More's the point, I'll have a placard with the words, Meeting Sir Nicholas and Lady Helen Gavin-Wheeler from Dublin."

After the St Paul's service, they went to the George. James only had a half of bitter and Louise stuck to lemon barley water. Both planned to put in some serious revision when they returned to Cambridge. Over lunch, Donald asked, "Could I cadge a lift back to London?

When they reached the Thames, Donald directed him to his house. It was a three-story Georgian terrace on Danvers Street, just off Chelsea Embankment. After dropping him off they crossed town to connect with the A3 to Cambridge.

"You know, old Hutchinson does all right for himself, what with that large house in Chelsea and the Packard. I'll wager he didn't buy those on a civil servant's salary. You realise, we know nothing about him apart from the fact he's a kind and gentle man who makes Bea happy. Actually, that's really all that matters."

"You're right of course, but you know, he can be a bit bossy. If he's wealthy, why on earth did he become a SIS wage slave?"

"Probably for the same reasons we did. I'll inquire on our trip to France as Bea's elder brother."

Louise gave him a puzzled glance and then stared out the car's side window.

"By six minutes."

34

TUESDAY, FEBRUARY 26ᵀᴴ, CAMBRIDGE

At his regular tutorial, Richard assigned questions from past part III Tripos papers and suggested he attend several lectures relating to Algebraic Geometry and specifically, curves and their Jacobians.

James said, "I've a couple of questions?"

"Do continue."

"Since you seem to know almost everything before it happens, I expect you're aware my sister Beatrice and Donald Hutchinson are now a couple."

"He asked MI6's permission to include her in his confidences as regards the Lebensborn investigation and recruited her to MI6. Is that a problem?"

"Not at all. They're both very happy and will be joining us in France during the vac."

"I'm aware of that, as well. Donald has arranged informal meetings with Lebensborn investigators in France, Austria, Belgium, and Holland."

"Louise and I would like to know more about him, you know, his background and so forth."

"You really should ask."

"I will, but could you steer me in the right direction so I don't embarrass myself?"

"I was teasing. His family is part of the aristocracy. They have a large estate in Yorkshire where he spent his early childhood before going off to Harrow. At Oxford, he was awarded a first in Modern Languages and a boxing Blue. His father is a hereditary peer and, as the eldest son, he'll inherit the title."

By telephone, James suggested they meet before the Mitre's opening time at a jewellers he knew on Fitzwilliam Street. Once there, they opted for plain platinum wedding bands. After sizing their ring fingers, the owner said he could have them ready in three weeks, but required a deposit. James wrote out his cheque for the total amount made payable to Joseph Libowitz and Sons, (Jewellers) Ltd.

They walked to the pub and secured their usual table in the snug.

"I've been invited to another meeting of the Apostles on Saturday. I'd like to attend to see what mischief they might be concocting."

"I've a golf match this weekend for the ladies Cambridge team. Shall we go to Woburn the following weekend?"

35

FRIDAY, MARCH 8TH, WOBURN

A fortnight later, they motored down to Addlestone. The family were in the library chatting to a girl in Orphanage uniform. Bea made the introductions. "This is Alice Ogden. She's a close friend to Lily and is now a Prefect. I've asked her to copy out your wedding guest list with columns to record whether they're friends of the bride or groom, whether they'd attend, and numbers in their party. She's also made a second list to record the wedding gifts as they arrive. Look what she's managed."

Louise admired her script, which was up to the standard of a professional calligrapher. "Where did you learn to do such high-quality work?"

"Miss Harcourt-Heath leant me some books on penmanship and secretarial duties. I've practiced as best I could in our library."

James took charge. "Tell you what, let's employ Alice as our wedding secretary. She can help Dorothy with the organisation and get some on-the-job experience. Bea, would she be able to get away from the orphanage during the day?"

"Alice is respected and trusted by Matron and the staff."

"Right, let's make it official. Alice, how 'bout a salary of five bob a week?"

"I'd be grateful for the chance to help out. I expect I could even get a reference when I leave in August and try to find a proper job."

Dorothy was impressed by her foresight. "After lunch, we should write down addresses so Alice can prepare the invitations. We can mail them from here and your Cambridge friends should receive theirs in the next day's post."

As they were doing this, Alice prepared a sample invitation. The envelope was addressed in her beautiful script and she'd printed the return address on the back flap. Inside was a second slightly smaller envelope containing the engraved invitation on which she'd written the guest's Christian names. Also, inside were the printed map and a list of local inns along with yet another smaller stamped RSVP envelope. Alice would cycle to Woburn each morning and work in the library until lunchtime. She'd return to the orphanage for her midday meal and in the afternoon work from two to six, Saturday being her half-day.

Over supper Donald discussed their French trip. "Bea and I have some work-related meetings on the continent so we can only spend a few days in Burgundy."

"Ours will be short, as well. I've got my Boat Race training and both of us have academic deadlines. Grandpapa, I expect you and the Gavin-Wheelers will explore other wine areas afterwards."

"That's our mission. Nicholas and I plan to go to Bordeaux for claret, Reims for Champagne and the Loire valley for whites."

Donald said, "My father has given me carte blanche to re-stock our cellar in Yorkshire. He said it's especially important since the European situation is rapidly deteriorating. I expect you've noticed, last week Hitler ordered the reestablishment of the Luftwaffe under Generalleutnant Walther Wever. Although this was not unexpected, it should be a wake-up call to those still hoping for a diplomatic solution."

James decided this was a good opportunity to inquire about his family. "I say, Donald, are you close to your parents?"

"Very much so. My father, Gerald, is Lord Hutchinson of Whorlton and my mother is Lady Mary. After our European trip, I'll accompany Bea on her training course. After that, we'll drive to Yorkshire so she can meet my parents and siblings."

"So you've brothers and sisters?"

"One of each. Walter read Philosophy, Politics and Economics at Oxford and is now a research fellow at Balliol while he works on his doctorate. My sister Florence read English at Edinburgh University. She's just passed the Civil Service exams."

36

FRIDAY, MARCH 15TH, WOBURN

He spent the final week of term training daily on the Great Ouse, attending maths lectures, and solving problems from past papers. When they arrived at Woburn, Alice was in the library addressing envelopes while Bea folded maps and the printed list of local inns and hotels.

"My oarsmen pals have received their invitations, so your system is working."

Alice said shyly, "As your grandparents will be away for a few weeks, I expect I won't be needed."

James said, "If you continue your secretarial studies, we'll maintain your wages."

"I'll work on my shorthand. Miss Harcourt-Heath purchased a Remington typewriting machine and I can try to improve my speed and accuracy while they're away."

After a light midday meal, Louise said she was tired and went upstairs. Humphrey asked James if he could join him in the library.

"What's on your mind grandpapa?"

"Now that you're about to meet the Gavin-Wheelers, I'd like to tell you a couple of things about them. Nicholas has been one of my closest friends for the last forty years. He saved my life when I nearly bled-out after taking a Boer bullet in the shoulder at the siege of Mafeking. I was a Captain and he held the rank of Major. Our commanding officer was

Colonel Baden-Powell. Every November 11th, Nicholas and I join him at Lutyens' Cenotaph in Whitehall. I'm sure you're aware, he's now 1st Baron Baden-Powell and holds the rank of Lieutenant General.

"After the Great War, Nicholas settled in Dublin where his wife has family. Apart from Armistice Day, we don't see much of him these days. We telephone occasionally but write almost weekly. It wasn't always like this. In the months following your father's death, he provided steadfast support. What I wanted to tell you is that Nicholas is your godfather and his wife, Lady Helen, is your godmother."

"Hang about. I thought, you and grandmama are our godparents."

"Before leaving for America, my son asked me to approach them to see if they'd act as backups in the event something happened to us. Remember I was a serving officer and we were at war. What's more, your father was a lawyer and they've a well-earned reputation for caution and probity. When they renewed their wills, it's possible their solicitor suggested reserve godparents. Now we'll never know. All present at that meeting are long gone.

"After the Lusitania was torpedoed and our only child murdered by the Germans, Dorothy and I were barely able to function. Nicholas and Helen arrived at Woburn and took charge. His London solicitors dealt with the probate, set up the trust for you and your sisters, and transferred the ownership of Woburn and the London residential properties to your name. Through his contacts, he arranged for your admission as a border at Dulwich College. He did the same for Bea and Margie at James Allen's Girls' School in nearby East Dulwich. Over the years, he's kept close contact with the Dulwich Master and the JAGS Headmistress. I expect he took such an interest in your lives because both his sons were killed during the fierce battle of Arras in 1917."

The family were in the library when they heard the throaty sound of an eight-cylinder motorcar in the front drive. James walked around the gleaming dark blue limo. "I say old man, she's a cracker. I expect you find left-hand drive a bit of a trial on our narrow country roads."

"I've the power to pretty much pass anything I want. In any case, in France, my car will be like the others and you'll be struggling to pass lorries and tractors."

As greetings and introductions were being made, Helen embraced Bea. "You remind me so much of your mother. She was a very beautiful lady."

Humphrey ushered the family into the library and said to no one in particular, "Sun's over the yardarm so we're allowed a spot of the preprandials, what?"

Jarvis handed Nicholas a crystal tumbler half-filled with Jameson 18-year-old Limited Reserve. It was the General's preferred pre-dinner drink. In the dining room, Clos des Chênes was poured to accompany the usual roast beef. Afterwards, port and coffee were served in the library.

Nicholas said, "We're both tired. It's been a long day and tomorrow promises to be another. Can your batman show us to our quarters?"

As if by magic, Jarvis appeared in the hall doorway where their luggage still rested.

"But first, I have a gift for my goddaughter."

Bea looked uncertain when Nicholas motioned her to sit next to him on the sofa. "Helen and I bought this for your mother's 10th wedding anniversary. At her memorial service here at St Paul's, I decided I'd give this to you when the time was right.

She opened a small box and inside was a pair of solitaire diamond earrings set it white gold.

Tears rolled down her cheeks. Bea rose and gave them both an embrace.

Humphrey attempted to take charge. "We should get some kip. It's a long drive to Beaune, you know."

Nicholas remained seated. "James, your grandfather has kept us briefed as regards your academic and sporting successes. Helen and I wished to be kept in the background, but we're both delighted to see what a fine young man you've become. This was your father's. It was being repaired when they left for America. I took the telephone call when the jewellers said it was ready for collection. With Humphrey's permission, I've kept it in safekeeping for the last twenty years waiting for the right time to pass it on."

James opened the heavy package. Inside was an elaborately engraved gold pocket watch with tiny diamonds set into the front cover. The gold chain held the winding key and the fob was a Sterling silver monogrammed seal with the initials H-H. On the centre of the watch cover were his father's initials, J.R.H-H.

Humphrey stood. "Now, it's indeed time for our beds. Up at seven thirty, breakfast at eight, and we'll be on the road at nine Ack Emma."

37

SATURDAY MARCH 16TH, MOREY-SAINT-DENIS

As they sat in the ship's café with mugs of tea, Donald put his hand on Louise's arm. "I'm afraid my Home Office search of your family name was a bust. There are a handful of de la Bere's in England and Wales, but none with the two diacritic acute marks attached to your surname. I did discover there'd been couple of spinsters with that spelling who lived together in Hastings. Both succumbed during the second 'flu pandemic in 1920 and left their substantial fortune to the Battersea Dogs' Home. I found no telephone listings, General Post Office mailing addresses, pension records, Inland Revenue filings, Local Authority tax records, or Land Registry entries for anybody with that name, apart from yours, that is."

"Donald, I'm truly sorry we seem to have got off on the wrong foot. I expect it's entirely my fault. I'm often suspicious of people's motives or am unable to understand their intentions. As a consequence, all my life, I've had difficulty making friends. Please forgive me and let me say, I'm exceedingly grateful for your efforts. I suppose I've always suspected I have no English relatives since I've had no contact with any family my entire life. I'm actually relieved that door is finally closed."

They felt the vibration as the ferry's engines reversed as it approached Calais harbour. That was their signal to return to the deck to be ready to claim their cars after cranes lowered them onto the quayside.

Once on shore, James said, "We know our way to Beaune so I suggest we drive in convoy. If we only stop for petrol and perhaps a quick lunch in Reims, we should arrive in time for the dinner service."

Louise had booked three double and two single rooms at the Hôtel le Cep. Donald requested a double when they arrived at the reception desk. Louise presumed Bea had discussed this arrangement with her grandparents.

Clos des Chênes was their first stop after breakfast. Using the brass hand-shaped knocker, Louise rapped on the front door. Louisa embraced her and they kissed four times, two on each cheek, which, in this part of France, is reserved for family and close friends. After the introductions, they were invited into the house to warm themselves in front of the open fireplace.

James said, "We arrived last night to begin a wine tour of Burgundy. Naturally, we wanted to stop here first. Could you show us 'round?"

Michel led them across the cobbled courtyard and up a slight rise to the left of the house. This gave them a panoramic view of the 12-hectare estate. Nicholas asked about what looked like dormant rosebushes at the end of each row.

Louise interrupted Michel's explanation. "In France it's called companion planting. It's based on the same principle as taking a canary into a coal mine. Roses act as a sentinel. Grape vines and roses are susceptible to the same diseases including downy and powdery mildew. If either is spotted on the roses at the ends of the rows, the vignerons know to spray the grape vines with Bordeaux mixture. Roses also attract ladybirds which are particularly fond of the aphids that can damage the vines proper."

Nicholas smiled, "Both practical and romantic. How very French."

In the barn, Michel explained the process of pressing and fermentation. Donald asked a couple of questions in French.

After Michel answered, he added, "I'm glad at least of two of the family have had a civilised upbringing."

He led them to the cave entrance cut into the hillside. The arched stone ceiling was festooned with cobwebs and both sides were lined with two-metre-high iron bottle racks. Michel lit a candle and disappeared into the gloom, eventually returning with a bottle in each hand.

Back at the house, Louisa invited them to sit down at their long oak dining table. Michel carefully opened both bottles, sniffed the cork and when satisfied, poured the contents into ten glasses. Neither bottle had a label but Louise knew that was one of the last steps before shipping. Louisa returned from the kitchen carrying a platter of sliced baguette, cheese, and thinly sliced smoked ham. The rest imitated Michel by warming the wine by holding the glass in both hands while swirling the liquid to release the aroma.

Louise stood, handed their wedding invitation to her aunt and raised her glass. "Here's to my two families."

Humphrey said, "I insist you stay with us. Why not take a few extra days in England after the wedding? Dorothy and I can show you around."

After a few minutes of conversation, Nicholas addressed Michel using his pigeon French. "Have you a decent restaurant nearby?"

"Monsieur, this is France. Bad restaurants simply cannot exist. They would be out of business within a week of opening."

"Then, can you tell us the name of the best local restaurant?"

"You should try Castel de Trés Girard."

"Would you join us tonight, say at eight? We'll book the table on our way back to our hotel. Just now, let's begin stocking our cellars."

Michel said, "Since you plan to lay down wine for aging, I'd suggest a range of years. Can I assume your cellars are sufficiently humid, say at about seventy per cent and maintain a constant temperature of around thirteen degrees Celsius?"

Louise translated and explained that was about fifty-five degrees Fahrenheit.

Michel then summarised the ratings of the various Pinot Noir and Chardonnay vintages going back to the turn of the century. The men took notes for future Burgundy purchases. In the end, each ordered sixteen cases of wine including four en primeur. Michel prepared their invoices after consulting a leather-bound journal.

"Normally, shipping and insurance would add about 10%. Because you're family, I'll pay that myself. What you owe is what you see on your invoices."

They'd come prepared with large denomination banknotes in their billfolds. Each owed slightly over 5000 francs.

"I have Humphrey's address but if Donald and Nicholas could give me your cards, I can add it to the invoice and arrange labelling and shipping next week."

In the tiny hamlet of Morey-Saint-Denis, they easily found the restaurant and made their booking. The sign outside said it had been an éstablissement vinicole in the 17th century.

Back at their hotel, they collected their passports and room keys and went upstairs for a rest. Once in their room, James commented, "I noticed you didn't mention our interest in funding and eventually purchasing Clos des Chênes."

"In Latin countries, business is never conducted in a social setting and certainly not with others present. I expect they've thought about our offer, but we must leave it to them to broach the subject."

They all met up in the hotel's reception and decided on a walk around Beaune before dinner. Nicholas asked about a shop that had wine bottles displayed in its window.

As they've come to expect, Louise provided a short lecture on the subject of Burgundy wine production. "This is a négociant. In Bordeaux they're simply merchants who find buyers for locally produced wine. In Burgundy, they might buy grapes for fermentation, must, or finished wines in bulk for blending and bottling. Most are themselves wine producers."

At the restaurant, they found Michel and Louisa already seated at a table for ten. Michel ordered a local Grand Cru he said was almost on par with Clos des Chênes. The group got on well as it turned out everybody had some French. Nicholas and Humphrey's language skills were based on their lessons at the Royal Military Academy, Sandhurst more than sixty years earlier. It turned out, Bea was also fluent although shy about speaking in public. James was able to follow most of the conversations based on his French lessons at Dulwich College when he was in Middle School. Throughout the meal, Louise chatted quietly to her aunt and uncle at their end of the table.

Nicholas summoned the waiter. "L'addition, s'il vous plait."

The others showed surprise, since his request, although perfectly understandable, had overtones of an Irish brogue. "What? I can get a drink, order a meal, and pay the bill in about twenty languages including Afrikaans, Zulu, Xhosa and, of course, Irish."

As they were leaving, Michel said something to Louise and they all shook hands or kissed as appropriate.

Back in their hotel lounge, Nicholas ordered two chilled bottles of Champagne.

Humphrey said, "Good man. What are we celebrating?"

"Ah, well now, me lad, don't you be knowing, it's Saint Paddy's Day?"

Humphrey raised his glass. "Here's to our family and an Ireland free of snakes."

Nicholas assumed command of what he termed Operation Burgundy. "If you've no objections, after breakfast, let's check out these négociant chaps. Donald and Louise can translate and we can sample a few more wines. Up at nine and a frontal assault by ten?"

Louise demurred. "I'm afraid James and I will have to beg off. We've an appointment in Nuits-Saint-Georges."

38

MONDAY, MARCH 18TH, NUITS-SAINT-GEORGES

Promptly at ten, James and Louise arrived at the Étude of M Le Rouvillois. Louisa and Michel were already seated in the notaire's office. On his desk, rested a large manila folder elaborately inscribed, de la Béré and underneath, Clos des Chênes. The civil servant began formally. "It is my duty to conduct property transactions in accordance with Code Napoléon. In doing so, I represent neither party. Michel and Louisa de la Béré have employed an avocat who has drawn up this contract."

He passed Louise an impressive-looking document, filled with strange legalese, hand written in elaborate and archaic French script.

"I'm afraid I've no knowledge of the law. We'll need to consult our own solicitor and go through this line by line."

M Le Rouvillois raised his right hand. "The bulk of this contract is absolutely standard for property sales and purchases. Let me summarise the contents and conditions so you understand the suggested arrangements.

"It is Michel and Louisa's wish, you become the eventual owners of their vineyard. However, they want to ensure you're serious about upgrading the operation. Their lawyer proposed the following conditions. They have agreed to transfer the ownership of the property to you over a period of ten years. During that time, you'll be effectively purchasing the vineyard in stages by investing capital to modernise the buildings and the equipment. Throughout that period, they will remain the sole arbiters as to how much capital is required and what improvements are necessary.

143

Furthermore, they insist they have the right to remain in their house and retain full control over the winemaking operation during this transition period. After ten years, when both have turned seventy-five, the property will be transferred to your names or before then in the event both are deceased."

James said, "I'm sure you will live longer than that. I'd like to insert a clause stating they have the right to remain in their house for as long as they wish after March, 1945. I'd also like to stipulate they'd receive 50% of the annual profits for as long as they live. That would provide them with a pension after they retire."

When Louise translated, both smiled and nodded. The notaire added these detail to a handwritten addendum to the final page of the contract.

"It's been our life's ambition to achieve a Grand Cru classification. Louisa and I believe this would be possible with modern equipment. That will be our legacy."

M Le Rouvillois continued, "There's one further aspect I'm obliged to explain. This is a legally binding contract. If either party reneges on the conditions, the contract is void and the other can successfully sue for damages."

The agreement with the changes and additions was placed before them and the notaire asked each to then initial each page of the document and then write the words, lues et approuvées and then sign and date their signatures on the final page.

Their business concluded they went to a nearby café. Louise asked Michel to order a bottle of the best wine in the district.

"They don't stock ours."

"Then ask the waiter for the wine list and choose a Grand Cru from Morey-Saint-Denis."

Michel outlined his plans for modernising the equipment and replanting some of the less productive sections.

James replied, "That's why we're here. Have you thought about what you'll need?"

"Bien sûr, but it'll be expensive. You might prefer to make improvements a bit at a time."

"Let's start as we mean to continue so everything is ready for the harvest in September."

"I'd hoped you'd say that. We're both getting on and we'd like to bequeath our vineyard as a profitable business. If you come back to our house, I've a schedule of what I'd like to purchase and estimates of the cost."

"We're the amateurs. Go ahead with the upgrades. Have you a rough idea how much money you'll need to prepare for the September vendange?"

"I'd prefer we start with the best equipment rather than make do and replace poor quality or second-hand machines later. First, we'll modernise our outbuildings. Then, we need a new press, an automated conveyor to take the grapes up to the press, two new oak fermentation vats, a pump to take the juice to the great vats, and new American and French oak barrels for aging. I'm afraid that will cost about a million francs."

James did a quick mental calculation. A franc equalled approximately thruppence ha'penny, so 1,000,000 francs was a bit over £15,000.

Although both realised this was an enormous sum, James and Louise agreed to the expenditure. James asked for their banking details and noted them in his diary. "It'll take a few weeks to arrange the transfer. When we return to England, I'll have my bank send £3,000 or just under 200,000 francs to your account. Louise will ring next week to ensure it has arrived. A similar tranche will follow within a month and the balance will be at your bank before summer. One final thing, when you come over for our wedding, could you tell us how the work is progressing?"

"Don't worry, it'll be ready. I've already made inquiries with suppliers. Given the current Depression, they've assured me everything we need is in their warehouses ready for delivery. All they require is a 10% deposit before releasing the machinery. I've also approached a reliable building firm in Beaune. They could begin immediately once they receive an initial deposit to cover the cost of materials. To oversee the renovations, I've enlisted an architect who specialises in établissement vinicole."

Before they left, Louise turned to Michel and asked him a question to which he answered with a nod and a smile.

Back at their hotel, they found the others in the lounge holding glasses of red wine.

Nicholas said, "There's enough left in the bottle for you two to have a taste of one of our purchases. What were you up to?"

Louise smiled. "We've signed a contract whereby we'll become the eventual owners of Clos des Chênes. I've also asked Michel to give me away and he's agreed. And you?"

"The forces are advancing. We've each purchased four cases of Nuits-Saint-Georges Grand Cru from a producer called Les Cailles, two en primeur and two of their '24. That's what you're sipping just now. You know, as a sporting man, I like these arrangements. Buying en primeur allows the grower or these négociant chaps to cover some of their costs. It's a bit like a futures market. Both sides are accepting risk. We're hoping it'll be a great vintage but the producer and the négociant won't know until it's aged and been judged by experts. If it's average or substandard, we'll have paid too much for some plonk. But if it's a great vintage, we'll have secured a bargain we can drink for years to come."

Louise asked him, "What's on the agenda tomorrow?"

"South to Puligny-Montrachet."

"Count us in. I adore that wine."

Over a light lunch of smoked trout and salade niçoise, Humphrey mentioned he'd purchased Saturday's Daily Telegraph at a Tabac. "Hitler has just reintroduced conscription, yet another violation of Versailles. Ramsey MacDonald's so-called National Government continues to dither. A Labour Party colleague described his latest speech as confused and unintelligible. It's obvious, his physical and mental health are failing. If there's a change in leadership, let's hope that brings a shift in foreign policy."

Nicholas said, "Since Hitler took full power in May 1933, I've been flying from Dublin for monthly briefings at the MOD. They believe a European-wide conflict is now on the cards which is all the more reason we should be restocking our cellars to prepare for one of the worst aspects of war."

They all looked puzzled.

"Surely, an embargo on French wine would force us to drink brown ale and scrumpy."

When they arrived in Puligny they stopped at the walled vineyards of Château Montrachet. All were familiar with this appellation. After tasting the '24 and the '29, each purchased two cases of each year and four more en primeur.

As they walked to their cars, Nicholas was a bit unsteady. He mused, "You know, any bargain struck where both parties are pleased, adds to the happiness of the world."

After the evening meal, Nicholas continued to take charge of what he termed, the expeditionary forces. "I've looked at the Michelin map and reckon we should continue south to Mâcon. I'd like to add some more whites to my cellar. I've always enjoyed Pouilly-Fuissé."

"An excellent choice. It's another pure Chardonnay varietal. But south of that, I doubt you'd find the wine suitable for cellaring. Beaujolais, is based on the Gamay grape and is usually best drunk young."

"Thanks for the advice. Let's spend tomorrow night near Pouilly and see what's on offer?"

"Unfortunately, James and I must leave in the morning. We've our studies and he's training for the Boat Race."

Nicholas asked, "How's your crew shaping up?"

"If you were a betting man, you might put a bob or two on Cambridge. After all, we've won every race for the last decade."

Donald added, "Bea and I must be off as well. We've a few errands to run this week and I promised to be back at my desk Monday morning."

39

WEDNESDAY, MARCH 20TH, WOBURN

When they stopped for petrol in Lille, James telephoned Woburn and advised Jarvis of their intended arrival later this evening.

After a restful night in their own bed, they discussed plans for the rest of the vac. "The Boat Race is less than three weeks away. I'll let Ran know I'm back and see if I still have my place in the first boat."

"I'm seriously behind on my reading of 19th century European literature. What shall we do with our last free afternoon before the Easter term begins next month?"

"What say we walk towards Weybridge to view the ruins of Oatlands Palace?"

When they returned, Jarvis helped them with their coats. James said, "We've not given the household much warning so we'll take potluck for dinner."

"I'll see what Cook can manage."

"While you're here, I'd like to mention several other matters. You should expect various shipments of wine to arrive over the next few weeks. We did some buying in Burgundy and my grandparents are continuing on to Bordeaux, Reims, and the Loire. The deliveries will be insured so do check there are no breakages before signing."

Jarvis stiffened when James mentioned this obvious precaution.

"Humphrey is purchasing quite a lot so you'll need to make room in the cellar. Will you manage that while keeping up with your household duties?"

"Certainly, sir. With the family away, I've already set aside a couple of bins. Since wine is coming from four regions, I'll have to rethink my current arrangements. Will there be anything else?"

"Wedding acceptances should start arriving. Could you contact Alice Ogden at the orphanage and ask her to cycle up here to record these? She might also help you reorganise our wine stocks."

Again, the butler looked a little sniffy.

"Look here, we're paying her a weekly wage and she's eager to learn. Humphrey and I know how well you've trained in Peets after he left the Addlestone Reformatory School. We'd be obliged if you could help Alice with her preparation to be my grandmother's secretary."

"Now that you put it that way, I'm sure she could be more useful to Mrs Harcourt-Heath if she understood my arrangements."

"As you know, my grandparents are getting on in years. Apart from his angina, both are still fit and healthy. Remember, they're in their mid-seventies and will need our support as the years go by."

"I'll do whatever is necessary to ensure my Colonel and his lady have an easy retirement."

"That brings up another matter. Can you let staff know Louise and I will be living here after our honeymoon? I'll be taking charge of the estate so my grandparents can begin their retirement proper."

"Very good, sir. Excuse me while I discuss dinner arrangements with Cook."

The starter was battered deep-fried wild mushrooms and the main course an array of tiny spring lamb cutlets, boiled new potatoes, and baby carrots.

"Jarvis, if this is potluck, we're seriously impressed."

"I've decanted a wine I thought might go well with the lamb."

As Peets poured an inch of the light red liquid into their fishbowl shaped Burgundy glasses, James caught the aroma. "Isn't this is from our vineyard?"

"James dear, you're finally developing a nose."

Jarvis left the cork on the table and Louise noted the imprint of Clos des Chênes, 1900. She'd keep this on her desk while she burned the midnight oil.

"You know my darling, when I first saw you at the '33 Boat Race, it was love at first sight. I'm sure you didn't know I existed."

"Not true. I had my friends ask around. They said you'd been seeing a final year student at Corpus Christi. Since you were there watching, I just had to get up the nerve to ask you out."

40

FRIDAY, MARCH 22ND, CAMBRIDGE

After dropping Louise off at Newnham, a King's porter handed him several messages slotted into his pigeonhole. One was from Guy Burgess inviting him to an Apostles' soirée tomorrow night. He was exhausted and certain he'd decline. A second was a request from Richard to meet immediately he returned to college. The third was a curt message from Ran Lawrie: Where the devil are you?

Richard's took priority. He walked across Back Lawn and entered his second floor study in Gibbs'.

"So, you're back. Is it to play at being a student or might you decide to get down to some serious work?"

James remained silent accepting the rebuke in silence.

"Here are the last two year's Part III Tripos papers on the topic of calculus. I'd like you to provide solutions to all twenty questions for next week's tutorial. Do you think you can manage that, what with your pressing social commitments?"

His sarcasm was hurtful but deserved.

"Two areas you need to revise are Differential Geometry and Topology and Number Theory. Write a summary of each and their possible practical and theoretical applications."

"Just to be clear, isn't that three topics?"

"James, you're proving my point. Differential Geometry and Topology is one and Number Theory a second."

"Oh, right. Is that all, sir?"

"No. We'd like you to attend the Apostles' meeting tomorrow evening."

"But why? I thought you had a mole in place and regard their activities as schoolboy role-playing."

"MI5 has provided three reasons. First and foremost, our man has been chucked out of the Apostles. We don't yet know why. Secondly, it's highly unusual for a meeting to be called during the vac. Finally, we believe some Trinity Angels plan to attend. Meet them and try to gain their confidence."

Richard rose and offered a curt dismissal. "I'll expect you at our usual time Tuesday next."

Back in his rooms, he wrote a note to Guy accepting the invitation and another to Ran promising to be at Sunday's training session. After his uncomfortable tutorial, he made a start on the calculus questions.

By midnight he'd found solutions to three. This was hardly encouraging. Under examination conditions, he'd only have three hours to accomplish the same task.

After a quick breakfast in dining hall, he returned to his desk, checked his solutions and then scanned the rest of the exam. One of the questions required a proof. Two hours later, he thought he'd devised a less than elegant method he hoped would demonstrate the conjecture. The others looked impossible. Before he got further involved, he telephoned Louise.

"Hello, my love."

"Do you always answer the 'phone that way?"

"Our Head Porter recognised your voice. To what do I owe this call? Have you found another? Am I to be cast aside like a secondhand motorcar?"

"Steady on. Vintage bangers have numerous attractions. They're reliable and have classic lines."

"So that's how you see me? An aging but still somewhat stylish lady who can be counted on to take you on romantic journeys with just the push of a button?"

"I wouldn't part with you even for a new Railton. Wait now, I hear tell they're coming out with a more powerful model next spring. Perhaps I should reserve judgment."

"Please don't trade me in. I can still offer you plenty of exciting trips."

James was finding this a strain, primarily because he could detect the underlying jealousy in her teasing banter.

"I'm ringing because Richard has given me oodles of work and I'm also instructed to attend tonight's Apostles' meeting. Shall we meet up Tuesday evening at the Mitre?"

"I'm afraid I've had other offers from those who'd like to examine my chassis. Out of loyalty to you, I've sent them packing."

He was left totally bemused by her unexpected repartee. It was completely unlike her usual literal seriousness.

By dusk, he was exhausted but had found solutions to three more questions. He took a walk along the Cam to clear his mind ahead of tonight's Apostles' meeting.

In Guy's rooms, most present were strangers. However, he recognised Anthony Blunt from his first year math's lectures. James had heard he'd eventually read Modern Languages for his first degree. Blunt introduced Leo Long, John Astbury, Michael Straight and several others from Trinity and Trinity Hall.

Flutes of Champagne were refilled while Donald Maclean stood and delivered this evening's discussion paper. It was titled, How to preserve our English way of life under changing European conditions.

James could hardly disagree with his opening assertion. "Britain deserves a government whose primary goals are the interests and well-being of the British people."

Unfortunately, the prescription he offered was to convert the UK into a Marxist state with centralised control resting with the intelligentsia. Maclean suggested this would be based on Thomas Jefferson's principles whereby government should be run by a trained intellectual elite. Cynically, James expected they had themselves in mind.

Politics was Maclean's next topic. After a rambling tirade, he concluded, "To provide an effective bulwark against German and Italian Fascist ambitions, Britain should align with Joseph Stalin and offer matériel support to the Soviet Union."

Turning to economics, he offered a long-winded defence of central planning. "Detailed production targets should be allocated to every industrial sector. Seven years ago, Russia adopted their first five-year plan. It was designed to promote productive and allocative efficiency. The developed world recognises it's been a resounding success."

Finally, he presented his views concerning the causes of UK mass unemployment and mediocre long-term growth rates. "Both problems are only partially attributable to the Great Depression. It's the immigrants who are taking scarce jobs from British workers. Residency should only be offered to those who are educated or possess specific skills. This would increase labour productivity and go a long way towards improving our long-term growth rate. It would also reduce the lamentable unemployment figures."

When he finished, there was desultory applause. What followed was a brief question and answer session, focussed on fleshing out the practical implications of this New Britannia as he called his proposed Marxist state. It was generally agreed elections should be temporarily suspended and martial law initiated to ensure an orderly transition towards an egalitarian society.

Leo Long stood and suggested the voting hiatus would likely need to continue for some years. "That would give the government an opportunity to educate or, if necessary, isolate dissidents who were always trying to disrupt progress. He asserted that in order to deliver a consistent message to the voting public, control of the press would be essential. Debate, contrary opinions, biased and downright false reporting only served to confuse the electorate."

Another member introduced himself as Kim Philby. "Donald's spot on. Centralised decision-making would, at a stroke, raise output and productivity." He paused for dramatic effect making eye contact with the members. "By its very nature, free-market capitalism leads to wasteful duplication of productive resources. This directly results in a loss of efficiency by missing out on potential economies of large-scale production. What's more, unfettered competition causes smaller firms to go to the wall. In bankruptcy, machinery is scrapped and plant abandoned. This represents a further loss to society. Thirdly, this evolutionary process embodied in the capitalist model, results in either the strongest firms becoming dominant monopolies or provides them with a strong incentive to join with competitors to form collusive oligopolies. Doing so, enables them to extract economic rents by exploiting consumers and society as a whole."

James thought these were interesting arguments that had elements of truth. While the discussion continued, he turned towards Guy and asked about Philby. "Two years ago, he earned a 2:1 in Economics. After that, he spent a year in Vienna helping refugees from Nazi Germany. He returned to England, married and is now studying Russian at the UCL School of Slavic Languages."

James decided to enter the fray. "Limiting immigration is obviously essential in these times of mass unemployment. But what are we to do about the unskilled and unemployable foreigners already settled here?"

Blunt stood to address his question. "Central to our policy would be to offer financial incentives to encourage voluntary repatriation of recent immigrants who possess only limited specialised skills. Eventually, mandatory exclusion would likely become necessary."

"I can see the sense in that, but what about unskilled UK citizens who are, shall we say, of differing cultural or racial backgrounds?"

There was a shout from the back of the room, "Send them back to where they came from." Gales of laughter and the clinking of Champagne flutes accompanied this outburst. Eventually all agreed they should be deported without specifying exactly how or where they would go.

James decided to test the strength of their anti-Semitism. "Actually, I was thinking of the Jews."

Blunt again rose and moved to where Maclean was standing. "Like Gypsies, Africans, Asians, or those of mixed races, Jews aren't really British in any practical sense. Racial cleansing of our Anglo-Saxon nation must be both rapid and thorough if we're to move towards a true Marxist society."

James was astonished with the speed with which the discussion of improvements in labour productivity morphed into xenophobic rhetoric. He immediately recognised the obvious parallels with the Nazi party's manifesto, but the Apostles are supposedly opposed to Fascism. Because of their elite positions in society, now, for the first time, he accepted Keynes might be right. This lot potentially posed a serious threat to British democracy.

Formal discussion ended and the members broke up into small groups. Blunt came over with a bottle of Champagne and offered a refill. "James, I have to thank you for asking your subordinate questions. It allowed me to go into some detail as regards our goals. We must keep in touch. I'd like to pick your brains on a number of matters that'll inevitably arise during our transition to a Marxist-Leninist state."

They clinked glasses, after which Blunt moved on to another group to bathe in their admiration.

Back in his room, he wrote a summary of the meeting and the names of the Trinity and Trinity Hall Apostles. After an early breakfast in dining hall, he waited until nine before ringing Richard.

"What can I do for you?"

"I'd like to stop by if I may."

"Give me a few minutes."

When he arrived at his study, Richard invited him to take his usual seat. "What's gotten you into such a lather?"

"It's the Apostles. There's something very wrong there."

"Is this why you've disturbed me so early on a Sunday morning? We've already discussed this. They're a rather silly lot playing at embracing Communism. We feel their dalliances are a transient phase for these intelligent and privileged young men."

"They might appear to be Marxists, but they're hatching plans to take over the United Kingdom and replacing our government with something akin to Nazi Germany."

As soon as he blurted this out, he realised how ridiculous it sounded. Marxists embracing Fascist principles made no sense. Richard said nothing so James handed him his notes concerning the meeting.

Richard quietly read them and then asked, "Was this unlike previous evenings?"

"Absolutely. For one thing, earlier meetings were more like soirées focussed on flirting and pairing. A substantially different group were present last night."

Richard remained silent so James continued. "I didn't catch all their names, but MI5 should keep an eye on Anthony Blunt, Leo Long, John Astbury, and Michael Straight. I think Blunt is their ringleader as he's older than the rest. Also, two men from Trinity Hall, Donald Maclean and Kim Philby, apparently support a Marxist takeover."

Richard leaned back in his chair and closed his eyes before speaking. "In the past you've proved to have good instincts so I'll follow this up. Personally, I believe it's a storm in a teacup."

41

SUNDAY, MARCH 24ᵀᴴ, CAMBRIDGE

He met his crew on the Great Ouse. Ran Lawrie was not well-pleased by his disappearing act, but James convinced him he'd not miss any training sessions from now until the Boat Race. He knew this wasn't entirely satisfactory since the race was less than a fortnight away.

Monday morning, his first academic task was to summarise the two set subjects and reflect on their possible applications. At noon, he again trained with his crew. Afterwards, he stopped by his bank, Coutts & Co, and instructed them to wire funds to Michel's bank, Crédit Agricole. He also rang his other trustee, Sir Ronald Featherstonehaugh and received his verbal approval to withdraw capital to upgrade Clos des Chênes. Humphrey had paved the way by expressing confidence in his business acumen as well as the quality of the wine. By midnight, he'd managed to solve all the problems although he suspected several solutions were less than elegant and wouldn't please his tutor in the slightest.

At his tutorial, Richard spent about fifteen minutes absorbed in his work. "Well done. You've even solved those two our external examiners deemed unfair. For next week, here are two more Part III papers. Where are your summaries of the set topics?"

Richard studied them with apparent interest and on one occasion, actually smiled. He rose from his desk signalling their tutorial had ended.

James remained seated. "Have you found anything out about the Trinity Apostles I identified?"

"They've sterling reputations as both gentlemen and scholars. I caution you, don't let your imagination run amok simply because you're working for SIS. Whitehall believes they're a collection of rich and spoiled young men who enjoy wearing the Marxist hat while they're free to do so as undergraduates. After leaving Cambridge, they'll create productive lives for themselves appropriate to their station."

James thought Richard had ignored the fact that Blunt, Burgess, Long, and Philby had graduated several years earlier and were older than the rest.

"If you've no objections, I'd like to continue to attend their meetings."

"You must do as you please, just don't let it interfere with your revision programme."

James had a substantial lunch in dining hall before starting on the next twenty problems. He felt he was getting into the rhythm of the exams since potential solutions to the first five popped into his head after only an hour's thought. After taking a few notes, he went downstairs to the communal telephone.

"James, my darling. I hoped you'd call."

"I'm just reminding you about our supper date at the Mitre."

Once there, they exchanged kisses although it was quite a public place. James fetched drinks and they sat at their usual table in the snug. "I'm training mornings and afternoons. This weekend we'll work on stroke coordination and change of pace. Are you up for lunch next Sunday?"

"Let's try the Eagle. Afterwards, we can stroll along the Backs perfecting our SIS disguises as lovers on a day out."

42

FRIDAY, APRIL 5TH, RIVER THAMES

A college servant beckoned James to the communal pay 'phone on the ground floor of Bodley's Court. Humphrey was on the line. "The expeditionary forces have returned with the spoils of war. We're now fully prepared for enemy disruptions to our supply lines."

James asked about Nicholas and Helen. "While purchasing Champagne in Reims, we decided skip the Loire and return early to watch the Boat Race. I've booked two seats on one of those steamboats that follow the crews up the Thames. We've also reserved a suite at the Coach and Horses in Kew to host a party for you and your friends."

Both riverbanks from Putney Bridge to the finishing line at Mortlake were packed with an estimated quarter of a million race followers. The bookies offered evens since it was understood Oxford had made great improvements since last year's drubbing when they lost by four and a quarter lengths. After the steward flipped a coin, there were cheers from Cambridge supporters. By winning the toss, they were able to choose the more sheltered Surrey side of the Thames.

With the blast of a horn, the race began. Cambridge immediately adopted a faster stroke rate. They steadied at thirty-two while Oxford seemed to hold back employing a rate of thirty. At the milepost, Cambridge opened up a boat-length gap. By Hammersmith Bridge, the lead widened to three lengths and at the finish line at Chiswick Bridge, Oxford had been demoralised. The Light Blues had won by four and a half lengths. Apart from the two years when one of the shells sank, this was the largest winning margin in the 106-year history of the Boat Race.

After a few drinks with his crew at the Ship Inn at Chiswick Bridge, they took the tube to Kew. With Louise on his arm, he found Humphrey and Nicholas standing by the buffet set up in their suite. He thanked them for their generosity in hosting the party.

"Actually, my boy, turns out this is down to you."

"How so?"

"You told Nicholas he might place a bet on the race and I decided to have a flutter as well. We each put £50 on a Cambridge victory. The win should pay for this party with a fair bit left over."

"Will you stay the night?'

"Peets will drive us back before we overstay our welcome."

"In that case, we'll sleep here and keep an eye on things."

"Bea and Donald plan to drive down to Woburn for our usual Sunday customs."

"We'll join you but we'll be a bit late. We don't have transport here in London."

Donald was within earshot. "Sunday train schedules are always uncertain due to engineering works. We'll swing by in the morning. I'm sure you've a change of clothes at Woburn and can travel back to Cambridge by train later in the day."

On the way down to Addlestone, James asked Donald about their trip to European capitals. "We shared confidential information with our SIS counterparts concerning UK Lebensborn activities. This was done face to face since we didn't want details to be leaked to the Germans via the open ICPC meetings."

"Any further developments?"

"Girls' orphanages in France, Austria, Holland, and Belgium have experienced similar disappearances. They've rescued scores of young blonde women and authorities have made a number of arrests. Danish and Finish authorities have also reported missing teenaged girls but it's rumoured that Norway is central to their programme. There's also speculation that suitable male toddlers are being kidnapped in Poland and placed in communal homes to be indoctrinated in what they're calling Aryanisation therapy, whatever that might mean. Those passing the course are apparently put up for adoption with Nazi families. We've no idea what happens to the infants they might reject as being incompatible with their racial or behavioural objectives."

Louise said, "Donald, this is an utter disgrace. Can't you persuade the Foreign Office to do something?"

"Since Hitler took power, German borders are on lockdown. They've begun the process of issuing identification documents to all residents and random checks by the Gestapo are now standard practice. SIS believes this is primarily aimed at identifying anti-government protesters. Nevertheless, Jews, Romas, and Slavs are being caught in their net. Our job has now been made much more difficult. Few of us are able to pass as German, even with papers that are undetectable forgeries. Over the last year, several of our leading agents in Germany and Italy have been arrested, interrogated, and shot as spies. We've absolutely no idea how their covers were compromised."

Upon arriving at Woburn Hall, they joined the family in the library. James asked Nicholas for a full account of the rest of their French trip. "After stocking up on Pouilly-Fuissé, we headed to Bordeaux for claret. We spent the first night in Limoges and after lunch, made the shorter drive to Bordeaux. From our hotel, we drove north to the Médoc, south to Graves and east to Saint Émilion. Each of us, and Donald, I include you in this, purchased fifty-five cases of wine, some ready to drink now and others left to mature in our cellars."

Donald asked Nicholas for his bill and scanned the contents of an envelope containing receipts. "What an impressive array. To whom do I owe the dosh?"

"I've been your bank manager. You'll find my details in the envelope. But you don't have to wait until it arrives. We returned with a few bottles of two of our favourites which should go well with Woburn beef."

The discussions of finances reminded James he should ring Michel to see if his bank's telegraphic transfer had arrived. Louise joined him since his French wasn't up to dealing with a poor international connection. They returned after a few minutes with the latest news. "Michel has put down deposits on new equipment. The builders have started clearing out the old machinery and are laying down a new concrete floor and installing wiring, plumbing, and drains. The architect's survey showed the barn and cave to be structurally sound. He suggested they place the old beam press in the courtyard, as it's an interesting eighteenth century artefact."

Humphrey continued the travel narrative. "We next went to Reims to replenish our cellars for future celebrations. Donald, you'll also find an invoice for ten cases of Champagne. For the wedding, I ordered another twenty. We'll save the Loire for another trip."

James asked his sister, "When do you begin your training?"

"I've already started. I've hired a tutor and I'm studying German two hours each day."

Louise gave James a quick sideways glance and then stared intently at her wine glass.

Donald said, "Tomorrow we'll drive north to the MI6 training centre based in a manor house just outside Leamington Spa. It's a two-week intensive course after which she'll be certified to carry her handgun. After that, we'll motor to Yorkshire to visit my family."

In bed he asked why she went quiet when Bea said she was studying German.

"You should do the same."

He started to object but she gently put her hand on his lips. "I mean after our exams. For now, let's speak German when we're alone." She smiled and teasingly said, "Playtime is Spielzeit, auf Deutsch."

Little verbal communication followed as they fell into each other's arms.

43

MONDAY, APRIL 8ᵀᴴ, CAMBRIDGE

In the morning, they boarded the early commuter train at Addlestone station and took a taxi from Waterloo to King's Cross to catch the train to Cambridge. At the porter's lodge, Powell passed him an envelope. Inside was an invitation to an Apostles' meeting Saturday week. He planned to accept since he wasn't at all satisfied with Richard's assurances.

In his rooms, he worked on the twenty questions he'd begun prior to the Boat Race. Solutions leapt into his mind. By late afternoon, he'd completed both papers and decided to telephone Louise.

"I hoped you'd call, I'm seriously fed up with French literature."

"Let's go into town and collect our rings. I'm in desperate need of some female companionship."

"You're in luck. I find myself free this evening."

Unwisely, he decided to continue the flirting banter that so surprised him on their 'phone call two weeks ago. "That is indeed fortunate. Now I don't have an excuse to go on the prowl to search for a bit of crumpet with your ring size."

Louise was struck dumb. She hoped she'd got over her insecurity, but was gutted by his words. Her friends had often told her she was overly literal and totally lacked a sense of humour. She wasn't prepared to assume they were right. But if they were, it might be down to her lifelong habit of emotional detachment. What's more, she really hated to be teased.

James clicked the receiver a couple of times. "Hello, you still there?"

163

"Yes, my darling. I'll meet you straightaway outside King's."

After trying on their rings, they headed towards the Mitre. As it was midweek before the start of the Easter Term, the pub was half empty.

"Louise, let's take the weekend off and go down to Woburn?"

"I'd love that. Could you 'phone your grandfather and suggest a round of golf? I'm always rusty before the inter-collegiate competitions which begin in a fortnight. Anyway, I can take notes on boring novels at Woburn as easily as I can in my digs."

Over sherry in Woburn's library, Dorothy mentioned how much they'd enjoyed French cuisine. "I've asked Cook to try to be adventurous with her sauces. Would you believe, Humphrey has decided he likes garlic?"

Lunch was French onion soup and grilled lobster tails. Dorothy said, "We've a new fishmonger in Addlestone. He gets up with the sparrows and drives to the south coast. We'll be having seafood more often. We got into the habit in Bordeaux, where the daily catch came straight from the Bay of Biscay."

Louise asked Humphrey, "Have you managed to arrange a golf match?"

"We tee off at ten against the same opponents."

Nicholas said, "I wish I could stay to watch you scalp those spivs again. We must be off to London in the morning. We'll stay a few days at the East India Club in St James's Square. I have meetings scheduled at the Foreign Office and the MOD. While I'm busy, Helen plans to do some shopping at Harrods."

Dorothy stood. "Louise, I've something to show you."

She handed her two calfskin bound albums labelled Wedding Guests and Wedding Gifts. Each title was scripted in Alice Ogden's beautiful calligraphy.

Opening the first, it was an easy matter to identify those who'd replied and whether they'd attend. Another column showed if they were friends of James, Louise, Bea, Donald, Humphrey, or Dorothy. Finally, the number in the party was shown. Most were couples, but Bea's lady friends and most of their fellow students were attending as singles. The second folder had the same alphabetised list of names. There were red ticks in a second column alongside a brief description of the gift.

"This is a little different from what we'd discussed before Easter. Alice felt it would make things easier when you send out thank you notes. She also thought these would help with the seating arrangements at the reception. She even suggested Bea's friends might be placed at the same tables as your Cambridge men. Alice is a real treasure. She's updating these lists and also helping Jarvis organise and inventory the wine purchases. Louise, if you'd like to make a start on opening your wedding gifts, she can begin to fill out the second folder."

"No time like the present…Oops."

Louise really hated deliberate puns but at least this one was unintended.

The gifts were displayed on the deep shelf that ran around the entire perimeter of the billiard room. There were envelopes, small packages, and two large shipping crates sitting in the corner.

The wooden boxes contained the older generation's joint present. Peets fetched a steel jemmy. Packed in wood shavings, was a complete Limoges Haviland dinner service of over a one hundred and twenty pieces in the Harrison Rose pattern. Nicholas said it was by Theodore Haviland, one of the four Haviland family firms that produce fine china.

Amongst the rest were a mélange of useful and impractical items. Victorian silver candlesticks, a Searle & Co condiment rack, and a small but beautiful antique Persian carpet fell into the first category. A seriously ugly ostrich skin ink blotter, three cut glass ashtrays, and four silver plated cigarette boxes were relegated to the latter.

In bed, Louise continued to introduce the sounds and structure of the German language. He found it a distraction, but accepted the lesson, his reward being passionate Spielzeit.

Saturday morning, Louise dressed in a tartan skirt and Arran sweater and quietly left the bedroom to join Humphrey downstairs. She knew James would occupy himself with maths or farm business.

Their golf match resulted in another win for the Woburn pair. Humphrey was over the moon, primarily because their opponents insisted on placing sizeable wagers in an attempt to recoup losses from the previous match.

All James could remember of the rest of the weekend was excellent fare, good company, his German lessons, and some delightful intimacy.

Back in his rooms on Sunday evening, he spent an hour looking over the two past papers. He soon spotted solutions to five questions on the first.

In the morning, he wrote out formal answers and proofs, finally completing the first paper by one thirty. He'd missed lunch so telephoned Louise and asked her to join him at the Eagle.

After the ten minutes drinking-up time, they walked towards the Cam. The branches of the water-loving willow trees were a haze of tiny green leaves. Daffodils and tulips had emerged from the well-tended beds along the towpath. Louise translated everything they saw into German and began making complete sentences so he could get used to the sound and rhythm of the language. He wasn't confident this was going to work, but agreed it would be valuable for their MI5 roles.

He escorted her back to Newnham and returned to his rooms to continue work.

Reading through all the questions on the second paper, he saw the solutions the examiners were after for five. He wrote these up on separate sheets of foolscap and turned to the remaining questions. By midnight he'd solved four more.

The final question appeared straightforward which is why he left it to the end. **Prove that no three positive integers a, b, and c can satisfy the equation: $a^n + b^n = c^n$ for any integer value of n greater than two.** He gave up at two in the morning. He set his alarm clock for seven but again failed to concoct the requisite proof.

As he knocked on Richard's door, the thought struck him, Fermat's Last Theorem. Although this unsolved 300 year-old problem was famous, he couldn't believe examiners would insert it into an undergraduate examination.

Richard complimented him on his efforts and was mildly amused he'd struggled with Fermat's Conjecture. "That was a bit naughty of us. In our defence, candidates only need choose three questions from ten. Those who recognised this famous problem could move on and focus on the others. Only the weaker students might waste their limited time trying to devise a proof. You should think of the Tripos as a competition between staff and students where anything's fair game."

Richard gave him another two past papers to attack during the week and instructed him to attend the Apostles' meeting scheduled for Saturday evening.

Being totally exhausted, he slept until late afternoon. When he woke, he rang Louise to see if she could join him at the Mitre.

Once seated, Louise supplied the German word for everything in the pub. James suggested it was a bit like the child's game I spy with my little eye. He was building his vocabulary but it was mostly nouns, adjectives, and present tense verbs. He knew conjugations would be difficult, as would cases and genders.

"Look, you only need to speak German. Grammar will be correct because the phrases sound right. That's how children learn their first language."

He initially found it to be an ugly language as compared to Italian, Spanish, and French. Now he enjoyed listening to Louise speak it when they were alone. It was these times he cherished and would never forget.

44

SATURDAY, APRIL 20TH, TRINITY COLLEGE

As the Easter Term would begin on Monday, they attended several parties thrown by friends.

"James, isn't it time you got our tickets for King's May Ball? We could invite Donald and Bea and, if he's ashore, Jonathan and Margie. I'm sure your grandparents could mind the twins for the night."

"I'll run it past them when we go down next weekend."

Although it was only six in the evening, Louise called time, saying she had earmarked tomorrow for French novels. After escorting her back to Newnham, he enjoyed the mild spring evening and the sounds of music and laughter emanating from open windows as he passed Queens, St Catherine's, and Corpus Christi.

The Apostles meeting was, as usual held in Guy Burgess's flat in Trinity. Blunt and several other Trinity men were present along with the usual undergraduate crowd.

Leo Long's presentation focussed on voting restrictions. He began by asserting, "We can create a better Britain by limiting voting to only those with the intellectual capacity to appreciate the issues set out in the various parties' election manifestos."

Throughout his rambling diatribe, he neglected to address how or by whom the fitness to vote would be determined. The discussion that followed was cursory. Obviously, the Apostles didn't think much of either his arguments or his presentation.

As the Champagne corks popped, Blunt sat next to him on an overstuffed couch. "What did you think of Leo's paper?"

"Nothing wrong with an educated electorate, but it would be a political nightmare to attempt to interfere with voter registration."

"Let me explain how parliament works. The first thing our government would do is set up a standing committee whose objective would be to produce a White Paper which would set out conditions necessary to create an informed voting public. It would eventually be published, debated, and in due course, a commission would be established with powers to determine the parameters necessary for individuals to be placed on the electoral register. It's that simple. All our side needs to do, is ensure like-minded people serve on the newly established Electoral Commission. Once we have the principles accepted into law, then, step by step, we'd expand the conditions until those remaining on the electoral rolls would pretty much support anything we propose."

James was appalled by his arrogance but had no idea if parliamentary democracy could be perverted in this way.

Blunt continued, "I know you're busy with exam preparation and I wouldn't wish to interfere. A number of us would like you to deliver a paper at our May 4th meeting on the subject of voter eligibility. By the way, you're right, Leo ignored the practicalities. Perhaps you could address those in a fortnight's time."

45

SUNDAY, APRIL 21ˢᵀ, CAMBRIDGE

Today and Monday were spent completing the two past papers. At his Tuesday tutorial, Richard showed him the mathematics Part III Tripos timetable. Exams would run from May 28th to June 8th. James had a wide choice of topics and after some thought, ticked two on statistical theory and six on pure maths. He was given two more past exams to tackle for next week.

Before leaving he said, "Blunt wants me to deliver a paper at the next meeting. I'm to devise a programme to effectively disenfranchise a significant proportion of the British electorate."

"As long as it doesn't interfere with your revision, you must do as you please. You're aware of my views on their dalliances."

During the week, he toyed with the problems on past papers, lacking either the interest or success in discovering solutions. Instead he purchased a German grammar at Heffers and studied verb declension and conjugation and noun genders and cases. He thought to himself, 'If only there weren't so many exceptions.' He found genders to be particularly problematic. 'Why was the German word for girl neuter and a door feminine?'

Friday morning, he collected Louise who was waiting outside Newnham College with her overnight bag and clubs.

He asked, "How was yesterday's tutorial?"

"Fine, I suppose. How 'bout you?"

"No problems there, but I'm not making much progress with my German."

She gave him a teasing smile. "We'll need to practice more when we're alone and in a quiet place. Anything else bothering you?"

"Blunt asked me to deliver a lecture at the next Apostles' meeting. I'm a bit concerned about where it might lead."

"Explain when we're alone. Your car is so noisy, it's difficult to concentrate on anything."

Donald's Packard was parked in the circular drive. In the library, the family were holding flutes of Champagne.

James asked, "What's the occasion?"

Bea held out her left hand, "I'm now official."

Her engagement ring had a large deep blue star sapphire surrounded by a circle of tiny diamonds.

"We'd like to be married here at St Paul's in October and our grandparents have offered to host the reception."

Humphrey said, "Dorothy and I thought your nuptials might be imminent so, in Reims, I ordered an additional twenty cases of Champagne. I'm sure Jarvis will devise a plan to keep 240 bottles chilled for each wedding."

Over lunch, James asked Donald and Bea if they'd like to be his guests at the King's May Ball. "It's a formal dinner dance on Saturday June 22nd. If you're free, I'll arrange tickets. You won't need rooms since it's an all-nighter."

Donald said, "I'll have to check our MI6 work schedules, but I'm sure it'll be OK."

Louise caught the plural usage. "Bea, how did your training programme go?"

"Fine. It covered general spycraft including codes and cyphers, miniature cameras, and blind drops. Armed and unarmed combat were also part of the course. I'm now certified to carry my Walther."

James asked, "Grandpapa, do you think Margie and Jonathan would like an invite to the May Ball?"

"God knows if he'll be home. Only one way to find out."

James went into the hall 'phone and returned after a few minutes. "It's all set. He'll be ashore and Margie has accepted."

Louise stood and said she and James would like to take a stroll in the fresh air. As they were putting on their coats in the mudroom, they overheard Bea suggest they inform Alice she has another commission.

"That'll mean Dorothy and I will need to employ her full time since she leaves the orphanage in August when she turns sixteen. I suppose she could stay in one of the servant's bedrooms on the top floor."

They walked towards Victory Park. Outside the newly formed Bowls Club, she asked, "So, tell me about your Apostle's paper. Couldn't you have declined?"

"I still might. When you hear the topic, you'll understand why I should accept."

James explained Blunt's ideas.

"What did Richard say?"

"He believes these privileged young men will leave their political speculations behind when they find their niche in society."

"You know, your paper might separate the wheat from the chaff. I'm certain MI5 would be interested to learn which of the Apostles find your voter registration proposals abhorrent and by elimination identify those who might support a Marxist takeover."

"I'll work on it tomorrow if you don't mind being on your own."

"Don't worry about me. Anyway, we should be getting back as it's approaching the cocktail hour. But, we mustn't neglect your German lessons. I'll make sentences relating to what we see and you listen to the sounds and try to translate what I say into English."

They were walking down Station Road. "Auf Deutsch, Dies ist die Bahnhofsstraße. Train ist Zug and railroad ist Eisenbahn."

Over pre-dinner drinks, James mentioned to Bea his attempts at spoken German. She said, "Vielleicht solltest du einen Lehrer finden oder mit Louise sprechen, wenn du alleine bist."

James actually understood. Louise could be both his teacher and conversational partner when they were alone.

Donald and Louise agreed Bea had mastered the German accent and had a good ear for languages. Louise knew she'd attained Distinctions in her Higher School Certificates in Latin, Greek, and French at James Allen Girls' School.

Over dinner, Bea asked Louise about their honeymoon plans. "James, we really should decide so you can make reservations and let Michel and Louisa know our dates."

"I've already made the bookings."

"And?"

"And, it's to be a surprise."

Louise shrugged and turned towards Humphrey. "Any chance of a round of golf tomorrow?"

"Actually, a couple of chaps asked me if I'd be available. They're ex-military and gentlemen of the first order."

"Excellent, I was beginning think Surrey golfers were cads and bounders, although that's an impossibility given the origin of the phrase."

"Eh?"

"A cad or caddie was a shortened name for the conductor on a horse-drawn trolley. In the last century it became a challenge with upper class young men to try to jump on the tram while it was moving to avoid buying a ticket. Hence, it's not possible to be both a cad and a bounder."

Humphrey shrugged and rose to make his telephone call to arrange their golf match. Louise accepted he had little interest in etymology.

Not for the first time, Donald thought Louise was showing-off. And what's more, he had serious doubts about the alleged origins. He had discussed her behaviour with Bea and both thought it was her insecurity that made her boastful. They said nothing, as it was not their place to be critical.

46

SATURDAY, APRIL 26TH, WOBURN

Over breakfast, the family discussed their plans for today. Donald and Bea thought they would take a long walk towards Ottershaw and have a look at Christ Church on the Foxhills Estate. Dorothy said she would be meeting some of her bridge friends for tea in the village and Louise and Humphrey had their golf match. James was glad he would be left on his own to concentrate on his Apostles' paper. With a second cup of coffee, he settled himself at the library table.

The golfers returned just as he completed his draft. He asked, Louise, "How was your morning?"

"We'd such a splendid time out in the spring air and didn't bother to keep score."

After a light lunch, Louise gave him a teasing smile and suggested he join her for an afternoon rest. "Or I should have said, ein Nickerchen machen?"

As they settled into their bed, he passed her his discussion paper. She propped herself up with several goose down pillows and read in silence. "James, you've created an appalling vision of Britain under your One Nation Party. I seriously doubt anybody could think this way?"

"For a start, the Germans are in the process of implementing many of those very same proposals with the almost universal approval of their truncated electorate. And don't forget about the Americans."

James retrieved his draft paper, kissed her neck, and proposed Spielzeit.

His Tuesday morning tutorial went as expected. "For my part, I believe you're ready for your exams. Having said that, I'd like you to continue to work on past papers so you don't lose your touch. Here are two more I trust you'll find challenging."

James wasn't sure he liked that description, but accepted the assignment in silence. As their academic business was completed, he passed his Apostles' essay across the desk. Richard read it with a wry smile James was unable to interpret. "Nobody would fall for this nonsense. Not only would it be politically impossible to achieve even a tenth of what you suggest, the general public wouldn't stand for the removal of their voting rights not to mention their civil liberties."

"I know it's seriously over the top, but my aim is to gauge their reactions. If there are dissenters, it might separate the fascists and the Marxists and from those who support British democracy. Those who find my proposals abhorrent or remain silent are likely the ones who were playing at being committed to one or other of the extremes. I expect I'll get the boot for taking the Mickey. In any case, exams begin in a few weeks, so I expect this will be my last Apostles' meeting."

47

SATURDAY, MAY 4TH, TRINITY COLLEGE

When flutes were charged with Champagne, James stood to deliver his paper.

A fortnight ago, Leo offered some intriguing proposals designed to ensure our electorate is sufficiently well-informed to make rational choices in both general and local elections. Tonight, I'll attempt to flesh out some of his suggestions. Let me begin by saying, our primary goal should be to create a fully-engaged constituency capable of understanding the social, political, and economic challenges currently facing Britain.

I'm certain all would accept my initial premise that universal suffrage is essential for a robust democracy. Obviously, this doesn't mean every man, woman, or child present in the UK on Election Day is granted the right to vote. As of seven years ago, a British citizen must have reached the age of twenty-one to be placed on the Electoral Register. Prior to 1928, the voting age for women was thirty. Additionally, current rules also require women to be property owners. Clearly, it's a well-established precedent, in both civil and common law, voters must be both mature and conversant with the issues of the day **and** have a stake in our economy.

Clearly, voters should have both an interest in and commitment to British society. Those deemed otherwise, must obviously be denied the vote. I'd not only exclude minors but also the mentally impaired and criminally insane. Recidivist miscreants and convicted felons, whether in prison or released having served their custodial sentences, have correctly and permanently lost their franchise under current electoral rules. I'd now like to propose we extend these restrictions to cover those committing lesser crimes such as public drunkenness, vagrancy, or obstructing the police in the execution of their lawful duties. Additionally, I'd apply it to members of the press should they publish stories containing anti-government propaganda. Such fake news can incite the general public to stage unlawful assemblies or demonstrations.

Next, I'd like to propose an immutable principle: Voting should be restricted to those who understand and actively embrace our British psyche. On this basis, we should withdraw the franchise from first generation immigrants even if they're naturalised citizens. If earlier arrivals have failed to adopt our way of life, they too must be excluded. It would be a simple matter to discover how successfully foreigners have assimilated. We could require they pass an English literacy examination before being placed on the Electoral Register.

It is interesting to note, a literacy test is currently employed in many American southern states where it has been particularly effective in disenfranchising racial minorities and poor whites. Our test should contain questions about British law, customs, and history. Adjusting the pass level, the difficulty of the questions, or even the intricacy of the wording could limit the amount of, shall we say, foreignness and ignorance that is allowed to influence our electoral outcomes.

We should also investigate the primary language used in their household. That question presently appears on the US Federal census. If it is not English, that in itself, could justify their removal from the voting lists.

There are also good reasons to exclude others even though they might have lived here for generations. I'm thinking about those the Irish call the tinkers and we refer to as travellers, Gypsies, or Romas. Their allegiances are to their families and their clans. Because they have their own language, they've effectively isolated themselves from the general population.

Using the same rationale, I propose we exclude the Jews. Like the Romas, they maintain a closed society, speak their own language, Yiddish, amongst themselves, and patently have no interest in assimilation. What's more, they dominate financial sectors such gold and diamond trading, banking, and insurance as well as professions such as medicine, law, and the performing arts. They conduct their businesses solely for the benefit of their own people rather than the collective welfare of British society. To be Jewish, one has to have had a Jewish mother. They use this genetic requirement, to exclude ordinary British people from participating in the professions they've effectively monopolised.

With these parameters in mind, I'd like to propose the establishment of a permanent government voting commission with powers to vet the electorate on the grounds of their commitment to our society. We should suspend or remove voting rights of any who failed to meet our criteria of having their loyalties to the Crown or who are unable to speak the King's English properly. Electoral fraud is a persistent threat to democracy and must be taken seriously. Once again, I've found contemporary precedents. In the southern US, the so-called Jim Crow laws have been highly effective in preventing the darker races from participating in federal, state, and local elections. Voting must be considered a privilege and not a birthright.

Earlier, I suggested potential electors must understand the issues facing our society from both current and historical perspectives. Eventually, we could add to our list of exclusions those who are not overtly feeble-minded but who are, shall we say, not sufficiently intelligent to appreciate the subtle and intricate nature of our current economic and political difficulties. As a rough guide, we might exclude those who've only gone to state schools or left school at 15. We should unconditionally include those who've attended private boarding schools such as Eton, Harrow, Westminster, or Dulwich.

In order to implement this principle, I propose a national examination for all children at the age of ten or eleven. My aim would be to segregate youngsters primarily suited to manual labour. Those below the pass level would be sent to Industrial Schools. These would adopt military style discipline and provide their charges with training. This would increase productivity and expand the employment opportunities available to the young. Obviously, our ultimate goal would be to produce a docile, obedient, and skilled labour force.

Next, I'd like to take this proposal to its logical conclusion and exclude trade unionists. Apart from a few exceptions, they'd not have achieved their School Certificates of Examinations. Like the Jews, they have their own narrow interests at heart, that is to say, more pay for less work. Although many are rabid nationalists when it comes to regional loyalties or football teams, I've seen no evidence to suggest they have the overall welfare of the United Kingdom as a priority. What's more, the better-educated trade unionists would likely be the most dangerous should they become bolshie union organisers and strike leaders.

Moving on, I can see efficiency arguments for a single party state. Just to be clear, I'm not, for a moment, suggesting we embrace the structure of our current and dysfunctional National Government coalition. The Labour Party has always been the mouthpiece of the unions and by definition, has failed to represent the interests of our country as a whole.

Next, I propose we reintroduce a poll tax. It's been successfully used three times to raise money for the Hundred Years' War. To soften the rhetoric, we might rename it a Community Charge, payable at voting stations before receiving a ballot. Judging by the turnout on a rainy day, the rate could be set at a fairly trivial level relative to the wealth of our class. Presently, a number of US southern states have a poll tax in place which has been highly successful at disenfranchising the poor and the coloureds.

Additionally, I can see no objection to returning to the situation where the vote is limited to landowners who, after all, are the ultimate stakeholders in our society. This system was in place for hundreds of years until fifteen years ago when, unfortunately, property ownership was removed as a voting condition for men after the Great War.

To ensure we have a truly United Kingdom, I propose anti-government protesters are identified and arrested as actual or presumed anarchists or traitors. To accomplish this, we'll need to establish a second tier of policing which would be given expanded powers of search and arrest. I suggest we use the non-uniformed framework of the Special Branch of the Metropolitan Police Service. They could enlist the general public's assistance to identify and report criminal activity. Loyal citizens could send photos, names, addresses, or descriptions of miscreants to the police or perhaps even to the Mail and Mirror. I'm certain Lord Rothermere would gladly publish these in a weekly column perhaps called something like Criminals at Large or Have You Seen This Man? Indeed, rewards could be offered to those informing on their neighbours.

To monitor our citizenship laws and prevent voter fraud, we'll need to introduce identity cards. Obviously, doing so would require enormous manpower. It would also necessitate the establishment of a new Cabinet post as well as an entire civil service department devoted to gathering and updating birth and death records, addresses, and ethnicity. I should note in passing, the costs of creating this register would be both one-off and short-term. Logistically, this doesn't present a problem. Currently, 20% of our labour force is unemployed and millions more are only in part-time employment. This programme would provide a much-needed Keynesian inspired stimulus to aggregate demand and help Britain out of the current Depression. What's more, these newly employed civil servants would be beholden and therefore loyal to what I would now like to christen our One Nation Party. Additional legislation must be introduced as regards identity documents. British passport holders who are Jewish or Roma should surrender their documents so the first page could be stamped in red with either a **J** or **R**. At the same time, any Jews with unpronounceable non-English Christian names should have either John or Mary inserted to replace their first names on their identity cards.

To enforce our citizenship laws, we'll need to establish resettlement camps. These could be in the Highlands of Scotland, on remote Scottish isles, the Isle of Wight, Anglesey, or even the Channel Islands. Dissidents accused of hatching anti-government plots or organising protest marches could be incarcerated in these holding centres. Once voting registers are in place, the prosecution need only show the defendant is, for example, a trade unionist, a Gypsy, or a Jew. Following the guilty verdict, these convicted enemies of the state, would be transported to camps for re-education. If rehabilitation is not possible, they would remain indefinitely at His Majesty's pleasure for the protection of British society. Their children would either be imprisoned, put up for adoption, or summarily deported. We need to adopt a zero-tolerance policy towards terrorists.

Next, I'd like to consider religion. The Church of England has been our established doctrine for the past 400 years. If Catholics are prepared to go along with our policies, I suppose they could be left alone. I'm sure you're aware that, because their loyalties are to the Bishop of Rome and not our monarchy, they had been denied the vote until about 100 years ago. This should remind us there is an historical precedent whereby religion has been and could once again be used to limit suffrage. For the same reasons, British citizens who follow other fanatical sects, Jews, Hindus, and Muslims, should be stripped of their franchise and their heathen places of worship torn down. We would justify this because these quite ugly buildings would likely be breeding grounds for anarchists and terrorists.

We might also consider uniforms and badges. To identify and reward loyal citizens, I propose we design and commission an enamelled Union Jack lapel pin. This could be judiciously and ceremoniously awarded to those loyal to our One Nation Party. At the same time, we'll obviously need to identify dissidents. I propose they be required to wear a different sort of badge or perhaps wristbands to make their foreignness obvious to the authorities and other loyal citizens.

Orientals and Blacks are easy to spot. Some Jews wear a yarmulke and Hasidic Jews wear black hats and have long curls. Muslim women wear headscarves. Muslim men sport beards and Sikhs wear turbans. A word of caution, potential terrorists could always dispense with their traditional garb and infiltrate our society to wreak havoc as they pleased. To combat this, I recommend we require those who wish to reside in the UK, sign a sworn declaration avowing they are Christians and will adhere to the principles of the Church of England. Once they do so, it would be a simple matter to enlist the clergy to monitor church attendance.

I recognise the need to protect our borders. As an island, we are fortunate to have an effective barrier against any who wish to enter our country illegally. Nevertheless, I'd recommend Customs and Excise and the Royal Navy be granted additional resources to ensure our borders remain impregnable and under our control.

Furthermore, it's obviously not in our national interests to be involved in a war with either Germany or Russia. I suggest signing a mutual defence treaty between us and one or possibly both countries to underscore British neutrality.

Finally, let me say, my long-term goal is to return our country to the essence of Anglo-Saxon life. I hope some of my proposals will achieve that end. As we enact our plans, expediency must trump bleeding-heart liberal objections. We need to find and support a strong Conservative leader who isn't afraid to say what he thinks or who he offends. By draining the feral swamp of political cronyism and lobbying, we can make the United Kingdom a truly Great Britain again.

While delivering his paper, he looked up from time to time and was surprised he had their full attention. Instead of laughing, being outraged, or simply chatting or joking while they smoked and sipped Champagne, the Apostles remained silent. Blunt and several other Trinity men were actually taking notes.

When he'd finished, they stood and applauded his performance. Animated discussion continued for the next hour and it appeared most agreed with his proposals. Their overwhelming preference was for a mutual defence treaty with the Soviet Union, which was consistent with their alleged Marxist leanings.

As more corks popped, three members stood, found their coats and left without a word. After a few moments, they returned and joined James who remained standing at the front of the room. They were silent until they had the group's attention.

"Xenophobia is not consistent with our role as the head of the British Empire. Presently, one-fifth of the world's population is loyal to King George V. If we were to profile members of our Commonwealth according to religion or skin colour, it would be overtly racist and Britain would lose all international credibility. You do realise, this dreadful paper proposes we strip United Kingdom citizens of their civil rights. I hardly need remind you, over 400,000 Muslims and 60,000 Jews fought bravely and many died for Britain in the Great War. Judging by your collective reaction, we're resigning from the Apostles forthwith. Good evening, gentlemen."

James was embarrassed but didn't dare show he agreed with the speaker.

Later, Blunt cornered him and asked for a copy. "I've only the one. I'll have a scribe make another."

"I'd like to introduce you to a friend who's an influential civil servant. You could present your ideas to someone with some political clout."

"I'd be delighted. By the way, I recognized David Champernowne who spoke for the others. He and Eric Hobsbawm are both at King's. Who was the third?"

He knew David well as he was reading Economics and Mathematics. Eric was an historian and he had spoken with him in dining hall on numerous occasions. He was Jewish and James guessed that was why he walked out of the meeting.

Blunt said, "The third man was Alan Hodgkin. He's here at Trinity reading Physiology and Biophysics."

"Why do you suppose they resigned?"

"I suppose they were just playing at being Marxists. Your paper forced them to reveal their true colours."

48

SUNDAY, MAY 5ᵀᴴ, CAMBRIDGE

Louise and James arranged to meet at King's Backs. They strolled past Trinity and Magdalene colleges, eventually arriving at the Bridge of Sighs. Louise fed the swans and Muscovy ducks with breadcrumbs she'd filched from Newnham kitchens. The rest of their walk was devoted to his German lessons. Louise insisted he repeat phrases and eventually complemented him on his developing vocabulary and pronunciation.

"James, I expect you know tomorrow is a national holiday to celebrate King George's Silver Jubilee. Fancy lunch at a country pub?"

"Leave it with me. I'll swing by at ten."

After escorting her back to Newnham, he went to the King's communal telephone. After several unsuccessful attempts, he eventually secured a table at The Crown at Shillington in Bedfordshire.

In the morning, James met her outside Newnham gates. "Choose any route you wish as long as we make it to Shillington by midday. Our reservations are for one o'clock, but I'd like to have a walk around the village first."

It was a glorious spring morning that showed England at its finest. With the end of the drought, fields were emerald green in the bright sunshine and cattle grazed knee deep in lucerne and clover.

"James, do you know Shillington?"

"Never been. I did a little research in King's library. It dates back to the Saxons and is mentioned in the Doomsday Book. All Saints church is grade-A listed and mostly 14th century."

The church and the common were the centre of the celebrations. Bunting adorned elm trees, lampposts and shop fronts. Trestle tables were being set up on the village green. Numerous High Street shops were open and doing a roaring trade since country people had taken the day off for the celebrations.

They entered an antique shop and Louise offered her hand to the owner. "We're looking for a wedding present, perhaps something in silver."

From her accent and demeanour, the shopkeeper recognised her as a serious buyer. "I've the very thing. It was owned by a local family for generations but death duties forced them to part with some of their heirlooms."

In the back of the shop he showed them a beautiful set of George III fish knives and forks nestled in a mahogany canteen. Under the lid, held in place by blue velvet straps, was a matching serving knife and fork. Louise carefully inspected each of the twenty-six utensils for damage to the ivory handles or the silver patina and found them to be pristine. She knew they were Sterling. Each had the lion passant and the anchor showing they'd been assayed in Birmingham. When she admitted she didn't have the knowledge to decipher the date or the maker's marks, the shop owner offered his loupe and his book of British hallmarks. The lowercase **m** indicated they were assayed in 1767. When she asked about the scripted HB, he told her these were made in the workshops of Hester Bateman, one of the finest silversmiths of the 18th century. With this pedigree, she knew these would be very expensive.

Louise began the haggling process. "I notice there's no tag. Can you tell me your best price?"

"I paid £50. To cover my overheads, I'm asking £75."

She knew they'd be twice that in a London shop. Nevertheless, she felt obliged to make a counter offer and suggested £60. He paused and proposed she make it guineas, which would just about split the difference. When she nodded her agreement, he wrapped the box in brown paper and string while James made out his cheque.

The highlight of lunch at the Crown was fresh asparagus, a Cambridgeshire speciality this time of year. Over coffee she asked, "So how was your fanciful paper received last night? I don't see any bruises so I guess you weren't slung out on your ear."

"Quite the opposite. They were awed by my eloquence and forward thinking."

"You're not serious. Are you? You know I can never tell."

"It went down as if I'd proposed the abolition of exams. Blunt asked for a copy and invited me to meet a friend who's apparently an influential civil servant. Do you think we should invite Blunt and this other chap to our wedding? That would give Richard and Sybil a chance to give them the once-over."

"You must. After all, covert intelligence gathering will soon be our second profession, vineyard owners being our first."

After their meal, they walked around the village to view the preparations for this evening's celebrations. Young children were running around chasing balls and each other. On the common, older boys were playing football, using coats as makeshift goal posts. Teenage girls were helping their mothers with the meal while men congregated around the beer tent. Whole spring lambs on spits were being cooked over open fires and stews bubbled away in large caldrons.

Louise said, "This community spirit could easily be destroyed by another European war. Villagers look after each other and that's the essence of English life."

He put his arm around her waist and found she was shivering. "Let's go to the Backs. There'll be parties, dancing, and a bonfire."

Once there, Louise said, "It seems so long ago we stood here on Guy Fawkes Night. So much has happened and yet everything seems the same."

"I'm sure we dwell on the prospect of war more than most, doubtless because of our work for MI5. A European conflict doesn't enter most people's thoughts. I say, fancy a Woburn weekend?"

"Yes, please. I so miss our time alone." She added with a teasing grin, "And you need your German lessons in the comfort of our bedroom."

He was glad they were parting on a positive note. He returned to his rooms and, as it was still early, copied his paper in case Blunt arranged a meeting for later in the week.

49

TUESDAY, MAY 7TH, CAMBRIDGE

Richard complimented him on his solutions and proofs and handed him two more past exams to work on during the week. He rose from his desk signalling the tutorial was at an end.

James remained seated. "I delivered my discussion paper to the Apostles Saturday evening and I fully expected they'd laugh out loud. Instead, they applauded my performance. In my experience, that's a first for this cynical lot. There were three dissenters who walked out of the meeting and resigned. Afterwards, Blunt asked for a copy and invited me to meet a friend he described as an influential civil servant."

"Now, you've got my full attention. I know it'll make little difference, but you should put at the top of your discussion paper: Not for publication or quotation without the expressed and written permission of the author. That might stop your xenophobic essay from becoming an overnight sensation in the gutter press."

James was delighted Richard felt he might be on to something. Since they were going down to Woburn this weekend, he decided to make an early start on his latest assignment. He was making good progress when interrupted by a knock on the door.

Anthony Blunt entered and sat on the sofa. "I'd like to know a bit more about you. I've discovered Keynes put you up for Apostles' membership, which should be a good enough sponsor for anybody. Who are your people?"

"My family are landowners in north Surrey."

"Ah, so you're a stakeholder committed to maintaining the status quo. Right now, I'm a Trinity Fellow teaching French. Two years ago, I received a first in Modern Languages. My inquiries suggest you're in line for one as well."

"We'll see about that in June."

"Have you a copy of your discussion paper?"

James passed him a sealed envelope and Blunt slipped it into his inside coat pocket.

"If you're free mid-week, I'll arrange a luncheon in town so you can meet my friend."

"My tutorials are Tuesday mornings so that would suit."

As Blunt rose from his chair, James passed him a second envelope. "You might have heard, I'm getting married to Louise de la Béré in July. She's in her final year at Newnham. We'd both like you to attend if you're free that weekend."

"Of course I'll reply formally, but wouldn't miss it for the world. Would you mind if I brought along my friend, Leo Long?"

50

FRIDAY, MAY 10ᵀᴴ, WOBURN

Over breakfast, Louise asked Bea, "Have you settled on a wedding date?"

"We're hoping for October 5ᵗʰ. We'll approach the vicar after Sunday's service to see if that's available."

"That timing would be perfect for us. The harvest will be completed and the must fermenting in the great vats. We'll have had two months of honeymoon which is more than most couples could expect."

Donald asked, "Does that mean you'll spend the entire time with your aunt and uncle?"

"We're planning on having a week or so at some romantic destination, but James is keeping me in the dark. After that, we'll motor to Berlin to see what progress he's made at convincing the Germans he's an Aryan. His appearance should pass muster but his accent will be odd. I don't expect you realise how heterogeneous the German language is in Europe. There are all sorts of enclaves in the east including Poland, Czechoslovakia, and eastern Prussia where German is spoken but with some strange pronunciations. In Switzerland, Austria, and Lichtenstein, they are almost different languages. Closer to home, even the Bavarian dialect can be unintelligible to Germans living in the north."

Donald made eye contact with Bea. He chose not to comment on her impromptu lecture on regional German differences. Louise surely was aware he'd been awarded a first in Modern Languages at Oxford.

James asked Donald, "Have you managed to find anything out about those names I gave you last week?"

"I ran them through SIS files. The Home Office and even the Met allowed me access. Nothing was flagged but I noticed your tutor made similar enquiries earlier this year. As far as we know, they are what they appear to be; rich, upper class, well-connected members of the Cambridge academic community."

"Anthony Blunt asked for a copy of my Apostles' paper and invited me to meet a friend he described as a senior public servant. I have the essay with me if you'd like to have a look."

"Thanks, we'll read it tonight in bed."

For dinner, Cook prepared sea bass fillets.

"Grandmama, I see you're still using the local fishmonger."

"Portman's doing a cracking business. His seafood is always fresh and top quality. We're lucky he's settled in Addlestone."

Humphrey said, "Louise, we tee off tomorrow at ten past nine. Is that too early?"

"I'm always ready to join my grandfather on the golf course."

In the morning, he continued to work in the library. Donald entered the room. "Bea and I are off to the old barn for some target practice. You game?"

"Absolutely. Any excuse to avoid maths."

"Do you keep your Beretta here?"

"I'd have no reason to take it to King's. It might be nicked by a student or servant. I keep it in the desk drawer in my study."

They practiced for about an hour, first taking snap shots with their guns in their coat pockets and afterwards taking careful aim at a bull's-eye target pinned on a hay bale. Donald showed James a few tricks to make the draw smoother and shots more accurate.

On the way back to the house, Donald mentioned his discussion paper. "Bea and I couldn't help but notice your obvious allusions to Nazi Germany. I'm surprised your Marxist Apostles didn't twig to your subtext."

"People hear what resonates with their prejudices."

He returned to the library to work while Donald and Bea left Woburn to walk to nearby Liberty Park.

When Humphrey and Louise entered the room, he asked about their match. "Another Woburn victory. I'll have to start offering handicaps. Louise was amazing. She went 'round in one under."

After lunch, Humphrey said he'd take his usual nap. Louise caught James's eye and he knew she expected him to join her. Upstairs, it didn't take much persuasion for him to focus on her instead of his Tripos preparations. He woke an hour later, quietly dressed and headed towards the door to return to the library.

He heard her says in a soft voice, "Thank you for putting my desires ahead of your exams."

He wasn't sure if she was being ironic, romantic, genuinely pleased, or simply talking in her sleep.

When the cocktail hour arrived, he'd written out formal proofs or solutions for three questions on the first paper. He was tired, but glad he'd made this much progress in only two hours. Returning to their room to change for dinner, he embraced her and gave her a lingering kiss.

"What's that for? Not that I need a reason."

"I can't tell you how happy I am we are about to spend the rest of our lives together."

"I'm ever so pleased you volunteer such loving thoughts on the spur of the moment."

After dinner, Dorothy proposed a game of bridge. Donald said he'd pass as he had a couple of things he wanted to talk over with James. They sat on the sofa while Jarvis set up the bridge table.

"So, Donald, what's on your mind?"

"Do you remember my second in command, Harry Pearce? He telephoned this afternoon with an update on Blunt. We're aware he's a wealthy, cultured intellectual, and an inspirational tutor. His interests range from Mathematics to Modern Languages to Art and Art History. Trouble is, he keeps some strange bedfellows."

"Such as?'

Donald consulted his notebook. "Have you heard of John Warburton Beckett, Arthur Chesterton, William Joyce, Robert Burton-Chadwick, Harold Philby, Donald Maclean, or Guy Burgess?"

191

"Burgess is a bit of a toady and a social climber intent on acquiring Cambridge connections. He read Modern History at Trinity and now holds a postgraduate teaching position there. I met him and Philby last March at the same Apostles' meeting where Maclean proposed a Marxist takeover of the UK. Philby has adopted his childhood nickname Kim, and like the others are active members of the Apostles. Weren't several of the others Members of Parliament?"

"Beckett was a Labour MP a few years ago. Currently, he's a leading light in the British Union of Fascists. Burton-Chadwick was also an MP and on the radical wing of the Conservative Party. He's active in Mosley's BUF and the Middle Class Union. Chesterton is a director and organiser for the BUF and a close friend to Oswald Mosley. William Joyce is one of the BUF's regular speakers at their mass rallies. Unfortunately, they run a closed shop. MI5 and the Home Office know virtually nothing about their aims, activities, membership, executive committee, or affiliates. What my controllers find puzzling is Blunt seems to be connected to Marxists through the Apostles and Fascists by way of the BUF. My guess, one's a cover for the other, but we've no idea of his true allegiances."

51

MONDAY, MAY 13TH, CAMBRIDGE

When he arrived at King's, a porter handed him an envelope. Blunt's note invited him to lunch on Wednesday at the Regent Hotel. He scribbled his acceptance and asked the servant to deliver it at his earliest convenience.

His Tuesday tutorial was exhausting, lasting nearly two hours. Richard stood and handed him a manila folder. "Here are two more past papers to keep your powder dry."

The following day at the Regent, he was shown to a table where two men were smoking cigarettes and drinking cocktails. Across from Blunt sat a well-dressed, balding gentleman sporting a bushy chevron moustache. Blunt introduced him to Captain Archibald Maule Ramsay, MP.

"It's a great pleasure to meet you, sir."

"You're amongst friends. I insist you call me Jock. Anthony showed me your Apostles' essay and I have to tell you I was mightily impressed."

"I thought of it as an intellectual exercise aimed at achieving our mutual goals. I accept many of my suggestions are likely out of reach. Others, if even partly adopted, would make some options redundant. I simply tried to set out the choices facing government should it decide to reinstate core British values."

"As it stands, I found it extremely useful. I particularly liked your historical and contemporary justifications and your American references

193

gave added credence to your proposals. I expect my associates could use many of those ideas to influence parliament and the electorate. I have to tell you, your focus on the Hebrews is what really caught my attention. It won't be difficult to disenfranchise the loonies and that Romany crowd. Jews are a different kettle of gefilte fish."

He loudly guffawed at his attempted witticism. "Raghead Muslims and Hindus are totally alien. I know India is member of our Crown Empire, but it's a damn shame those little brown buggers have been offered citizenship and residency rights. I've read Muslims believe in something they call the Jihad that commits them to wage war against unbelievers. Just now, they're minor players, but that could change if we don't take steps to block immigration. Our real enemies are the Kikes. As you pointed out, they are thoroughly intrenched in British society, control substantial wealth, and have developed powerful political and financial connections. Any further thoughts as to how we could emasculate the Yids?"

James was appalled by the bigotry of his language. Before he could answer, the waiter arrived to take their orders. That gave him a chance to consider his reply. "From my understanding of Political Economy, Adam Smith, John Stuart Mill, and David Ricardo foresaw the economic damage that inevitably results from restraint of trade, restrictive practices, and the monopolisation of markets. Indeed, the Labour Government's proposal to nationalise the coal industry, directly reflects those concerns. I'm thinking of the way mine owners colluded to restrict supplies and raise prices over the last few winters when demand was at its peak and young and old were dying from hypothermia."

"Careful. Coal barons are major Tory contributors."

"What I'm getting at is that we might use the same arguments to nationalise the Jewish dominated banking and insurance sectors. There's nothing in British law that requires full compensation if an enterprise is being run contrary to the public interest. Better yet, the Lord Chancellor has the power to determine Jews have embarked on a criminal conspiracy. We could, at a stroke, arrest and try the bank owners. After securing a conviction, we could confiscate their assets and replace them with state run banks and insurance companies. They could then operate for the benefit of depositors, insurance policy holders, and Britain as a whole."

"Steady on. Nationalisation will never form part of our Tory manifesto. We regularly beat our drums for small government and free market capitalism. Interestingly enough, to marginalise the banking Shylocks, we'd consider your argument. I expect we might convince the Ministry of Justice they've developed an unlawful scheme designed to undermine the working of Adam Smith's 'invisible hand' of market forces. It would be particularly useful and, indeed ironic, to charge the Jewish merchant bankers with violation of the 1660 Usury Act. Vigorous enforcement of the rule of law is always central to mainstream Conservative philosophy."

The entrées arrived and conversation moved on to lighter matters.

"James, tell me a bit about yourself. Anthony said you're financially well-placed and have no need to earn a crust following your degree."

"That's not quite right. I have my family's properties, financial investments, and our Surrey estate to manage. My fiancée and I just purchased a vineyard in Burgundy which we plan to run after we're married in July."

"What I meant, is you'd have time to develop arguments we could put to the electorate."

James knew he had to be careful. The last thing he wanted was to become visible as a recruit to Mosley's British Union of Fascists. "I'm not much of an orator. I believe my strengths lie in formulating strategy."

"We've a number of speakers who can fire up a crowd. What they need are clear proposals with background justifications. Your paper has that in spades. Would you be interested?"

"Always glad to help."

"Welcome aboard. We'd like you to be on hand as a consultant when we present our ideas to the public. Our MP's also need clear arguments they can use in parliamentary debates and Select Committees. Emasculating the Jew-boys will remain our primary objective."

"For the next few months, I'll be pretty busy preparing for finals. Just so you know, I'm no starry-eyed idealist. I'm well-aware enacting even a tenth of my proposals would represent an important victory for our class. You set the agenda and once I know BUF strategy, I'll provide tactics and justifications."

"That's what we need and your timing suits. May I offer my early congratulations and wish you and your bride a happy life together."

James reached into his coat pocket and pulled out an envelope containing a wedding invitation. "We'd like to welcome you and your wife to our ceremony. Anthony and his friend Leo Long will be there so it wouldn't all be strangers."

"I'll consult Ismay and let you know in the accepted manner."

Jock stood, paid the bill and left to catch the train back to London. James and Blunt remained seated finishing their brandies. He saw this as an opportunity to ask Blunt about his politics.

"Think of me as a facilitator. I bring people together who can benefit from each other's skills. I'd say you and the BUF have a lot in common. As for me, I'm a committed Bolshevik. What I found interesting about your paper is that many of your proposals fit nicely into my Marxist world."

"That can't be right. Marxism and Fascism are opposite ends of the political spectrum."

"Come now James, you're being naive. As a matter of course, politicians of every political persuasion employ contrasting rhetoric to enthuse and persuade their unsophisticated rank and file. If you examine Marxism, Fascism, and for that matter, Capitalism, you'll discover their political goals are identical as are their strategies and tactics. Each creates and supports a dominant bureaucracy run and controlled by a powerful financial and military elite. To survive, every political system requires a skilled and docile working class. Dissidents are counter-productive and must be emasculated through civil and criminal laws and, if necessary, by military force."

"So, you've no problem with a foot in both camps?"

Blunt downed the remainder of his brandy and rose from the table. "It's always nice to be on the winning side, whatever the outcome."

When he returned to King's, he rang Richard, Donald, and finally Louise about his meeting.

"Hello, my darling. What can I do for you?"

"I've rung to tell you about my lunch with Blunt."

"Let's take a walk, you can enlighten me along the way."

"What about your tutorial?"

"It's been cancelled. Sybil said I should just keep reading and I'd be fine."

"I'll be 'round in two ticks."

"My luncheon was curious. Blunt seems to be playing for both the Marxist and Fascist teams. I was introduced to a Member of Parliament, Archibald Ramsay who took a shine to me due to my anti-Semitic stance in the Apostles' paper. He's a dreadful man, a racist, and a xenophobe. Anyway, I'm now a consultant to the BUF with a commission to provide arguments their public speakers can use to promote UK Fascism."

"I wouldn't advertise that amongst our friends."

"Certainly not. I'll always be in the background and my name won't appear on any of their propaganda sheets or membership lists."

"Apart from ploughing through European literature, I'm now free of college commitments. Could we have a long weekend at Woburn?"

"I can work on maths there as well as in my rooms. There'll be one additional but welcome distraction, especially at night."

"I expect you mean your German lessons."

52

FRIDAY, MAY 17ᵀᴴ, ADDLESTONE

Over lunch, Louise asked Dorothy how Alice was progressing as her secretary. "I know the girl is only sixteen but she's an absolute wizard at organisation. I just hope she stays after the wedding. By the way, Jarvis is in complete agreement."

Humphrey said, "Louise, I almost forgot. The Club's Captain has asked if we could join him and Vice-Captain on the links tomorrow morning."

James and Louise spent the afternoon strolling around the estate and practicing German. He learned when it was appropriate to use the familiar or 'du' form and when the polite or 'Sie' form of address was needed. She explained how each could affect verb conjugation. Louise spent little time with formal grammar. Instead, she made him repeat phrases until he got used to the rhythm and pronunciation.

"Just remember, if it doesn't sound right, it isn't right."

James thought to himself, If only my Latin, Greek, and French masters at Dulwich had her teaching expertise. Classroom motivations to learn grammar rules were underpinned by the threat of detention and ultimately a liberal use of the cane. He enjoyed the fact that Louise's teaching incentives were rather more intimate in nature.

After dinner, Louise asked Humphrey about the Captain and Vice-Captain. "Both are ex-Indian Army and know how to keep the Pavilion running smoothly. I have to warn you, they've scratch handicaps on a good day and know the course like the back of their hands."

First thing in the morning, Louise quietly dressed and went downstairs for breakfast. James woke when he heard the longcase hall clock chime ten times. After he finished breakfast, he went into the library to work on what would be his final two past papers. By noon, he'd completed the first and made a start on the second. As had become his habit, he read through all the questions and zeroed in on those he thought he could solve. He'd written out another three solutions when Dorothy came into the room.

"Am I disturbing you?"

"Not at all, grandmama."

"Humphrey and Louise have been invited to dine at the Pavilion restaurant, so we'll be on our own for lunch. Could you drive me into Addlestone so I can see what our fishmonger has on offer?"

When they entered the shop, they were no other customers. After scanning what was on display, James asked Portman to make up a plateau de fruits de mer.

Dorothy said, "I don't know what that is, but it sounds exotic."

"It's just various shellfish served on a bed of crushed ice. Let's have that for Saturday lunch when Bea and Donald are down.

Turning to Portman, he said, "Right, two dozen oysters, half a pound of shrimp, a dozen of those large prawns, six langoustines, two dozen scallops, and six medium sized lobster tails. Could you have our order ready for collection later this afternoon?"

"No need to drive in again, sir. I'll have my lad deliver it to Woburn Hall, say, 'round tea time."

"That's good of you. How much do I owe?"

"I'll make up your bill with the delivery and you can settle at your convenience."

"Grandmama, anything else you need while we're in the village?"

"I'd like to show you something I've found curious."

"Ah, a mystery. I always love ferreting out clues and discovering whodunnit."

"Stop teasing, James. This is serious and I'm really worried. Do you know Green Lane?"

"Doesn't it run between the High Street and St Peter's Way?"

"Yes, it's a long road with a few cottages at the upper end."

He turned into Green Lane and approached the crossroads with the A317.

"Stop here. See those houses on the left?"

The semi's looked pre-war. The front doors had stained glass panels in the Edwardian geometric style.

"Do you see they have names as well as house numbers?"

One was called Dunroamin' and another Dam Breezy.

"Until last year, number 11 was called Swastika. Now its Wisteria Cottage and there's absolutely no sign of wisteria. When I asked our postman, he said their surname is Messer."

James now understood her concerns. Messer was the German word for knife.

"Perhaps they felt embarrassed by the house name. Before Hitler co-opted the symbol and renamed it the Hakenkreuz, it was a sign of wellbeing and good luck especially in the Muslim world."

He'd picked up that bit of trivia somewhere over the last couple of years, perhaps at one of his Politics' lectures.

"Grandmama, this is definitely suspicious and worth looking into further. Just now we should be getting back. Cook will have our lunch on the table."

As they were finishing their meal, the golfers returned and appeared to be in a celebratory mood. Humphrey asked Jarvis for a chilled bottle of Champagne.

"Are we celebrating your victory?"

Louise said, "Actually, we lost by one hole. The good news is, I've been invited to become the first lady with seven-day membership at St George's."

Humphrey added, "I knew something was afoot when they asked us to lunch. Apparently, the executive committee voted last week. She's been appointed Lady Captain with the task of recruiting more ladies for full membership. Their decision was based on her sportsmanship and playing skills."

Later that afternoon, Donald and Bea arrived and the two young couples walked into town.

James asked, "Have you learned anything about Ramsay?"

Donald extracted his notebook from his breast pocket. "Some of it makes my blood boil. He's a Scottish peer, married to Lady Ninian Crichton-Stuart, herself the widow of a titled MP. Ramsay was elected to Parliament in the 1931 General Election as a Conservative representing Peebles and Southern Midlothian. He holds a comfortable majority and has begun to express his virulent brand of anti-Semitism as he gains confidence in his position within government. MI6 has flagged him as a xenophobe with Nazi leanings."

"We've invited him to our wedding so you can see if your background checks are accurate. By the way, since you've apparently got access to Home Office files, can you see what you can find anything about a family called Messer who live at 11 Green Lane here in Addlestone? Dorothy is concerned they might be Nazis, but between you and me it's a fool's errand."

"I'll follow up on this when I get the chance. No doubt she sees the enemy 'round every corner because of our jobs."

For lunch, Jarvis and Peets brought out the enormous silver platter of shellfish and placed it in the centre of the dining table. The wine was '24 Puligny-Montrachet, the Chardonnay they'd purchased the previous October.

53

MONDAY, MAY 20TH, CAMBRIDGE

He worked in his rooms and by midnight, completed his final two past papers. He was quietly confident his results wouldn't disappoint Richard. For himself, he wasn't particularly bothered since his livelihood didn't depend on gaining a first. His pride was another matter. He telephoned Louise to suggest a drink, but she was immersed in reading 19th century French novels and presently taking notes on Émile Zola's *Germinal*. They agreed to meet tomorrow evening at the Mitre.

When his Tuesday tutorial ended, Richard shook his hand and wished him well in the exams. "By the way, I've asked around about Ramsay. Few Conservative MPs regard him as a likely candidate for a cabinet post. They acknowledge he's an inspirational speaker and a very personable chap, but Tory grandees don't altogether trust him. We'd like you take that consultancy."

"I intend to do just that. By the way, Louise tells me Hitler plans to make a major speech this afternoon."

"Sybil and I will be listening on the shortwave wireless. I expect Louise will do the same but doubt your German is up to following his ranting style. The SIS is particularly interested to hear if he reveals anything more about his Eastern European ambitions."

That evening, there was a raucous crowd in the Mitre, the air thick with cigarette smoke. Once they were seated, James said, "So, tell me about Hitler's Reichstag speech."

"Actually, it was distinctly odd. It was as if he there was an impending election and he was trying to rally his supporters. But that makes no sense. Since the passage of the Enabling Act in March 1933, he's ruled by emergency decree without reference to either the electorate or Reichstag approval.

"Anyway, he made a number of placating assertions. Initially, he said he hadn't the slightest thought of invading other nations. He kept repeating the assertion, Deutschland braucht Ruhe and den Frieden will! Germany needs peace and desires peace! He stressed that for the last sixteen years, they'd adhered to the onerous conditions of Versailles. Germany had disarmed while other countries had increased their tanks, ships, aircraft, and standing armies. He promised to personally guarantee the French borders and cede Alsace-Loraine to France forever. He offered to sign a similar treaty with Poland guaranteeing their sovereignty over their current post-war borders. Finally, he asserted, that as socialists, his government is focused solely on domestic policies, especially those aimed at creating full-employment and prosperity. He repeatedly attacked the Bolsheviks for openly promoting their international mission to dominate the world."

"What's your take on that?"

"To my mind, he correctly dismissed Versailles, arguing that nearly seventeen years after the end of hostilities, Germany should have the same rights as other nations to raise an army and protect and defend her borders. What's more, he's spot-on about the Russians. Stalin regularly highlights the Communist's international ambitions, centred on invading neighbouring countries.

"On the other hand, this is likely a load of codswallop, designed to placate and confuse Europe, Russia, and the US while they arm themselves to the teeth. He's a pathological liar and I simply don't trust the man. Given the tightness of German border security, I doubt the rest of the world is aware of what's happening there. As we both know, the international press has been denied unfettered access.

On Saturday, they met at the Backs and walked along the Cam towards the Mill Pond so Louise could feed the ducks and swans. They spent the next three hours quietly speaking German, even over lunch at The Mill.

"My last maths exam is next Friday morning so let's escape to Woburn in the afternoon."

"I so miss our Spielzeit. It'll have been two weeks of abstinence what with these retched Tripos."

"We can return the following week for the results and the May Week fun. You know I'm committed to the Bumps."

"I watched that silly boat race last year. Your crew didn't do all that well. Every time a following boat barged into you, they passed you easily."

"The race can be chaotic, but if there are any rules at all, that's it. If your boat is touched by another, you must let them pass or be disqualified."

54

FRIDAY, JUNE 7ᵀᴴ, WOBURN

They arrived at midday. After lunch, Dorothy said she and Humphrey would take an hour's rest in their room. James saw a twinkle in Louise's eye and said they'd like to take a nap as well. They were awakened when they heard talking and laughter coming from downstairs. James rose first. "Donald and Bea must have arrived. We should get dressed and join the family."

"You go down when you're ready. I'd like a quick bath."

As Louise descended the stairs, she heard the pleasant sound of a cork exploding from a bottle. All had raised glasses to toast the two students.

Donald asked, "When are the results announced?"

"They're posted at Senate House Friday next for all the disciplines apart from maths. For us, there's a bizarre tradition whereby the Senior Examiner reads out the Tripos results from the balcony, after which printed copies are hurled down to the students. Candidates who achieve a First are called Wranglers and the top scholar is called Senior Wrangler."

"Why Wrangler?"

James shrugged. "No idea."

"I expect it stems from the debating term to wrangle with an argument."

Louise took a sip from her flute and starred out the window. "Donald, that's rather obvious, don't you think?"

After dinner, while the rest of the family chatted about the wedding preparations, James asked Donald if he'd learned anything more about

Ramsay. "He's on the radical fringe of the Conservative and Unionist Party. While he's well-connected amongst the British upper classes, he and his wife's anti-Semitic views have made enemies such that they've been excluded from some functions associated with the social season. There are unconfirmed rumours he's connected to the White Knights of Britain."

"What's that when it's at home?"

"They're a secretive organisation also called The Hooded Men. Apparently, they model themselves after the American Ku Klux Klan. SIS are aware of their anti-Semitic aims but unfortunately we know nothing about their membership or the composition of their executive committee."

Dorothy must have heard Donald mention his name. "Archibald and Ismay Ramsay have accepted your wedding invitation. James, how is it you know a Scottish Member of Parliament?"

"Through a friend at King's. By the way, Donald, I've got something for you."

He reached into his jacket pocket and gave him their May Ball tickets. "It's a fortnight Saturday. I've booked a table at The Blue Boar on Trinity Street for six o'clock. Travel up in the afternoon and after the meal, you can change into formal attire in our respective rooms. At nine, we'll meet up for the dinner dance."

"I see they cost you ten guineas."

"Consider it a wedding gift."

"Then let me pay for drinks."

"You're outta luck there, old man. Unless you want to bring a flask, Champagne, wine, beer, and soft drinks are included."

"Well then, I'll spring for dinner."

55

SATURDAY, JUNE 8TH, WOBURN

At breakfast, James asked Donald if MI6 had found out anything about the Messer family.

"I did try. There's no Home Office record of a family by that name in Surrey. I expect that's because they're residents but not citizens. My staff is digging deeper and will contact the General Post Office and the Inland Revenue. As far as the house name goes, they probably changed it when Hitler co-opted the symbol for the Nazi party."

Dorothy overheard this. "Donald, please keep looking. I'm frightened there might be more Nazis lurking in Addlestone."

"You mustn't worry. We got rid of that lot last February."

Louise asked Dorothy, "Can you tell me where Alice would be just now? I'd like to have a look at our wedding books and the latest gifts to arrive."

"Jarvis has set up a table for her in the billiards' room."

Bea joined Dorothy and Louise while the men remained in the library. Humphrey said to Donald, "I've heard rumblings from my contacts in the Foreign Office that we're about to sign a maritime accord with the Nazis. From the Admiralty's point of view, it's intended to limit their build-up of naval tonnage. All it really does is rubber-stamp the current illegal expansion of the Kriegsmarine."

"MI6 presumes Hitler is worried about the treaty signed last month between France and Russia. Our analysts are convinced he's trying to cement closer relations with Britain in the event both countries declare war and he's forced to fight on two fronts."

Humphrey was dismissive. "This is Stanley Baldwin's first decision as prime minister in our National Government. After replacing Ramsay MacDonald, I expect he's trying to put his stamp on his premiership. If this is his strategy to avoid war, it's a damp squib. Hitler's as slippery as an eel and will renege on agreements at the drop of a hat. What's more, negotiating and potentially signing this treaty would only give international credence to his Fascist regime."

The ladies re-joined them in the library. Louise said, "Our wedding list is almost complete with only a few stragglers."

Bea approached Donald. "My dear, you'll need to write down the names and addresses of your extended family members, your Harrow and Oxford friends, and your MI6 colleagues so we can finalise our own guest list. We can use theirs as a starter since many of the same people will be invited."

After lunch, Donald and Bea went into the library to work on their own wedding guest list. Humphrey and Dorothy took a short walk to the Mill Pond, leaving James and Louise on their own.

"James, can you show me the Messer house?"

"There's not much to see. It's just a non-descript Edwardian semi."

They walked towards Addlestone station. Louise said, "By the way, I rang Michel last evening."

"Well done. It keeps slipping my mind what with the Apostles and our exams."

"Apparently, it's been a splendid spring and the grapes are setting nicely."

"And the building work?"

"Nearly complete. Michel assures me it'll be ready for the harvest. He told me he'd spent the first tranche of money so I've sent the same again from my trust. I discussed this with my guardians and since it's an investment, they've no reservations about invading the capital. In any case, it'll be dissolved next June when I turn twenty-five."

"You needn't have done that. I've also secured permission from my trustees."

"Please pay attention. We're about to enter into a lifetime partnership. I insist you regard me as an equal in all senses including the funding of our vineyard."

"Understood. We're both loners and there'll probably be times when we plunge off in some direction without discussion. I'll do my best to ensure that doesn't happen."

"As will I. Equal partners? Pact?"

"Pact! And if you don't mind, I'd like to seal it with a kiss."

"James, we're in a public place."

She was too late. He embraced her under the station's new Belisha beacon. Arm in arm, they continued their walk to the upper end of Green Lane. Just as they arrived, a black Austin Ten-Four stopped in front of Wisteria Cottage. Four men got out and entered the house.

James said, "One used a key so they must be part of the Messer family, perhaps with some pals."

A few minutes later, the same men got into the car and drove off towards the town centre.

"That man with the flat hat is Portman our fishmonger. I expect they're his drivers."

Two more men left the house and drove off in a Ford Popular which was parked across the road.

"You know, James, there's a lot of coming and going in that little two-up two-down. Let's see if he's in his shop."

An assistant stood behind the counter. "We'd like three dozen fresh oysters."

She went out back and returned with a wooden box packed with seaweed. "These were in the channel yesterday so should be perfect for the Harcourt-Heath family. Will be there anything else?"

"Actually, I wanted to have a word with Mr Portman about providing a shellfish starter for our July wedding"

"He's gone to the bank to deposit the week's takings. I'll tell him you stopped by."

"It'll be a large order. Will he be back later this afternoon?"

"I expect he'll run some errands while he's out and about."

"Not to worry. We'll pop 'round next week."

He paid for the oysters and they left to walk back to Woburn. "You know James, banks aren't open Saturday afternoon so she wasn't altogether straight with us. Have you met her before?"

"Never."

"I wonder how she knew who you were?"

Jarvis met them at the front door. "Could you ask Cook to prepare these oysters as a starter? We'd like a drink when you've got a moment."

The rest of the family were in the library when they entered the room.

Louise spoke first. "Donald, do you remember Dorothy's concerns about the house on Green Lane? James and I walked by this afternoon and to my mind there was some unusual activity. I've memorised two license numbers. Could you check on these when you have a chance?"

"What am I looking for?"

"There was an Austin Ten-Four and a Ford Popular, both black. Six men left the house and the cars headed towards Addlestone centre."

She wrote down the registration numbers and Donald excused himself to use the 'phone.

The starter was a hit. Thirty-six fresh oysters each in their half shell were served on a bed of crushed ice with quartered lemons on the side.

Back in the library for coffee, Jarvis called Donald to the telephone. When he returned, he was frowning.

James asked, "Bad news?"

"In a way. The registration numbers Louise gave me are associated with different makes of vehicles. Louise, you sure you've not made a mistake?"

"I don't make such errors. I leave that up to you and MI6."

"Right, it's now a police matter. I'll pass this on to the local constabulary in the morning."

James asked, "Aren't they taking a chance using false plates?"

"Not really. They're only at risk if they have a prang or get stopped for some Highway Code violation. Any dodgy garage can make plates if they're offered the readies. Criminals sometimes do that when planning a robbery."

Before they left for St Paul's, Donald rang the local police station and reported the false number plates. He identified himself, gave details of the cars to the constable on duty, and asked to be kept informed.

56

FRIDAY, JUNE 14ᵀᴴ, CAMBRIDGE

Several hundred students milled around the Senate House notice boards. James fought his way to the front and saw Louise had been awarded a 2:1. The Senior Examiner stood on the balcony and called for silence before he began to read the Mathematical Tripos results. After each name, he paused before announcing the class of degree awarded.

"William James Rawnsley Harcourt-Heath, First Class Honours with distinction."

After the final candidate's results were announced, printed results showered down on the students. James was 12ᵗʰ Wrangler just as Keynes had been thirty years earlier. Louise put both hands on his cheeks and kissed him in front of everybody. A number of friends shook his hand and offered their congratulations. An attractive blonde grabbed James's shoulders and planted a kiss on his lips. She whispered something in his ear, gave him a sultry smile over her shoulder, and disappeared into the mass of raucous students. Louise was livid and was certain she'd confront him about this embarrassing display.

James felt a tap on his shoulder. Richard grabbed his hand and pumped it vigorously. "Please accept my congratulations."

"I have to thank you for your faith in me and your hard work."

"If both of you could turn up to my office at our usual time Tuesday next, I have a proposal that might be of interest."

As he melted into the crowd, they headed to the Mitre for a celebratory drink with friends.

After a couple of hours, Louise stood. "I'm fed up with this smoky atmosphere. I wish I could hold you close to me in our own bed."

"Then let's escape to Addlestone."

"Are you fit to drive?"

"I've only had a couple of pints. If we have a meal before we leave, I'll be fine. What say we grab a bite at The Blue Boar? I can confirm Saturday's reservations."

When they arrived at Woburn, Humphrey was at his writing desk in the library. "We thought you might turn up. How'd you do?"

"I was awarded an upper second and James got a first and a rowing Blue for his participation in the Boat Race."

"Louise and I are tired. We'd like to take a nap before supper."

Pleasant and relaxed lovemaking on this warm June afternoon cleared their minds of all thoughts of essays, deadlines, tutorials, and examinations.

Later in the library, they chatted while enjoying flutes of Champagne. James raised his glass to his grandparents. "I have to thank you both for putting up with me during all these years of education."

Humphrey said, "Now you're free of academics, I trust you won't forget Woburn."

"No fear. After the May Ball, we'll move our belongings into our room. Actually, we've both packed some suitcases filled with books and odds and ends. I'll ask Peets to take them to my study."

Over a light supper, Dorothy asked Louise about their plans for children. Her heart skipped a beat. "Not just yet. We'd like to get used to being married without the distractions of academia."

She deliberately steered the conversation away from childbearing. "If you plan to take a winter holiday, you might think about making a booking after Bea and Donald's wedding. The Burgundy harvest will be over and we'll be here to look after things."

"You know, I've already made a few inquiries with Thomas Cook about Cunard cruises."

Dorothy looked up from her knitting. "I didn't know that. It would be nice to avoid some of our dull winter weather."

"I'd thought about asking Nicholas and Helen."

"You must. Apart from our French trip, we've been encamped here since before the war. Mind you, I'm not complaining. I'd just like to see a bit of the world before I'm too frail to travel."

Saturday morning, Donald and Bea arrived and went directly to the billiard room to discuss wedding invitations with Alice. After lunch, the family decided to stroll into the village.

James asked Donald, "Did you manage to follow up on those dodgy license plates?"

"Actually, I've heard nothing back from the police. Tell you what, let's pop by now. It's on Station Road, isn't it?"

The sergeant was behind the front desk. Donald showed his credentials and asked about the two cars he'd reported with false plates.

"That's news to me. Hold on a tick and let me find out what's what. When did you ring?"

"Last Sunday morning."

He licked his finger and flicked through the station log until he arrived at Sunday the 9th of June.

"Well now, there's nothing here. Who'd you speak to?"

"I didn't ask. I gave my name, my Secret Service designation, and said I was staying at Woburn Hall."

The sergeant pulled out another ledger. "PCs Adler and Galvin were on duty that morning but they're off just now. You can be certain I'll ask them about this when they clock on."

"No hurry, but could you keep me posted?"

The sergeant saluted, "Certainly, sir."

They continued their walk and Dorothy suggested a detour towards Green Lane.

"Capital idea grandmama. It's only fifteen minutes away and I'm sure Donald and Bea would like to see the site of the Highway Code infraction."

When they arrived at Wisteria Cottage, Louise noticed a distinct twitching of the net curtains behind the bay window. She said, "Neither black motorcar is parked nearby."

Donald replied, "It all appears perfectly normal to me. I'll follow up when we're next down."

James pointed out, "That won't be until after the May Ball, you know." He said, sotto voce, "I rather doubt it's urgent."

Over cocktails, James asked Donald what he was working on just now. "We're still trying to identify the young women who were abducted. Regional Missing Persons have asked for our help so they can remove them from their lists. No doubt Bea's two orphanage leavers are amongst the group of thirty-six confirmed kidnapped girls. Apart from that, we occasionally catch a German trying to pass muster. They don't manage the language, accent, or idioms. All have been minor field agents sent over by the Abwehr."

"Richard mentioned that organisation in connection with the Lebensborn kidnappings."

"Abwehr means defence. Their role is to gather strategic military intelligence. Himmler and Heydrich have tried to take control, but Hitler's been loyal to Admiral Wilhelm Canaris. It's our understanding, political machinations have prevented them from recruiting effective operatives and, as a result, their agents are easily identified. We've even turned a couple and sent them back to Germany as doubles."

"I expect you've only caught the stooges and the rest are out and about getting up to mischief."

"Louise, just so I'm clear, our senior analysts have totally discounted that scenario. Those we've questioned, admit their training was minimal and all they needed was some practical knowledge of English."

57

SUNDAY, JUNE 16TH, CAMBRIDGE

They enjoyed their usual Sunday rituals including St Paul's, the George, and roast beef. While Bea went upstairs to pack, Donald said they'd leave after lunch. "Bea needs to prepare for work on Monday. She now has her own office and secretary at the Government Code and Cypher School. She seems quite talented in that direction and has come up with some useful ideas for our own codes. Many of her cyphers are based on combining her skills as a musician, artist, and linguist."

When Bea joined them, James said, "If you need help with your codes, remember, I can wrangle solutions."

No way would Bea rise to his whimsical suggestion.

Tuesday morning, Richard directed them to sit in the leather chairs in his study. "James, GC&CS has formally instructed me to offer you a position in their coding programme. It's become a tradition to invite some Wranglers to apply. You might remember Alan Turing. He's accepted our offer in principle although this year he's taken a King's fellowship. Are you interested?"

"We've too much on our plates. And, of course I know Alan. His rooms were just down the corridor from mine. We talked maths at meals and after lectures."

"I told them you probably wouldn't be interested but it's an open offer. You can take it up any time in the future."

"I expect you're aware my sister is working there on cyphers? Jokingly I suggested I could lend a hand."

"SIS is hoping for something like that. I'll have Donald persuade her to enlist your help. If there's anything else you'd like to discuss, I'm always available."

"Dr Chillingworth, might I raise a hypothetical."

"Louise, from now on, address me as Richard. You're no longer students and we work for the same organisation."

"Richard it is. Donald told me, Whitehall's view is that the Abwehr, under Admiral Canaris, is a corrupt and inefficient organisation. He said, they've been overwhelmed with infighting and intrigue such that their agents are ineffective and easily identified."

"And so they are."

"It's occurred to me this might be a smokescreen put out by the Abwehr. MI5 might have only spotted the amateurs and there still could be active cells getting up to mischief."

"A logical possibility, but, in our view, that's highly improbable."

"With the Lebensborn kidnappings, we encountered a professional network that remained undetected for eighteen months. If you recall, they were only exposed by chance."

"Have you anything to support your concerns?"

Louise shrugged her shoulders.

"Bring me some evidence and I'll follow it up."

Louise remained silent and stared out the window. She thought his reply officious and condescending as was Donald's response last weekend.

They left Gibbs' and decided to take tea at the Regent Hotel. James said, "I'll need to excuse myself this afternoon. I'm meeting my King's crew to prepare for this evening's Bumps."

"It was really quite hilarious last year, but I guess you enjoy your schoolboy silliness."

"Excuse me. May Bumps are deadly serious. Every college and a number of social and sporting clubs field crews. Because the Cam is winding and narrow, races are conducted in series rather than in parallel. Eights start off at set intervals and the challenge is to try to touch the boat ahead. If your crew manages that, they must yield and let you pass.

Competitions begin at six in the evening and continue until dusk. The next afternoon we start again, the previous day's results deciding each group's starting order. There's substantial betting and rankings are published daily in The Times and The Telegraph. Since exams have finished, the river's lined with thousands of raucous supporters, many wearing silly costumes and most having had substantial amounts of drink taken."

"I still don't see the point." With that, she turned and departed towards Newnham to sort out her belongings.

Before going to the Boat House, he visited a couple of jewellery shops in town without spotting anything that caught his eye.

Arriving at the starting point at Baits Bite lock, she watched the King's crew flip their scull into the water.

The first race began with a deafening explosion from a small brass cannon. Louise collapsed on the footpath and blacked out. She was grateful to some passing students who helped her to her feet. "I must have tripped on a root or something."

She was fifty yards up the river when she heard another cannon explosion which caused her to shiver. As the second division race progressed, she saw James chivvying his crew. It wasn't long before they made a delicate contact with the boat ahead. At the finishing line near Chesterton Footbridge, King's crew had passed another and were now in 4th place.

After the race, he was soaked, but elated. "We made a double overbump!"

They'd agreed to meet at the Penny Ferry public house. After a few drinks with his mates, he escorted her back to Newnham. The sounds of student revelry, crickets, and nightjars filled the balmy evening air. As usual when they were by themselves, they chatted in German.

"I know you like surprises. Tomorrow I've planned an outing."

"James, do tell."

"Then it wouldn't be a surprise."

58

MONDAY, JUNE 17TH, GRANTCHESTER

———————

He arrived at Newnham's gates wearing a striped blazer and straw boater. "We're punting to Grantchester. I've booked a table at the Green Man."

They walked east to Scudamore's rental site adjacent to The Mill. She sat in the bow while James skilfully took his position at the stern without causing so much as a wobble.

Louise wondered how many ladies he'd escorted along the Cam since October 1932. That idle speculation led her to think about the blonde who kissed him in front of Senate House. She put these jealous twinges out of her mind and let her hand skim along the water while watching James's powerful and relaxed punting skills. She was aware he had an amatory past but she also knew he loved her and wanted to marry her. That was all that really mattered. Intellectually she regarded jealously as akin to envy, one of the seven cardinal sins. She didn't really understand that emotion. In novels, it was invariably self-destructive and more often than not, poisoned loving relationships. To her mind, love involves a mutual commitment freely offered and has nothing to do with possession, ownership, domination, or control.

He tied up at the Grantchester dock. After a leisurely pub lunch of Welsh rarebit, they returned the punt to Scudamore's and strolled to Baits Bite lock. She walked quickly along the towpath, ensuring she was nowhere near the starter's cannon.

King's crew achieved another double overbump so would be in second place for Thursday's race.

They had a light meal at The Anchor, just around the corner from King's.

"You know James, apart from having family down for the May Ball, I'm in limbo."

"Cheer up, old girl. After that, we'll have our whole lives together."

"You're right, of course. A good night's sleep will see me sorted. By the bye, tomorrow's junket is down to me. Don't worry, we'll be back for your precious Bumps and I'll loyally cheer you on at the finish."

In the morning, she was waiting by the Newnham gates. James asked, "Where're we bound?"

"Not far. It's only about seven miles away. I've reserved a table in Hardwick."

"Hardwick?"

"My Newnham friends tell me the Blue Lion is an ancient pub with gobs of atmosphere and excellent fare. As we're getting an early start, I'd first like to go to Ely. We can walk along the Great Ouse and perhaps visit some antique shops. You know I always like browsing."

Ely was a pleasant escape from the boisterous atmosphere of Cambridge May Week. It was compact and little more than a small town, but because of its cathedral, it is classified as a city. They discovered a good selection of antique shops and visited several without making any purchases. At the fourth shop, Louise wandered towards the rear to examine ceramics. In a glass case, James spotted a bar brooch he thought might possibly be Edwardian. The proprietor claimed it was made up of diamonds, sapphires, yellow gold, and platinum. James was dubious, primarily because the broach had no obvious maker's imprint. He knew it was silver as there was a faint hallmark. They agreed a price and the shopkeeper placed it in a small box. James slipped it in his pocket when he spotted Louise returning.

Afterwards, they walked around the majestic Cathedral. James focussed on the intricate and varied ceramic floor tiles. They embraced for some minutes in the light of the beautiful west-facing stained glass window.

At the Blue Lion, they held hands across the table while the waiter took their order for shepherd's pie. "As this is my day out, I insist on buying lunch, unless that would offend your male prerogatives. I expect you've forgotten it's my birthday."

"Actually, I thought you might like this."

After a careful inspection, she put it on her lapel. "Thank you, my darling. This is such a beautiful Tiffany brooch."

"Is it by Tiffany?"

"I can just make out a faint T, some other letters and then & Co. When we're next in London, let's ask about its history. I've read they keep detailed records of their creations."

Returning to the Bumps, he parked near the starting line and rushed off to join his crew. When the King's shell came around the final bend, they were some ten lengths ahead of the nearest competitor. James and his teammates were shouting in celebration accompanied by some quite disorganised rowing.

They met before he changed his clothes. "We've made the First Division. It's the first time in a couple of decades."

59

FRIDAY, JUNE 21ST, CAMBRIDGE

After spending the morning packing, they met at the Mitre for lunch. Louise realised this would likely be their final drink at what had become their local. At five, they walked to the lock for the start of the final May Bumps competition. At Top Finish, King's had moved into 5th place in the First Division.

"This is our best showing this century. We plan to get a blade, record the date and our names and hang it in our dining hall."

"That's a bit like retiring one's putter after a match play victory, which would be just plain silly."

They celebrated the final day of the 1935 Bumps at the Penny Ferry. James and his crew remained until last orders.

"Good thing we walked. No way should I be behind the wheel."

When they got to King's, he noticed the Porter's Lodge was empty. He grabbed her hand and hurried her along the walkway to Bodley's Court.

"James, this is very bold."

"We're adults of voting age with Cambridge degrees. I can't see the harm. It's quite a distance to Newnham and we're in no condition to walk that far."

"Speak for yourself. If we're to inaugurate your room, I'd better use your loo to freshen up before joining you in your tiny single bed."

James stood guard while she visited the communal facilities.

In the morning, he asked a porter to fetch the Edinburgh telephone directory. When he disappeared into the back office, he gave her the thumbs-up. She nipped through the gateway and walked quickly down King's Parade.

Returning to his rooms, he laid out his white tie clothing for this evening. After a light lunch in the dining hall, he continued packing his belongings. Remembering his bedder and gyp, he slipped crisp ten-shilling notes into two envelopes.

After the three couples finished their meal at the Blue Boar, they separated to change into formal attire. At nine they met up outside the marquee. Once inside, they claimed a table with the ladies' shawls.

Louise thought: 'Tonight is the denouement of my student days. From now on I'm going to be a faithful wife and an amorous lover.'

They danced to some old favourites interspersed with some popular songs that had come out this spring. The dance floor filled when Charles Kunz and the Casani Club Orchestra played 'One Night in Chinatown' and again when they belted out 'Okay Toots'.

At midnight, the musicians took their second break. The dining hall was arranged with circular tables, tablecloths, and linen napkins. Champagne was freely available on each table. Starters were boar's head, suckling pig, or Scotch salmon with mayonnaise sauce. The main course was served cold with a choice of roast chicken or roast turkey plus cold ham or cold tongue salad with new potatoes. Anchovy eggs, lobster, and chicken vol-au-vent followed. Finally, there was fruit salad with fresh cream or coffee mousse.

By two in the morning, they were back in the marquee. More popular songs were played including 'I've got a Feelin' you're Foolin'', 'How's Chances', and 'With My Eyes Wide Open I'm Dreaming'.

At four, Louise stood and said she was returning to her room. Bea and Margie also rose and collected their shawls. Jonathan explained he'd only had barley water since supper so they'd drive back to Woburn. Donald added that he'd tapered off and they'd spend the night in Chelsea.

James said, "We'll pack your daytime clothes and bring them down tomorrow. If you set off now you can be in your beds before dawn."

60

SUNDAY, JUNE 23RD, WOBURN

Powell, the Head Porter, allowed James to park on King's forecourt to load his car. His servants brought boxes of books along with his trunk and suitcases. They bowed slightly and thanked him for the generous gratuity. He drove straight to Newnham to help Louise pack her Hillman but needn't have hurried. Bea and Margie's cases were stowed on the front passenger seat and the rest of her belongings were piled on the back seat or crammed into the boot.

After turning through Woburn's front gates, they parked next to Donald's Packard and Jonathan's Alvis Firebird. The entire family were assembled on the manicured front lawn. A wicket was set up and Jonathan was throwing a tennis ball overarm towards Peter while everyone else was fielding. Louise presumed this idyllic scene was being repeated all over the country. Three generations of her family were enjoying the quintessential game of cricket on this tranquil June day.

They approached, intending to join in the fielding. Before they could exchange greetings, a black Austin Seven sped through the front gates, spraying gravel as it turned and came to a sliding halt. A uniformed police constable stepped out of the left passenger seat and donned his custodian helmet.

The driver saluted and flashed his warrant card in Humphrey's direction. "I'm DS Mahoney and this is Police Constable Adler."

Humphrey smiled and asked, "What can I do for you Detective Sergeant?"

Instead of answering, Mahoney sneered at James. "You bloody well took your sweet time."

Turning back to Humphrey, he began to give orders. "Tell your bleedin' family to do exactly as I say."

"Now, hold on there. You can't come on an Englishman's private property with that attitude. I don't care if you're police. We've a right to be treated with respect. Let me have a proper look at your warrant card so I can lodge a complaint with your Chief Constable."

"Have a butchers at these why don'tcha."

Both drew guns from their coat pockets. Mahoney said, "You lot, into the library. Now!"

Just then, two more automobiles pulled into the drive and four armed men got out of each.

Louise recognised these as the same ones she had spotted on Green Lane, but now they had different registrations.

The twins were at first confused because their game had come to an abrupt halt. At the sight of guns and angry voices, they began to wail.

Mahoney snarled, "Do something to muffle those little toe-rags."

In the library, Jarvis and Peets were standing by the piano. Two men held them at gunpoint. Yet another escorted Cook and both kitchen maids into the room.

Donald asked, "What do you want from us?"

"We've been keeping an eye on you lot since you scuppered our orphanage project."

At that point, Sprott entered the library holding a luger. "That's the lot, sir."

Mahoney said, "I recruited her last February to be our eyes and ears in your household. She's Scots but has German ancestors from a village called Sprotte in Westphalia."

"So you're another Abwehr cell."

"Good guess, Hutchinson. I hope you enjoyed your poncey May Ball."

Bea asked, "But why us?"

"Look bitch, when Portman's wife spotted you lot walking by our house, I knew we didn't have much time before Hutchinson called the Old Bill about our car registrations. By the way, PC Adler was on duty when you rang the copshop. After your follow-up visit, he persuaded his sergeant to ignore the matter saying you'd returned and admitted you'd made an error in writing down the numbers. And Beatrice, you can stop playing the innocent. We know you and Hutchinson work for MI6 and the other two are MI5 agents. I'm sure the Colonel and his wife are fully aware of your activities and no doubt uses his MOD connections to help out from time to time."

He pointed his Mauser at Jonathan. "I don't know much about you, but bagging a naval commander has got to be a bonus."

Mahoney's use of their names and SIS connections succeeded in taking the wind out of their sails.

"What I don't understand is what you're doing in Addlestone."

"Jimbo, I'll satisfy your curiosity since it no longer matters. We speak like locals because some of us were born here. I'm from Irish stock. My parents came over in the last century as navvies to work on your sodding railways. When I left school at fifteen, I went to the old country and proudly served with the Dublin Brigade of the Irish Republican Army. After we lost the six counties to you limey bastards, a number of us IRA soldiers were recruited by the Germans. Anything that buggers the English, is Ireland's gain. We moved to Munich, learned their lingo and received Abwehr training. Adler and Portman are locals but Portman's wife was born in Ebersberg in Bavaria."

"I can understand why the Abwehr wants retribution but you could have us killed us with snipers or paid assassins?"

"Of course, Jim lad, but that would have attracted unwanted attention. We've another mission."

"What can that be? Addlestone is an inconsequential little Surrey village where nothing much happens."

"Now you're being as two-faced as your toffee-nosed slag of a sister. Our senior Abwehr agent based in London has informed Berlin that Brooklands is the design home of a new Supermarine fighter aircraft. We plan to kidnap Mitchell and Wallis to secure the blueprints. From the test results our man has obtained, it looks like it will be a fast and manoeuvrable short-range fighter. It will have a higher top speed than your British workhorse the Hawker Hurricane and apparently will be superior to the current performance specs of our Messerschmitt Bf 109s."

With the knowledge he'd freely imparted, James accepted it was now certain their lives were forfeit.

"Sprott tells me your cellar is the best place for you while I finalise my plans. We'll feed you and give you water. If you wish to cheer yourselves up, you could always crack a bottle or two of bubbles."

James couldn't understand why they were being kept alive. It would have been easier just to lock them in the cellar and kill them like shooting fish in a barrel. He immediately realised, that might be Mahoney's intention and didn't want to panic the family into doing anything rash while still upstairs.

The cellar had a stout oak door with an ancient but functional lock. Dorothy helped Margie and Nanny comfort the boys who were still whimpering. The family were lost in their own thoughts as they found seats on empty wine crates near the bottom of the stairs.

After a few minutes, Humphrey stood and assumed command. "Let me summarise our position. When I'm finished, any of you, and I include my staff in this, can correct any errors or omissions and suggest ways forward.

"We're being held by thirteen armed men plus Sprott. Mahoney is obviously their leader. That we're still alive suggests three things. Firstly, their plot to capture Wallis and Mitchell is still in the planning stages. Secondly, and it directly follows, we'll be needed to give the appearance of normalcy while they prepare for the kidnappings. Finally, we could be useful as hostages down the line. We've no weapons to match their firepower, although there are guns in the house, assuming Sprott hasn't found them. I have my Webley, Donald and Bea have their Walthers and James and Louise have their Berettas. Mine is in our bedroom in the right-hand bedside drawer. Ammunition is stored on the top shelf of our wardrobe. We're trapped here in the cellar with only a single exit. The door is stout, locked and presumably guarded. If we're to believe them, we'll be fed and watered. I'll ask for buckets so we can see to our ablutions."

Donald responded immediately. "Humphrey, that was exceedingly useful. Our Walthers are in our bags along with spare ammunition. We're seriously outmanned and outgunned, but I expect we've seen the entire cell. Most will be out and about, especially at night. They'll be at their homes and staying at Wisteria Cottage. If we can secure our weapons and get a chance to confront the gang, we may only have to deal with a handful of guards."

Louise disagreed. "Humphrey, you're forgetting Portman and his wife. James and I saw him leaving their house with some of these men. The minimum number is sixteen. By the way, our Berettas are in our bedside tables. Several boxes of ammunition are in the top drawer of the bureau to the right of the door."

After that, Louise remained silent. She sat and stared at stacked boxes of claret.

Bea said, "I don't know if this helps, but I know PC Adler. He's the officer who poured cold water on my concerns about my missing orphanage leavers when I approached him last October."

Jarvis stood. "Begging your pardon, Colonel, but there might be something else you'd like to include in your planning. Mr Peets and I found it when we were rearranging the bins for the arrival of your French wine purchases. On my days off, I regularly visit The British Library Reading Rooms at St Pancras. My hobby is to research the history of Chertsey Abbey which owned these lands in medieval times. Woburn Hall is Georgian, but I have discovered that it was constructed on the site of the 7th century monk's living quarters. It is my belief that this cellar dates from that time. When Henry VIII disbanded the Catholic Church in the 16th century, his men removed cut stone arches and oak beams for his new palace at Oatlands, a few miles east of here. In the Middle Ages, Abbeys were usually constructed with secret passages so monks and abbots could escape religious persecution and Viking invaders. I believe we've found one but haven't investigated since it wasn't relevant to our immediate duties."

"First I've heard of this. Show me."

Jarvis led Humphrey to the south corner. The light was dim but they could just make out a stone arch. It had been neatly filled in and blended perfectly with the surrounding walls which were darkened by mould and cobwebs. On either side at floor level were two foot-square rectangular cast-iron Victorian grills.

"Right, get busy and pry out the stones."

Jarvis and Peets separated and scoured the perimeter looking for abandoned tools.

Louise was certain the plan was a non-starter. Even if there had once been a passage, it was highly unlikely a medieval tunnel would be open and intact. Nevertheless, she thought it might be good for morale if the family had a goal in mind rather than dwelling on their obviously hopeless situation.

"As head of the household, they'll need Dorothy and I upstairs to greet estate workers and visitors and to accept deliveries. I'll work out a plan whereby I can fetch my Webley."

"My dear, you must leave this to me. You have to take your heart medicine every day. I'll tell them the stress of our captivity requires you to have your digitalis capsules and your nitro-glycerine tablets to hand should you feel angina pains."

Peets returned with some broken iron barrel straps and an ancient club hammer. After several hours, he and Jarvis pried out stones and made a sizeable hole. Jarvis found several tallow candles on an empty oak barrel. He lit one with a match he extracted from the small silver box he always kept in his waistcoat pocket. Holding it up to the opening, the flame was drawn towards the exposed gap.

Jarvis said, "There must be some sort of exit. Tunnels are like chimneys. Stale and damp air is removed so cellars remain dry. That was obviously the purpose of installing those grills when the manor house was constructed. I'd like to volunteer to investigate."

"Begging your pardon Colonel, it rightly should be me. I'm smaller, younger, and fitter than any of you."

Humphrey was exceedingly pleased Peets stepped up so readily. "Take a few more candles and the match case and see how far the tunnel goes. If it's blocked, return immediately. Don't take any chances."

Jarvis produced a large spindle of twine and suggested Peets let it out so he could find his way back if the candle went out.

Humphrey added, "If you discover an exit, tie a knot and ball it up again so we can estimate the tunnel's length. It's essential you return to report. Your absence would alert our captors if they decided to do a head count."

Peets put the spare candles in his waistcoat pockets and clambered through the hole. The passage was narrow and only about five feet high. Although he was less than 5'6", he still had to crab his way along. After a few hundred yards, the way was partially blocked by a landfall. He crawled on his belly over the rubble and pressed on. Tree roots hung down like snakes from the arched stone ceiling, casting eerie shadows in the flickering candlelight.

After twenty minutes of slow progress, the corridor widened. He entered a room constructed with large sandstone blocks. The arched ceiling was about seven feet high at its peak so he was able stand upright for the first time since leaving the cellar.

To his left he saw about two dozen slate alcoves each containing a skull. He was seriously shaken by this ghoulish display, made even more eerie in the dancing candlelight. He forced himself to look away. On the opposite wall, he spotted a grey slate shelf with a number of two-foot tall brass candlesticks. He grabbed one since the dripping tallow had repeatedly scalded his hand.

Holding it aloft, the first thing he noticed was a full skeleton collapsed over a rotting oak table. The jawbone had separated from the rest of the skull and it appeared as though it was grinning at him.

Disturbed by his presence, mice scurried everywhere including in and out of the eye sockets of the skulls to his left. Only the security of the candlelight kept him from panicking.

Rats scuttled around his feet nipping at his ankles and scores of bats circled overhead. Despite their creepiness, he was actually reassured. He realised there must be an exit so the bats could escape during the night to feed on flying insects.

He left the room and worked his way forward, now encountering massive spider's webs attached to roots dangling from the ceiling. While shuffling along and waving his left arm to make a passage through the cobwebs, the candle went out. In the pitch dark he fumbled with the matches but couldn't manage to get it relit. He panicked and began to fight for breath. He'd had enough of this and decided to return to the cellar.

Instead, he inhaled deeply, wiped his brow with his sleeve and pressed on. He used his left hand to feel his way along the tunnel wall as he doled out the twine. He kept hold of the candlestick as it offered security despite being of no further use. After another fifteen minutes, he thought he could detect a faint glow ahead and felt the dank air flowing at the back of his neck. The tunnel floor started to rise but a barricade stopped his progress.

He kicked the rotting wood and peered into a large room. It was in semi-darkness but appeared to be constructed of black timber posts and beams filled in with daub and wattle.

He whooped for joy when he realised he was in the tithe barn. Acting on the Colonel's instructions, he tied a knot in the string. In the better light, he relit a second candle, placed it in the brass holder and worked his way back towards what he now thought of as the skull room. There he inserted a fresh candle and slowly crabbed his way back towards the cellar.

While Peets was away, Louise proposed an alternative plan. "I'm going to attempt to persuade Mahoney that Donald and I are working for the Abwehr. I'll ask for the promised food and water and some buckets. When I get a chance, I'll switch to Bavarian German and demand to speak with Mahoney. I'm banking on him being at least a bit curious as to what a German speaking lady was doing amongst this English upper-class family."

Dorothy said, "I'll go with her to fetch Humphrey's heart medicine and some coats for us and my grandchildren."

Together, they climbed the stairs and banged on the door. After a minute or two, it opened halfway. A guard pointed his luger at Dorothy's forehead. "Was ist los?"

"We were promised food and water and we need some buckets down here. I also need coats and blankets for my grandchildren."

Without saying a word, he slammed the door in her face. Five minutes later, another guard arrived and, in heavily accented English, asked her what was wrong. Dorothy repeated her request for buckets and water and this one seemed to follow what she was saying.

After a long delay, the door opened and the same guard placed two zinc buckets on the top step. Louise fetched them and a few minutes later the door opened and a three-gallon demijohn of water and several glass tumblers appeared. Louise brought these downstairs and returned to the top of the steps to wait for the promised food. When the door opened, the soldier was startled and pulled his gun.

Louise switched to Bavarian German. "If Mahoney is your leader, I must speak with him urgently."

The man was clearly surprised by her German as well as her use of the imperative. "Das wird nicht passieren."

"Tell him I can help him kidnap Wallis and Mitchell."

He nodded and was about to shut the door. "What about the old woman. If we're to succeed, we'll need her and the Colonel to be healthy and fit to greet visitors. He requires his heart medications and they both need overcoats."

Without uttering a word, he shut the cellar door. After twenty minutes he returned and pointed his gun at Dorothy. "You. Come here."

She was taken to the library where Mahoney and several men were sitting at the table apparently studying local Ordinance Survey maps. Dorothy explained she needed to fetch blankets for the children and medicine for her husband. Without looking up, Mahoney said something in German to her guard.

"I also need to visit the loo and I insist on my privacy."

"Get on with it, you old bat."

Upstairs, Dorothy went directly to the WC to take care of her immediate needs. The wardrobe door blocked the guard's view as she fetched blankets from the top shelf along with a box of ammunition. She took two winter coats off their hangers and slipped the heavy box of bullets into a pocket. Next, she went to the bedside drawer where Humphrey kept his heart capsules. She kept her back turned so her bundle of blankets and coats blocked his view. After slipping the Webley into the coat pocket, she selected the two bottles of heart medicine along with a small torch he kept in the drawer in case of power cuts. When she turned around, he escorted her back to the cellar.

Once down the slate steps, she handed the blankets to Nanny. She then gave Humphrey her bounty. After putting on the overcoat, he loaded the heavy pistol and slipped it into his waistband.

Now it was Louise's turn. She banged on the cellar door and finally got the guard's attention. He motioned her to follow him into the library.

Louise addressed Mahoney, "Soll ich dem Führer sprechen?"

"What's it to you, bitch? Of course, I'm the boss."

"I'm an Abwehr agent assigned to infiltrate the British Secret Service organisation, MI5. I've recruited Donald Hutchinson to be my counterpart in MI6. Apart from obtaining intelligence, we've been instructed to watch this family after their known involvement in dismantling our Lebensborn operation here in Britain. I've been told to only break cover if necessary to assist your team to complete your mission."

"That's a crock."

"I'm instructing you to pay close attention to what I say. I was born in Berlin and sent here to attend Cambridge University. My father is Generaloberst Johannes von Seeckt. He raised me bilingual in the expectation I'd be of future use to the Fatherland, believing there'd be another conflict with the English. I'm sure you're aware, he became chief of staff for the Reichswehr in 1920. My instructions were to recruit and create a cell of influential individuals who'd support our cause. As these would likely come from the moneyed classes, I targeted Donald Hutchinson. He was already with MI6 and his father is a peer. I seduced him, we became lovers, and now he believes in the ultimate destiny of our Third Reich."

"Hang about. Sprott tells me you're engaged to that tall pillock."

"What better cover than to be the wife of a country gent based in the Home Counties? This year, I encouraged my fiancé to be taken on by MI5 so he could pass on information he receives from his masters. Donald and I will remain lovers so I can continue to control him."

"You're some hard bint. I'm glad you're working with us and not for those limey bastards. You told my soldier you could help secure the fighter blueprints."

"Last summer I was briefed by Generalmajor Hans Oster and Admiral Wilhelm Canaris, chief of the Abwehr. He told me your scheme would involve a simultaneous frontal assault on the households of Wallis and Mitchell and you'd use one as hostage while the other fetched the plans. This would require perfect timing, knowledge of where both would be at a particular moment and, most importantly, their willingness to accept the other as hostage."

"Exactly. It's an excellent plan. Do you see a problem?"

With that question, Louise knew he'd taken the bait. "I met Wallis, Mitchell and their wives here on Boxing Day. The Colonel knows them socially as well as professionally from his stint at Brooklands. They could be invited to dinner on some pretext or other. Once here, you and your men could take charge. This would avoid running into guards who undoubtedly keep round-the-clock watch on their households."

From his reaction, it was obvious it hadn't occurred to Mahoney they'd have permanent security.

"The first thing you must do is let the Colonel and his wife upstairs to make the dinner party invitations. In the morning, they can deal with estate workers and deliveries. Cook and the kitchen maids will also be needed to prepare meals. I want Hutchinson released so together we can help refine your plans. From what I've seen, you've enough men to keep an eye on the kitchen staff and the old couple. The rest, including my simpleton fiancé, will remain in the cellar. To complete the charade between now and the dinner party, we'll need the butler and footman to cooperate."

Louise saw that Mahoney wasn't happy about all these people wandering around the house unsupervised.

"You must understand this is a very close family. Those two young boys make ideal hostages as they are the family's genetic future."

"Why the elaborate plan involving dinner?"

"You're really not paying attention. We're aware Wallis and Mitchell work in the same lab but we don't know if they're close friends. They might even resent each other. Their wives will be the critical hostages to get one of them to comply. Once we've got the plans, we'll kill the lot. The cellar would keep their bodies hidden for days if not weeks and that would allow your team to escape back to Germany. You could lock Hutchinson and I in another room so we can survive with our covers intact. An added bonus is that killing Wallis and Mitchell would set the fighter project back at least a year."

"Good thinking. When should we arrange the dinner?"

"Tuesday. We'll say it will be to celebrate their 45th wedding anniversary and they've only decided to invite family and a few close friends at the last minute."

"Anything else?"

"I don't want my position compromised. Return me to the cellar. Slap me about along the way so it won't occur to them I'm working with you."

After some thought, Mahoney decided to adopt her plan. He knew his scheme to kidnap the engineers was uncertain. Regardless of whether it was successful, the attempt would create a national uproar with police and military swarming all over Southern England. Escape might prove difficult, if not impossible. By following her proposal, freedom was guaranteed and getting a copy of the fighter's schematics might never be discovered. He'd kill all the witnesses including Wallis and Mitchell and their wives. Her suggestion of roughing her up went a long way in persuading him she was a committed Abwehr agent. Once he'd secured the blueprints, she and her lover would join the others as casualties of war. He smiled at the thought. In any case, his explicit instructions were to kill the entire household before returning to Berlin.

He quite enjoyed slapping her in the face. She picked herself up and a guard escorted her to the cellar door. At the top of the stairs, he shoved her with the butt of his rifle. She grabbed the banister with her left hand to break her fall. Her shoulder was twisted as it took her entire weight when she tumbled down the slate stairs. She landed badly on the flagstone floor.

When James tried to help her up, she screamed, "My arm."

Dorothy used her shawl to fashion a sling to ease the pain. "I believe it's only sprained or possibly dislocated but I'll treat it as if it's a fracture. Your face is abraded and your cheek has begun to swell. Without ice, there's little I can do." She paused. "Jarvis, go to the coldest part of the cellar and fetch a bottle from one of the lower racks and bring another for her shoulder."

When he returned, Louise held a bottle of sauterne to her cheek and another nestled in her sling. Despite the pain and the seriousness of their situation, she giggled at the thought of this unique medicinal use for 1921 Château d'Yquem.

Humphrey asked, "What's the situation upstairs?"

"Mahoney is indeed their leader. He's got plenty of men, but only a crude plan to procure the fighter aircraft's technical drawings by kidnapping Wallis and Mitchell. So here's what will happen. Jonathan, Margie, Nanny, and the boys will remain in the cellar as hostages the entire time. When you're taken upstairs, you'll invite Wallis, Mitchell, and their wives to dinner on Tuesday. Apart from that evening, James and Bea will also remain down here in the cellar."

"What about timing?"

"I expect some activity after Mahoney briefs his team.

She asked sceptically, "Any luck with the tunnel?"

"Peets just returned and found it ends in the tithe barn. He had to contend with every imaginable type of infestations and a partial cave in. I suppose that was to be expected given the passage is more than a millennium old."

They all looked at Peets in admiration for his bravery. He still clutched the brass candlestick as he described the room with a skeleton at a table and skulls in cubicles. Jarvis suggested the room might be an ossuary and the skeleton that of a monk assigned to say prayers over the departed abbots' mortal remains.

Humphrey ignored his speculations and again assumed command. "Right, we now know the tunnel can serve as an escape route. One of us should use the passage to alert the authorities. If they get their timing right, they could raid Wisteria Cottage and the fishmonger's and arrest constable Adler at the local nick. At the same time, they could surround Woburn. By then we'll be armed and ready to capture or at least neutralise the gang. I'll consider my timing when I see if I can lure Mitchell and Wallis to our dinner party."

James disagreed. "Surely there's no need to involve them. I expect the SIS could find middle-aged operatives to play their parts."

"That's not on. Mahoney will monitor my telephone calls."

"Tell you what. After the arrangements are finalised, I'll use the tunnel to alert MI5 and suggest they find surrogates to replace the engineers and their wives."

Just then, the cellar door opened. Mahoney stood at the top of the stairs, legs spread, hands on hips and silhouetted by the overhead pantry light. He ordered Humphrey, Dorothy, Donald, Louise, and Jarvis upstairs. Once in the library, he instructed Humphrey to ring Mitchell and Wallis.

The engineers were surprised at the short notice and said they'd need to check with their wives and work schedules and would get back by midday tomorrow. Mahoney had his ear close to the receiver and nodded his approval.

Donald and Louise went upstairs to their rooms. Louise attended to the abrasions on her face and then went to their bedside tables and found their Berettas still in place. When they met at the top of the stairs, she showed Donald she had them hidden in her sling and he patted his pockets in return. She slipped her right arm through his as they entered the library. Mahoney was asking Dorothy about visitors tomorrow morning. While he was doing this, Louise and Donald each handed Jarvis a loaded gun which he slipped into his pockets.

Dorothy continued her answer to Mahoney. "There's my secretary Alice, the postman, the baker's boy, and the milkman. Dustmen collect the bins Tuesday mornings. There might well be some deliveries from the village or London shops."

"You and the Colonel will deal with those. Remember, my men will be in the background so don't get clever."

Jarvis cleared his throat, "If we're to give a dinner party, we'll need to restock the kitchen."

He ignored him and addressed Humphrey, "Tell your flunky we'll be having seafood. Portman will supply the starters and main course and we'll leave it to your staff to provide desert. Wine will come from your cellar and your kitchen surely has potatoes and greens this time of year. When the time is right, I'll choose which wife will act as hostage."

Everybody apart from Louise and Donald were escorted back to the cellar.

Humphrey said, "Now we must wait until morning."

"Not quite grandpapa. At dusk, I'll use the tunnel to go to the kiosk is on Station Road. Bea gave me the direct telephone number for MI6 and I'll also ring Richard."

He waited until it was dark, took the torch, and disappeared into the tunnel entrance. It was after midnight when he returned and reported to his grandfather. "It's all set. They assured me they'd find agents to pass as Mitchell, Wallis, and their wives. I've told them we're armed but outgunned and outnumbered so they shouldn't attempt a frontal assault. By the way, I'm seriously impressed with Peets. That tunnel was an absolute nightmare."

61

MONDAY, JUNE 24TH, WOBURN

First thing in the morning, Humphrey, Dorothy, and Jarvis were led upstairs to deal with visitors.

At half eight, Dorothy greeted Alice at the front door. "You've worked so very hard these last few months, you deserve some time off. Here's a florin. Why not take the omnibus into Weybridge?"

"I would like to give presents to my friends when I leave the orphanage in August, but I've had no chance to get to the shops."

Mahoney sneered when Alice curtsied as she left. "You limey toffs make me want to puke. Just make sure you do the same with the next lot."

Those included bread, milk, the iceman, and the first and second posts at their usual times. Smalbridge arrived to discuss ordering lucerne seed for autumn planting.

At midday, Jarvis called Humphrey to the telephone. Mahoney listened as Mitchell accepted the dinner invitation for himself and his wife. He said he'd spoken to Wallis at work and they looked forward to helping them celebrate their wedding anniversary.

By early evening it was obvious there'd be no further visitors. Mahoney said, "Tomorrow morning it'll be the same dance. For the dinner party, I've arranged a shellfish starter and the main course will be wild salmon. Portman will deliver it in the morning and the kitchen staff can fix lunch and then sort out dinner."

Back in the cellar, Humphrey began to organise the timing of the possible armed confrontation at the dinner party. Louise interrupted. "Look here, some of us have experience with pistols, but I seriously doubt Jarvis and Peets have ever touched a gun."

"My dear, I believe you'll find Regimental Sergeant-Major Jarvis knows his way around weapons. He was my non-commissioned adjutant while I was overseeing Brooklands. Before that, his regiment was gassed on the Somme and he was given a non-combatant role the remainder of the war. I'm certain he'll instruct Peets as to the proper use of a pocket gun."

In the morning, Dorothy and Humphrey were escorted into the library to greet visitors and accept the regular deliveries. Jarvis, Peets, and the kitchen staff were also allowed upstairs to prepare the anniversary meal. Mahoney watched as Donald and Louise came downstairs holding hands.

The first and second post, bread, and milk arrived and the family fielded a few telephone calls in the morning. Several concerned golf matches and another was for Dorothy about arrangements for this afternoon's regular bridge club meeting. Portman arrived with the seafood and checked in with Mahoney. Unfortunately, Humphrey was unable to overhear where Portman planned to be when the dinner party began.

Lunch was served in the dining room. Guards took a platter of sandwiches and another demijohn of water to the cellar. Afterwards, Jarvis and Peets set the dining table for eleven using Woburn's finest silver, crystal and china. At dusk, the family were allowed upstairs to dress for dinner. At the same time, Mahoney slipped out to change into black tie.

When the front door bell-pull sounded, Jarvis showed their guests into the library. Right on cue, Humphrey made the introductions. "You've met most of my family on Boxing Day, but not Donald Hutchinson. He's engaged to my granddaughter, Beatrice. We've also an old friend visiting from Ireland. Mr Mahoney, this is Molly and Barnes Wallis."

He knew Barnes had married a much younger woman so he was able to distinguish them from the other couple. Next, he introduced Reginald and Florence Mitchell.

Barnes muttered an apology. "We'd no choice but to bring along a couple of minders. Would you believe, our latest War Office contract stipulates whenever we leave Brooklands, these chaps are at our sides? They even maintain a twenty-four hour rotation keeping watch on our houses."

Humphrey directed everybody into the library. "Jarvis, please serve drinks to our guests."

At the dinner table, James asked Barnes what progress they were making on the new fighter.

"It's all very hush-hush and walls have ears don'tcha know. I can tell you, we're set to produce a very fast and manoeuvrable short-range aircraft that'll give the Hun something to think about if push comes to shove."

"Does it have a name yet?"

"On the drawing board, it's the refined version of the Type 300. Some bugger at the Air Ministry decided to call it the Spitfire, just the sort of bloody silly name they'd give it."

Humphrey asked, "Is it in production?"

"Not yet. We're still tinkering with the prop design. The Rolls-Royce Merlin engines are being upgraded and bench tested in Southampton. I'd expect the prototype will be in the air early next year. I know you and your family, but I shouldn't be talking about this to the general public and certainly not to the Fourth Estate. Mr Mahoney, I trust you're not a journalist."

"Mr Wallis, I'm happy to say I've no connection with Fleet Street. The press regularly distorts facts and invents fake stories to titillate, influence, or outright deceive the general public in order to promote their own political agenda and, of course, to sell newspapers."

"How do you keep yourself busy?"

"Please, you must call me Seamus."

"Seamus it is. How do you earn a crust?"

"I suppose you'd call me a facilitator. I introduce businessmen who share a common interest so they can develop some profitable enterprise. For that, I naturally accept a consideration."

"What are you working on at the moment?"

"It's a long story, and I see dinner is being served. If you're interested, I'll explain over brandies."

When the meal was over, Humphrey rose to indicate they should adjourn to the library. Jarvis took drinks orders and as he left the room, noticed the engineer's two security guards were bound and gagged in the mudroom. He quietly reminded Peets to ensure the safety was off and to take careful aim so as to not to endanger the family. Eleven Germans were crowded in the front hall waiting for Mahoney's signal.

When Wallis pressed Mahoney about his current project, instead of answering, he stood and pulled a Mauser from his belt. "I'm happy to say, my present commission is to acquire your Spitfire drawings for Germany." He then shouted, "Jetzt Rein!"

His men rushed into the library and spread out, guns at the ready. Mahoney told his prisoners to line up against the wall by the fireplace. He pointed his pistol at Molly Wallis. Barnes said, "Don't hurt my wife. She's frail and has heart palpitations."

"She looks fit to me. If you wish to see your bit of crumpet again, go to your lab and fetch all the Spitfire blueprints you can manage to hide under your overcoat. One of my men will drive you there to make sure you return with the drawings."

"He won't be allowed past the gates."

"I know that. Give your totty a kiss. If you don't return with the plans, it'll be your last kiss from those pouting young lips."

James realised there'd now be only ten men plus Mahoney left in the house. He was sure the surrogate Wallis would, with the help of SIS agents, take care of his escort immediately they left Woburn. The proxy Mitchell would be armed but James thought the ladies would be a liability since they'd no place to conceal a weapon.

Nothing happened during the next half hour. Then the 'phone rang and Mahoney went to the hall, picked up the receiver, but remained silent.

He glared as he returned to the library. "That was Portman. He tried to meet us here but turned back when he saw the military in your front drive. I'm sure you and Hutchinson are responsible and I can promise you a painful death. I should have done that in the first place. Right now, we're in a hostage situation. Mitchell and your family will be my bargaining chips."

As he spoke, Jarvis and Peets entered the room and separated. Jarvis knelt and clinically shot a guard in the back. Another Nazi quickly turned and got off a shot in the butler's direction. It was later found imbedded in the doorframe about head height.

Bea grabbed Dorothy and pushed her behind the leather sofa. From then on, sporadic gunfire echoed in the room. Those still active tried to find cover behind furniture. Kneeling beside his writing desk, Humphrey spotted one of the gang crouched behind the chaise. Using his powerful Webley, he shot him through the settee back and dispatched another who was kneeling behind the leather sofa.

One of the Germans shot Peets in the right shoulder. He fell backwards, dropped his pistol and was horrified as it scuttled under the sideboard. Instead of crouching behind the piano, he rushed the Nazi and booted him in the groin. When the man doubled over, he followed up with a kick to his jaw.

After pulling her Beretta from beneath her silk dress, one of the MI6 agents shot Peets' assailant as he attempted to rise from the floor. James realised she must have had the pocket gun concealed in her garter. Bea crawled towards the sideboard and retrieved Peets' Beretta just as the second female agent downed another German with a shot to his temple.

Donald and Louise sought cover behind the sofa. From that position, they double tapped two others. Jarvis knelt by the sideboard to defend the dining room exit and shot another who was trying to leave the room. Only one more of the gang was still active. The agent masquerading as Mitchell shot him in the back as he tried to escape through the hall doorway.

The family relaxed and started to rise but they'd forgotten about Sprott. She entered from the hall and fired two shots in Humphrey's direction. He collapsed heavily onto the floor, blood staining his shirt front. Bea returned fire and the lady's maid was killed instantly by shots to chest and head. By this time, the gunfire had ceased and the room was filled with smoke and the smell of cordite.

When the shooting started, Mahoney ducked behind the second leather sofa. He watched, as his team were being killed or wounded. During the melee, he aimed his Mauser at Peets. His shot missed when the footman nipped behind the piano. He shifted his target to Louise. James saw Mahoney's intent and shoved her out of the way. She landed badly on her injured left arm and cried out in pain. Mahoney was momentarily distracted by her scream, but had enough time to alter his aim. He shot James in the midriff from a distance of six feet.

James crumpled to the floor like a rag doll. Blood immediately soaked his starched shirtfront. Although Louise was on her side, she still had her Beretta in her right hand and fired a single shot in Mahoney's direction.

He howled in pain so she knew she had scored a hit. He fell to his right but was now out of sight behind the sofa.

Being unable to take the second shot, she crawled to her fiancé. Pressing her shawl over the wound she shouted for somebody to call a doctor. Out of the corner of her eye she saw Jarvis had disarmed Mahoney who was moaning loudly and holding his shoulder. The room was now filled with soldiers and plainclothes agents who took charge of the weapons. The SIS had the foresight to order several ambulances to be on standby and a doctor rushed into the room to attend the wounded. He went first to Mahoney who was making the most noise.

"Leave him. He's the enemy. See to my James."

The doctor knelt by his side and visually examined the stomach wound. "There's nothing I can do. I'm afraid he is dead."

He started to rise to attend to the others.

"God Damn It To Hell. Don't leave him. Do something."

The doctor knelt again and held his wrist for about half a minute. Eventually, he was able to detect a faint pulse. Over his shoulder he instructed one of the soldiers to fetch the ambulance attendants. In the background, Louise could hear Donald rapidly barking orders.

Louise accompanied the stretcher-bearers and boarded the ambulance still holding James's hand. Gravel sprayed from the drive as it headed to the surgical hospital in Weybridge, its siren blaring. What was normally a nine-minute journey, took under five but to her it seemed an eternity. The attendant held a thick compress to his shirt front. It quickly became soaked with blood.

Someone, probably Jarvis, must have telephoned ahead since nurses and surgeons were waiting at the emergency admissions entrance. The ambulance backed up to the door and nurses lifted James onto a gurney and rushed him into theatre.

Matron prevented Louise from following and ordered her to remain in the dingy waiting room. She sat on a bench with shoulders slumped and tears in her eyes, her dress and shawl soaked with her fiancé's blood.

Twenty minutes later, Jarvis arrived pushing Humphrey in a hospital wheel chair and took him straight into the surgical ward. Peets followed, his arm in a makeshift sling.

Dorothy and Bea joined Louise in the waiting room. Dorothy put her arm around Louise's shoulder and muttered something inconsequential. Louise hugged her but was unable to either speak or contain the flow of her tears.

Bea provided the latest news. "Our family is safe. Five of the gang are dead and the rest are being brought here for treatment. James, Humphrey, and Peets' injuries will, of course, take priority. Portman, his wife, and PC Adler have been arrested along with another of the gang waiting outside our gates in a motorcar. He wasn't known to us and Donald thought he might have been there to provide Mahoney with an escape route whether or not he was able to secure the plans."

After a couple of hours, Humphrey was wheeled back into the waiting room. Dorothy bent down to kiss her husband and asked how he was feeling. "Never better. It was just a graze and will provide me with another interesting scar to go with my Southern African wounds. More's the point, how's James?"

Louise was unable to speak so Dorothy answered for her. "He's still in theatre so he's presumably alive and fighting for his life."

Louise listened to this with a spark of hope but couldn't take her swollen eyes off the green and white tiled floor.

At midnight, a surgeon met them in his blood-spattered gown. "Your grandson has survived. He's lost a lot of blood and his heart stopped twice during the operation for a bit over four minutes on each occasion. The bullet was lodged against his spinal column, so we might expect some degree of paralysis. We've removed the projectile and stemmed the internal bleeding. Right now, he's in intensive care and breathing with the help of a mechanical ventilator. Unfortunately, he's in a coma, most probably the result of brain damage caused by the cardiac arrests. I'm unable to offer a positive prognosis unless or until he regains consciousness."

Louise asked the surgeon, "May I see him?"

"Two at a time and only for a couple of minutes. He's neither awake nor aware of anything that happened after he was shot."

She sat by his bedside and reached for his hand. Almost immediately, Matron entered and instructed them to leave. She said they could return tomorrow during hospital visiting hours. Dorothy slipped her hand through Louise's undamaged right arm and led her back to the waiting room.

The surgeon was still there talking with the family. "It's best you all return home. Get some rest and I'll give you an update in the morning."

A junior nurse noticed Louise's arm in the makeshift sling and asked if she wanted it looked at. Louise shrugged, said nothing and stared at the tiled floor. While walking to the emergency room, Louise idly noted the nurse's nametag showed her name was Moira O'Sullivan. The attending doctor arranged for an X-ray. When that was done, he put it up to the light box.

"You've a hairline proximal fracture in your left humeral head. This will heal naturally, but for the next three weeks, you're not use your arm to lift anything heavier than a book. After that, have your local doctor arrange some physiotherapy so you can get the strength back in your left shoulder."

She stared at the illuminated X-ray in silence. She couldn't be bothered to tell him she didn't have a local GP but used her Harley Street doctor on the few occasions she'd been ill. After the doctor left the room, she adjusted her clothing and nurse O'Sullivan led her back to the family which was still in the waiting room.

Louise announced, "I'm not leaving."

Dorothy tried to dissuade her but saw she had made up her mind.

Jarvis was waiting with the Daimler to drive the family back to Woburn. Peets accompanied them after having his shoulder wound disinfected and bandaged.

Sitting down in the library, all were in a sombre mood. Although the kitchen staff had tidied the room in their absence, Dorothy shuddered when she noticed James's bloodstain on the Persian carpet. She moved towards the damaged chaise so as to be as far away from it as possible.

Humphrey asked Jarvis and Peets to join them in the library. "I want to thank you for your service to our family. Both of you were instrumental in securing our release and we are forever in your debt.

"Leonard, your resourcefulness with a simple thing like dry matches and your knowledge of the medieval origins of our house shifted the odds in our favour. What's more, your military training was crucial in taking out the enemy forces.

"Albert, our family will never forget your courage exploring the tunnel and your willingness to put yourself in harm's way. Rest assured, you've a position at Woburn for as long as you wish. By the way, we were all impressed with your bravery when you attacked that armed Nazi after you were shot. Where did you learn to fight that way?"

"Before I came here, I was living on the streets in Bethnal Green with my pals. At fourteen, I was arrested for petty theft and habitual street fighting. The juvie Court sent me to Addlestone Reformatory School as I was too young for Borstal. I may be a titch but I learned a few tricks along the way to deal with bullies."

Both Jarvis and Peets were surprised by the use of their Christian names, a first for both in this household. "On behalf of Mr Peets and myself, we're deeply moved by your words. We'll do our utmost to live up to your praise should you ever require armed assistance in the future."

This got a smile from the family who then stood and applauded the servants.

Humphrey rose using the cane the hospital had supplied. "You have my personal guarantee, you'll never again be placed in danger nor asked to raise a weapon on our behalf."

"If you'll excuse us, Colonel, Mr Peets and I have some chores to attend to. By the way, we'll need a new ladies' maid. Perhaps Miss Beatrice might make inquiries at the orphanage."

When they left, Dorothy asked the question that was on everybody's mind.

"What about the wedding? Should we send out cancellation announcements and return the gifts?"

Humphrey was resolute. "Nothing has changed. I insist we assume our grandson will be fit to walk down the aisle in just over three weeks' time. I'll not have anybody even consider the possibility he will fail to survive and eventually make a full recovery."

62

SUNDAY, JUNE 30TH, WEYBRIDGE HOSPITAL

Louise hadn't left his bedside apart from exchanging her bloodstained dress for a hospital gown.

When the surgeon entered to check James's wound, he noticed Louise was holding his hand. "I've recently read an article in The Lancet that might be of interest. Neurologists at Guy's Hospital have described two cases where previously comatose patients said they could hear sounds, understand conversations, and feel outside stimuli but were unable to respond. Try to encourage him to fight. I've no idea if it will help, but as things stand, you've nothing to lose."

Louise accepted the surgeon's final words implied James was in mortal danger. Instead of feeling defeated, she was filled with renewed strength and determination.

The previous Wednesday during visiting hours, Bea brought a small suitcase with some of her casual clothes. She changed, unpacked and stored the rest in the tiny wardrobe in the corner of the room. She wasn't hungry and during the week had picked at the hospital food the nurses provided. Bea insisted she eat the sandwiches Cook had prepared. She took a few bites but said they tasted like cardboard.

All week she chatted to James while holding his hand. She talked about Morey-Saint-Denis and their plans to design and build a stone cottage on the far side of the courtyard of Clos des Chênes. She talked about the glorious spring days they'd spent idly strolling along the Backs and feeding the ducks and swans. She talked about their nights at Woburn and their passionate love life, saying she knew it would resume once he returned home. She talked about their honeymoon at some mysterious destination.

She'd no idea whether he heard any of this but when she mentioned the honeymoon, she was sure his hand moved. She pressed the buzzer and asked the nurse to fetch the attending doctor. When he arrived, she described how James had responded to her words.

Without giving her eye contact or even examining his patient, he spoke as if he were lecturing a first-year medical student. "It's well-documented that comatose patients occasionally have autonomous muscle movements and sometimes display a flickering of the eyes behind closed lids. I should add, this is also true of those who have spinal cord damage. Remember, that was where the bullet was lodged and extracted during the operation. Every hour he remains in a coma, his already minimal chances of survival are progressively diminishing. Right now, his body is shutting down, starting with the kidneys and liver and then moving on to other vital organs. In the end, his heart will stop. Before one might have even a modicum of optimism, the patient needs to emerge from the coma. Let me remind you, there remains the virtual certainty of extensive and permanent brain damage and lower body paralysis."

Every day the family visited for an hour or two but the nurse only allowed one other in at a time. Louise had become a permanent feature of the room and the corridors, prowling them at all times of the day and night.

One evening when she was talking about their wedding day, she again felt him squeeze her hand. She could see from the dim light of the bedside lamp he seemed to have a faint smile on his lips. She didn't press the buzzer. She couldn't abide the doctor's views on involuntary twitches or whatever gibberish the man might spout.

Sunday morning she held his hand and began to speak to him in German. She had no idea why, except for the last few months that had been the language they used when they were alone and intimate.

This time the squeeze was much stronger and his eyelids fluttered. She continued to speak about their love life, their work for MI5, their success in disrupting the Lebensborn operation right on their doorstep, and their wedding.

Now she was sure he was responding. His lips were moving but no sound was coming out. She pressed the buzzer and asked the nurse to fetch the attending doctor. Louise recognised her from previous visits. She appeared surprised Louise was speaking German. At the same time, she observed the movements of hand, eyes, and lips. She took his pulse and saw it was over one hundred beats per minute, well above his normal resting rate of sixty-five.

"He's coming 'round and not before time. Keep doing whatever you're doing and saying whatever you're saying in whatever language you choose. I'm convinced you're the only reason he's still alive and finally emerging from his coma."

Tears rolled down her cheeks. She continued speaking in German, reminding him of their trip to Munich and Berlin, the frightening militarism, and the terrible food.

Although his eyes remained closed, James spoke for the first time since the shooting. "Wir müssen sie aufhalten!"

That was all. His breathing returned to normal and he turned his head towards the wall.

When the family arrived, the nurse allowed Humphrey and Dorothy into the room. "Don't stay too long but I think you'll find he's on the mend."

Louise told them he had spoken but the effort had been such that he was now resting, asleep but no longer in a coma.

"What did he say?"

"I was speaking to him in German about the Nazis. He said, We must stop them!"

"My family is made of stern stuff. I've taken a couple of direct hits from Boer rifle fire and been stuck like a pig with a Zulu assegai. That's not to mention the best Jerry could come up with last Tuesday evening. He'll be as fit as a fiddle in no time."

The doctor came in and told them she put his recovery solely down to Louise's encouragement and perseverance. "What's more, it appears there is no spinal cord damage as we'd feared. He has feeling and movement in his lower extremities."

Humphrey reached for Louise's hand. "Our only child died before his time. Dorothy and I have never recovered from that loss. In the grand scheme of things, children aren't meant to pass before their parents. I have to tell you, James is our legacy. As his wife, we rely on you to perpetuate my name and ensure our genetic immortality."

Louise was unable to respond. Tears rolled down her cheeks as she lowered her eyes to stare at the tiled floor.

The Head Nurse entered the room. "Visiting hours are over but doctor said Louise could stay as long as she wished."

When she resumed her bedside vigil, she continued in German. "We're a right pair. When we arrive at the altar, I'll have a sling and some substantial foundation on my face and you'll be in a wheelchair."

He opened his eyes and spoke in a rasping whisper. "After we tie the knot, I intend to walk down the steps of St Paul's with you on my arm. Don't forget, we have our first waltz to consider."

63

MONDAY, JULY 8TH, WOBURN

It had been hot and humid all week with summer thunderstorms almost every day. At 8:00am, the doctor signed the release forms. At the front desk, Humphrey instructed the hospital to bill him directly.

On the trip back to Woburn, they were caught in a downpour. Jarvis switched on the headlights. The sky was as black as night and the wipers were unable to cope with the torrential rain. He stopped the car under a railway bridge as the road was awash. Periodic flashes of lightning illuminated the countryside and the almost constant rumble of thunder could be heard even in the well-insulated interior of the Daimler.

Back home, Louise and Jarvis helped James upstairs to his room so as not to put strain on his stiches.

Peets tapped on their bedroom door and entered with a tray of sandwiches and a bowl of chicken noodle soup. "I trust you're on the mend, sir."

"I know you helped foil Mahoney's plans and were wounded defending us. I thank you on behalf of myself, Louise, and our entire family."

"The Colonel has already embarrassed us with his praises but it's nice to hear it from you, especially as you'd such a close shave from the best those Kraut bastards could manage. Begging your pardon Miss for my language."

James was propped up in bed leaning on several down pillows. Louise coaxed him to finish the second half of the sandwich. "You'll need your strength to cope with the rigours of our honeymoon."

He smiled at her somewhat risqué encouragement. Obediently, he finished eating, slid down under the covers, and immediately fell asleep.

She left his room and found Alice waiting at the bottom of the staircase. "I'm ever so glad Mr Harcourt-Heath is recovering."

"Thank you for your support. Is everything sorted for the wedding?"

"Yes, miss. The gifts are inventoried and on display in the billiard room. Mrs Harcourt-Heath and I have finalised the reception seating arrangements and I've scripted place cards."

She smiled shyly when she added, "I placed Bea's best friend, Rose Gregory at the same table as James's riding pal, Humphrey Paine. She told me they seemed to hit it off when they met here on Boxing Day."

She thanked Alice and entered the library. Humphrey asked, "How's he doing?"

"He's getting stronger by the day. Of course, he sleeps most of the time. The Weybridge doctor who visited today said that was perfectly normal due to the lingering effects of the anaesthetic. I doubt he'll be dancing at our wedding, but it won't be for lack of trying. He's anxious his life quickly returns to normal."

Louise asked Donald about the mopping-up operation. "Sir Hugh Sinclair, the head of MI6, told me to thank you for challenging our assumption that the Abwehr was staffed by amateurs. Like the gang involved in the Lebensborn operation, this one had detailed intelligence, excellent organisation, and plenty of manpower, which included native English speakers. What's particularly worrying, they had precise and detailed knowledge of the highly classified Spitfire programme. Our first priority will be to identify the source of that leak. It's most likely associated with Brooklands, but could be anywhere within the MOD or the War Office. Even worse, it might be somewhere within the SIS. The Home Office has instructed all military research agencies to tighten up on security and move subsequent Spitfire development, testing, and manufacturing elsewhere. Brooklands is now rather too well-known to the Germans."

"What about the Abwehr gang?"

"Mahoney was a mercenary pure and simple. He's already been charged with attempted murder. As a British citizen and a non-commissioned Wehrmacht officer, he'll also be tried as a traitor and a spy. With our evidence, I expect he'll be hung. Adler, Portman, and his wife will likely receive long custodial sentences. The surviving members of the cell were German and their trials will have full press reporting. The Home Office now accepts the general public should be made aware of the possibility of domestic threats from foreign infiltrators. They've issued a telephone number to the press so their readers can anonymously report suspicious behaviour. Most will be false alarms, but because of you, we're raising our guard."

Louise glanced at the floor where James had fallen. "Dorothy, what happened to the carpet?"

"The staff removed the stain, but every time I looked at that pattern, I thought of my grandson lying there bleeding to death."

She started to cry. Louise sat beside her on the leather sofa and held her hand. "You did the right thing. I can't bear to be reminded of that evening. What heartens me most is he's already forgetting about being shot and is looking forward to our wedding. I'm convinced both of you are responsible for fostering his pragmatism."

"You needn't worry about the arrangements for your nuptials. Alice is marvellous and I realise I can't do without her. We'll have to pay her accordingly to make sure some other employer doesn't poach her. The problem is, Addlestone has limited social opportunities for a pretty sixteen-year-old."

Louise started to rise. "If you'll excuse me, I'm going upstairs to see if he needs anything."

"Nonsense. You said he was sleeping. You've always been too thin and I can see you've lost weight with hospital food and worry. I'll get Cook to prepare a tray. You're family and in our world we look after each other."

Louise thought, 'I couldn't agree more perhaps because I've never been part of a family until now.'

The weather continued to be oppressive and there had been constant rumbles of thunder for the last hour. While she was waiting for the tray, rain and hail began pelting against the library windows. The outside temperature dropped and the room became gloomy. After another loud thunderclap, the power went. Jarvis and Peets entered the library with lit paraffin oil lamps. Just then, lightning hit the chestnut tree in the front drive. The library was illuminated with a bluish light accompanied by a deafening explosion.

Louise fainted and crumpled to the floor. Dorothy knelt beside her and put a cushion under her head. Jarvis instructed Peets to get Cook to prepare a pot of tea.

When she recovered, she was embarrassed and decided she needed to explain her reaction to loud noises. As she sipped the Darjeeling, she told them about the bicycle accident and eventually admitted she might be unable to bear children.

"You're family. Even if you are unable to conceive, Dorothy and I will still love you as our granddaughter."

64

SATURDAY, JULY 20TH, ADDLESTONE, ST PAUL'S

The service was to begin at one. As best man, Donald's role was to ensure James arrived at least ten minutes in advance. In his experience, the bride was always intentionally late. That gave the guests time to greet each other and find seats as either friends of the groom or friends of the bride.

James muttered, "What if she legs it?"

"Don't be daft. Louise intends to marry you even if you couldn't manage to advance down the aisle without a wheel chair, a saline drip, two nurses, and a bottle of oxygen."

"I'm glad to be alive. My family is safe and I'll soon have Louise as my bride. I'm also glad to welcome you as my brother-in-law. You and Bea are also lucky to have found each other."

"I've known that since last January when I heard her play Beethoven's Pathetique. That was the moment I fell in love. I think of it as being struck by Cupid's arrow. The Italians call it colpo di fulmine. One thing, as we intend to meet up in Berlin, I'll need to know where you'll be on your honeymoon. I might have to contact you if there's a change in plans."

James obfuscated lest his surprise destination be revealed by accident. "For the first week we'll be in southern Europe. After that, we'll drive to Morey-Saint-Denis to spend a few days with Michel and Louisa. We'll meet you in Berlin on the 3rd of August."

Donald wrote these details down in his diary.

James asked, "What hotel have you booked in Berlin?"

254

"The Grand Hotel Bellevue on Potsdamer Platz."

"An excellent choice if you like peasant food."

They waited on the steps outside St Paul's, greeting guests at the double doors while Jarvis, Peets, and Alice acted as ushers. It was fully a quarter past one when the organist began playing Wagner's 'Bridal Chorus'. Louise entered the church escorted by Michel on her right arm. Five Newnham ladies served as her bridesmaids. The guests watched as she slowly walked towards the altar, smiling radiantly towards their guests. Michel handed her over to James and sat next to Louisa in the left front pew.

The Rev Hugh Paterson waited for silence. "Dearly beloved, we are gathered here…"

THE END

HISTORICAL BACKGROUND

As this is a novel, the primary characters are fictional. Nonetheless, in the mid-30's, William Gosden was a builder in Addlestone whose office was on the High Street, Joseph Hodges was an Addlestone butcher whose retail shop was on Station Road, and Charles Hall was the landlord of the George Inn on Chertsey Road. A hand-painted sign on the wall behind the bar still informs patrons that during 1935, A.A. Collyer took over as the new landlord. The George is still a public house and is reputed to be the oldest building in Addlestone.

I've introduced two local characters to this novel, Rose Gregory and Humphrey Paine. Both lived in Addlestone in the 1930's. The inspiration for the Addlestone Chronicles came from their wedding in July 1937 catalogued in The Bride's Book that I mentioned in the forward. I've inserted them into the story as friends of the fictional Harcourt-Heath family. In the next book, they will court and in the third book, James and Louise will attend their society wedding at St Paul's, Addlestone that occurred on July 24th 1937.

I have James driving a 4.2 litre Railton Drophead Coupé. The Fairmile Engineering Company manufactured this marque between 1933 and 1938. The factory was located in the Fairmile ward of the village of Cobham, less than six miles from Woburn Park Farm. It was a British designed body incorporating the engine and chassis of the American Hudson Terraplane motor car. Railton 8's had a 0-60 mph time of 8.8 seconds.

In 1935, Addlestone had a population of some 7,000. This included approximately 500 officials and inmates of the Chertsey Poor Law Institution, a home for the mentally ill and insane. The census also included the permanent contingent at Brooklands and the staff and charges of the Princess Mary Village Homes Industrial School for Girls. While I have Bea volunteering at the fictional Addlestone Orphanage for Foundling Girls, it bears no intentional resemblance to the Princess Mary Home. The Reformatory School I have Peets attending is also a literary invention.

In 1935, the Reverend Hugh Edward Paterson was the vicar of St Paul's. In December 2003, a fire broke out early in the morning and the entire roof was destroyed and most of the beautiful stained-glass windows were damaged along with the box pews and wood flooring. The fire was likely the result of an attempted burglary of the church treasures. It was rebuilt with some modernisation but still retains the original architectural design. The centres of the stained glass windows were saved or replicated and returned to their original positions with new leaded glass above and below depicting images of flames.

Woburn Park is about half a mile to the northeast of the centre of Addlestone. Presently, the open spaces are filled with sports facilities including football and cricket pitches, all-weather tennis courts, a running track, and post-WWII housing developments. St George's College is also on the original grounds of Chertsey Abbey having moved from Croydon to Woburn Park in 1884. In the 1930's, apart from St George's, the fields were primarily used for grazing cattle. There is a large Grade II listed manor house on the site, which for a time was a hotel and restaurant.

Completed in 1907, Brooklands was the world's first banked racetrack. It inspired the construction of the Indianapolis Motor Speedway in America some two years later. From the outset, Brooklands was a front for the British aeronautical research and development. Barnes Wallis, Reginald Mitchell and the other engineers mentioned in this novel, worked there on the design of the Spitfire attack aircraft. In WWII aerial combat, it proved to be superior to the Messerschmitt Bf 109s.

It was the Spitfire and Hawker Hurricane aircraft and pilots who were primarily responsible for winning the Battle of Britain. This was the confrontation between Hermann Göring's Luftwaffe and the Royal Air Force under Sir Hugh Dowding's Fighter Command. This air battle raged over southern England and the Midlands between July and October 1940. Hitler's intention was to gain air superiority over England and the English Channel by decimating the RAF along with the British industrial heartland in Coventry and Birmingham. He regarded victory as a prelude to the invasion of Britain, the Nazis codenamed Sea Lion. The 1955 film, The Dam Busters, detailed Barnes Wallis's development of the bouncing bomb. It was successfully used in 1943 to attack and breach Möhne, Eder, and Sorpe dams in Germany. Despite being diagnosed with cancer in 1933, Reginald Mitchell continued to work on the Spitfire and a four-engine bomber called Type 317. In 1936, his cancer returned, he was forced to retire and died the following year. Barnes Wallis died at the age of 92 in 1979.

John Maynard Keynes was a Fellow and Bursar of King's College, Cambridge, throughout the interwar years. In 1919, he was part of the British delegation at the Versailles Treaty negotiations. Because of his outspoken views concerning the likely consequences of the stringent reparations, he was at odds with the British Delegation. He resigned in protest and returned to Cambridge where he wrote the influential pamphlet, *The Economic Consequences of the Peace*. In July 1944, he was Britain's lead negotiator at the Bretton Woods Conference in New Hampshire. At this stage, the Allies were winning the war in the European theatre. The objective of these talks was to liberalise tariffs and remove quotas, thereby increasing world trade following the end of hostilities. The aim was to remove the protectionist policies adopted in the 1930's, which saw world trade drop by more than 50%. The Conference was successful in establishing the International Monetary Fund, the World Bank, and the system of fixed but adjustable international exchange rates. Those arrangements survived for the next 25 years. Keynes died April 1946 of heart failure.

Alan Turing was an undergraduate at King's and a Wrangler having been awarded a first in Mathematics in 1934. He was also an oarsman, having competed in the 1935 May Bumps for King's second boat. He became known as the Bletchley Park Codebreaker for his work decrypting German radio messages and deciphering an Enigma machine captured from the Nazis in May 1941 from the U-boat, U-110. In 1952 he was charged with homosexual acts and accepted chemical castration instead of a long prison sentence. In 1954, at the age of 41, he committed suicide. A film chronicling his life appeared in 2014 called The Imitation Game.

John Tressider Shepherd was Provost of King's at the time this novel is set. He was also an Old Alleynian, the name given to a Dulwich College leaver. During both world wars, he undertook intelligence work for the British Government and was later awarded an MBE for his work as a classicist. In 1968, he died of natural causes at the age of 87.

In 1935, Miss Joan Pernel Strachey was Principal of Newnham College. Louise's tutor at Newnham, Miss Sybil Ferguson, and Dr Richard Chillingworth, James's maths tutor at King's, are both fictional creations.

A proof of Fermat's Last Theorem, also called Fermat's Conjecture, remained elusive for more than 350 years. In 1993, Dr Andrew Wiles, a British mathematician and Oxford professor, submitted his 150-page proof. For this, he collected numerous accolades, including a knighthood. He was awarded the Abel Prize by the Norwegian government in March 2016 and, in 2017, the Copley Medal by the Royal Society.

The Apostles was, and still is, a secret Cambridge society. In the mid-30s, members were primarily undergraduates from King's and Trinity colleges and were purported to be Marxists. Guy Burgess, Anthony Blunt, Leo Long, Donald Maclean, and John Astbury all were active members. Each eventually secured sensitive jobs within the British Secret Service. Burgess became an MI6 officer and Maclean worked for the Foreign Office. Adrian 'Kim' Philby was also a Trinity College member who received his degree in 1933. He was a close friend to Guy Burgess and by 1941, held a senior post within MI6. In April 2016, a film clip was released from Russian Stasi files in which Burgess told the audience he found it a simple matter to filch SIS files. He simply put them in his briefcase and walked out the front door of Broadway Buildings, the MI6 offices in London. He'd return the files the following morning after accomplices copied and photographed the documents. Apparently, this went on throughout WWII and continued during the Cold War period well into the 1950's. All those mentioned above were eventually exposed as Soviet agents. Burgess and Maclean fled to the Soviet Union in 1951 and Philby defected in 1963.

Anthony Blunt came under MI5 scrutiny in the early 50's. Despite that, in 1956, he was given a knighthood. In 1963, he was exposed as a Soviet spy by the American and former Apostle, Michael Straight. A year later, he confessed and gave up John Cairncross, Peter Ashby, Brian Symon, and his former lover, Leo Long. In exchange for his confession and the betrayals, his lawyers successfully negotiated immunity from prosecution for fifteen years. When that agreement expired in 1979, the Government, stripped him of his knighthood and released details of his career as a Soviet spy. This became an overnight press sensation and the British Secret Services became the butt of jokes detailing their incompetence. Blunt died of a heart attack in 1983.

Captain Archibald Henry Maule Ramsay was a Member of Parliament. He was also an outspoken racist and anti-Semite. In 1940 he was arrested, charged with high treason and disloyalty to the Crown and interned under Defence Regulation 18B. He was incarcerated in Brixton Prison and remained there for the next four years. This was despite the established principle of Parliamentary Privilege. This provides legal immunity against civil and criminal liability for actions and statements made during the course of their legislative duties. He died of natural causes in 1955.

Konrad Lorenz's research in wolf behaviour was used by the Nazi Party to justify their assertion of Aryan superiority over what they termed Untermensch (subhuman people). Lorenz was an Austrian who joined the Party in 1938 and was conscripted into the Wehrmacht in 1941. He was given the title Military Psychologist and assigned to conduct 'racial studies' on eastern Europeans. His published papers purported to demonstrate that interbreeding between different races would lead to serious dysgenic effects. He argued, the detrimental consequences would impact on later generations through the inheritance of undesirable traits. Referencing his own publications, he provided the requisite scientific justifications the Nazis needed to support their policies against miscegenation. He later studied German-Polish 'half-breeds', arguing their offspring would be psychologically and physically unfit and therefore shouldn't be allowed to reproduce. In 1944 he was captured on the eastern front and remained a Russian prisoner of war until 1948. Based on his work with animals and his popular publications, he became the joint recipient of the Nobel Prize in Physiology or Medicine in 1973. He died in Vienna in 1989.

The three men I have walking out after James's presented his discussion paper to the Apostles, were members in 1935. David Gawen Champernowne was a close friend to Alan Turing. In 1948, they developed a chess playing computer game. Later he became editor of the world's most prestigious economics' publication, The Economic Journal. His life's work culminated in the publication in 1998 of *Economic Inequality and Income Distribution*. He died in August 2000.

Eric Hobsbawm was also at King's and was an outspoken Marxist. As a child, he lived in Vienna and Berlin until Hitler's assent to power in 1933. When his Jewish parents died, he was adopted by an aunt and taken to England. After a distinguished career as a world-class historian, he became president of Birkbeck College, London. He died in October 2012.

The third member I have leaving the meeting was Alan Lloyd Hodgkin. In 1963, he became joint recipient of the Nobel Prize for Physiology or Medicine for research into synapses. He died in December 1998.

George Randal Mundell Laurie, known as Ran to his friends, led the Cambridge 1935 Boat Race crew. After graduation, he became a medical doctor. He served as stroke for Great Britain's eights at the 1936 Munich Olympics. When Olympic competitions resumed in London in 1948, he won gold in the coxless pairs with Jack Wilson. Ran's son is Hugh Lawrie, the comedian and actor. Himself, a Cambridge graduate of Selwyn College, he gained international fame in the US television series House.

In 1892, Francis Bellamy, authored the American Pledge of Allegiance, instituting the obligatory salute involving a raised right arm with palm forward. It was used every morning by primary and secondary school children prior to the commencement of lessons. Controversy arose in the late '30s, when fascist Germany and Italy adopted a similar salute derived from images from the Roman Empire. In December 1942, a year after the US entered WWII, Congress amended the Flag Code. The salute was replaced by the requirement students place their right hand over their heart as they recited the pledge.

There actually was a residence in Addlestone called Swastika. It was on Slade Road and occupied by a family called Luker. The house name hadn't been changed at the time of the 1939 Register. There's no suggestion they were ever involved in anything traitorous or illegal.

A final note on etymology. Louise's explanation of the origin of the phrase 'a cad and a bounder', sounds plausible but has no basis in fact, so again she was boasting.